The Moment
of
Now

Elizabeth Day

The Moment of Now

ISBN: 9798663403047

Blue Root Press

Bee on cover designed by
Arcadia_dreamstime.

For us

Before

Day 1, Tuesday

8:37 a.m.

When Ella's phone rang, she was turning off the heat under the whistling teapot, and it didn't register that her husband never called on Tuesday mornings because he was always in meetings then.

"Hey, Ella," Ben said. "I … uh …" It wasn't just that his tone was strained, a forced casual; he had hesitated, and the only time he paused heavily like that was when he knew his next words would be an upheaval—but he was going to say them anyway.

Ella left the mug with the dry tea satchel on the counter, pulled a chair from the kitchen table, and sat down. She knew, though she didn't know how she knew. This was one of those calls, like the one three and a half years ago: both of her parents on the other end of the line, hysterical, talking over each other. Hearing the unexpected had distorted Ella's ability to understand the simplest words—*your brother, accident, Pacific Coast Highway*. Before that call, she thought she understood how life could change in an instant. Afterwards though, she had experienced firsthand the emotional turmoil and mental vertigo that could uproot her reality, leaving a mess of pieces. Her mind had replayed that call again and again—*oh Ella, he's dead, Andy's dead*—until she learned that the need to repeat the trauma was a habit of her left brain. To interrupt it, her right brain needed to comfort her left brain like a child, saying, "Shhh ... it's okay. It's over now."

"Ben?" she said, fighting all the places her imagination was taking her. "Are you okay?"

"Not really. I mean, don't worry—there's nothing to worry about ... Shit. This isn't going how I planned."

Ella fought the nausea rising. No words came out.

After a loud, slow exhale, he said, "God, I love you, Ella. I love you and Izzy and Daxx so much."

"Why are you saying that right now? I love you too—you know that—but why are you saying that right now?" The sadness in his voice had jolted her, but the accompanying fear was replaced by a sudden knowing. "You've decided something," Ella said, standing up. "What did you decide?" *Without me.*

She pictured him holding the phone against his ear, looking down; he always looked down at his feet when making a big decision. When she pointed it out a while back, he had been unaware but loved that she noticed. He had smiled and asked, "What else do you notice?" The details came to her one after another—how he put toothpaste on her toothbrush for her because she used the sink right after he did each morning; how when they watched sunsets together, he was never the first to turn away from it; how… She could have said so many things. Instead, she laughed off the question and changed subjects.

Ben wasn't saying what he had decided—or anything else.

Ella swallowed hard. "Ben, what happened?"

When he didn't respond, she looked at her phone to make sure they were still connected. "Are you hurt?"

"No." His voice was so quiet.

Ella closed her eyes. "Oh thank God …" The relief was short-lived; Ella's mind snapped back to attention, a primal urgency propelling her words. "Was there an accident? Did something happen at work?"

"No, no … it's nothing like that. I just … I'm walking."

"You're walking?" *Breathe. Think.* "You're not at work?"

"I can't do this," he said.

"Do what? What are you talking about?" She stopped pacing. "Wait—what do you mean you're—"

"I'll call you back. I just … nothing happened. I just need to think—or no. Shit. I'm sorry."

Ella looked at the phone. Never before had he hung up first. Not once in the seventeen years they had known each other.

After three tries and leaving three messages, Ella sat down and put the phone on the table in front of her. He would call back.

Any second now.

Her legs were in constant motion, bouncing as she stared at the clock above the kitchen sink, focusing on the loud ticking. The second hand continued lugging itself around, its effort obvious. She and Ben had talked about getting a new clock, one that wasn't so loud, but she couldn't, she never would, because the one they had would always remind her of the conversation where she confided in Ben that she sometimes felt like that second hand, trying to keep up with the first hand—the first hand being who she thought she should be. After Ella detailed that person, Ben looked at her for a long time before saying, "Don't do that to yourself. You're neither hand, Ella. You're the entire clock, all of it, right on time."

With still no word from Ben, Ella decided to call her friend Charlotte. If she wasn't with a client, she would definitely answer.

When Charlotte picked up on the second ring, Ella said, "Oh good," and then choked back tears that suddenly sprang to life. "Something's wrong with Ben."

"What do you mean?" Charlotte sounded as nervous as Ella felt.

After Ella explained that Ben wasn't acting like himself, Charlotte said, "Jesus, you scared me. I thought something happened or—just please don't do that again. All right, I'm breathing now. Talk to me."

Ella walked out to the backyard as she started to share parts of the conversation she had with Ben. But the more she talked, the worse she felt. The words she was using … they felt skewed, and Charlotte's distorted responses convinced Ella she wasn't saying it right. It didn't feel like her words matched what was happening, and the urge to get quiet grew more insistent, so she wrapped up her explanation without finishing.

Charlotte said she was coming over, then quickly added, "The client whose house I'm staging—I told you about him, right? Jasper? He asked me to hold off a day, which is fine. It worked out actually. Right? I'm not meeting any other clients till this afternoon."

"No, I'll be fine," Ella said. "I just ... I don't know." She started walking the perimeter of the small yard. "It's like as soon as he called, I knew it was something I'd been waiting for without realizing it. I've had this feeling ..." Ella pulled her phone away from her ear and looked at the incoming call. "Hold on—that's him. I'll call you back."

"Okay, I'm hanging up. Call me as soon as you can."

Ella switched over. "Ben?"

"Sorry. I thought I'd be able to call back sooner, that I'd have a grip—because I'm trying, I really am, Ella. But I don't, and I'm not sure when I will, and that's what I need to tell you. I'm taking some time. I'm ... walking ... well, I might be hitchhiking. That's the truth."

"You're *hitchhiking?*"

"I can't stay here. I want to, but I can't. I have to go."

"Where? Ben! What happened? You have to tell me what's going on!"

"I'm not sure yet, but I can't think anymore. I can't think clearly."

Ella forced herself to calm down. "I can help you, Ben. It's okay. We can figure this out. Just come home. Or no—I'll come get you. Where are you?"

"*No.* I need some space, some time. It's not you, Ella. I promise it's not you. There's something wrong with me—not in a sick way—I'm not dying. It's my mind. It's in my head. I need to figure things out."

Ella's throat tightened. He sounded so different; she had never heard him so resolute and raw. *Except once. That day.* "I don't understand. Where are you going? How long—wait ... what did you tell the office?"

Silence.

She went back inside. Pacing the kitchen and living room, Ella said, "Ben? What did you tell them at work when you left? Did you say you'd be back later today? Tomorrow? When are you coming back?" She looked for her car keys. They were right there on the counter.

"I don't know. All I can tell you is that leaving is so hard. This is so ... I wouldn't do this unless ... I just can't think of any other way, and I've *got* to stop thinking."

She grabbed the keys. "I know, Ben. I understand. It's okay. We'll figure this out together. You don't need to leave. Where are you?"

"I never want to feel this way again. *Never*, Ella. I don't want to come back until I don't feel this way anymore."

"What way? What's this about?" she said, hurrying out to the car.

Silence.

She opened the door and slid in. "I don't understand. Did something happen at work?" Fumbling with the keys, her hand shook as she cradled the phone on her shoulder and tried to put the key in the ignition. "You can tell me anything. It'll be okay. I promise. I *promise* you, Ben."

"I just ... I'm so sorry. I'll call you when I can."

"Ben?" She looked at the phone. "Ben!" He had ended the call.

Her hands were still shaking as she opened the Where Are You app on her phone. Ben's signal was off.

No, no, no, no, no ...

How could she know where he was then? How could she possibly know?

No, no, no, please no ... It felt impossible to take a deep breath as she backed out of the driveway and started driving, not sure where she was headed, looking down side streets as she passed them, one block after another, trying to piece together what was happening. It began to sink in that something was in motion that she had no say over, that she couldn't stop it, this wrecking ball, shattering her sense of stability, leaving her stranded in an unknown that was closing in, without Ben, who had made a decision, a *big* decision, she could feel it, without her, without—

When the other driver slammed on the brakes, screeching across the intersection, Ella did too and then realized she had gone straight through a stop sign without pausing. After yelling out his window and giving her the finger, the other driver took off, and Ella pulled to the side of the road, profusely apologizing even though there was no way he could hear.

When the effects of the adrenaline started to wear off, her heart was still pounding so hard it scared her, and the nausea was growing stronger. She held the steering wheel tightly and focused on breathing ... one slow, deep breath at a time.

Gratitude overwhelmed her. She had missed that car by a sliver.

Breathe.

She was so lucky. She was *so, so* lucky. She almost just shattered someone's—possibly many people's worlds. Guilt started to creep in, its tentacles squeezing the life out of all the gratitude she had been feeling, and then it didn't take long for one question after another to find their way into the mix.

Ben's office was less than a mile from their house. How far could he have gotten if he just left?

What if she didn't find him before Izzy and Daxx got out of school?

What happened?

Why wouldn't he just talk to her?

Just one slow, deep breath at a time.

After making sure no one was coming, Ella pulled back on the road. She would drive until she found him.

But what if—

Just focus on the road. One block at a time.

* * *

Ella pulled into the driveway and turned off the car. The last thing she wanted to do was sit and wait, but she didn't know where else to look, and the near-accident just under two hours ago was still fresh in her mind.

It didn't feel right to go inside the house, because maybe Ben would come walking home, or maybe someone would drop him off. Or, even better, he would call and ask her to come get him. She'd be ready.

She sat on the front stoop and went over the past few days, looking for a catalyst, a sign, any shift in Ben's behavior or an explanation, but she came up with nothing—except a strong, terrifying feeling this was bigger than an event or a trigger, a single thing happening.

She checked her phone to make sure the ringer was at its loudest. He would call soon. She was sure of it. He had to. Otherwise she would have to call someone at Starfish to find out if they knew what was going on. And then Ben would be upset because she *knew* he didn't share anything personal with his bosses or coworkers. But she would justify it by explaining how worried she had been, and he would hug her for a really, really long time, not saying a word, letting the matter drop, not needing to be right.

It had been a while since a hug had lasted more than a few seconds. How long had it been? When did it change?

And their conversations. They used to last for hours, back when the two of them asked each other endless questions and were interested in the answers, answers that didn't always come easily.

She couldn't remember the last time she had asked him, "How are you?" and then waited for the answer, her mind open, wondering what he might say.

And was she *always* the one who ended a hug?

A car slowed a few doors down, and her heart surged. She stood and craned her neck to get a better look at whoever would be getting out of the car once it stopped. But then it kept going, right past their house, no passenger in the back or front.

She sat back down. Where was he? He really needed to come back before it was time to pick up the kids from school.

It was different when Daxx and Izzy were around. She and Ben would catch each other's eye and smile at something Izzy said or something Daxx did. Ella's entire world would feel like it was spinning right again—and Ben's world would seem in sync with hers; she could feel it. But then, when it was just the two of them again, something would feel off-kilter. Was it Ben? Was it *her*? Why hadn't she said anything? Why hadn't she asked him if he felt it too? Why hadn't she asked him how he was *really* doing?

Until now, the distance between them had felt like a dull knife, harmless and not capable of cutting. She thought of Daxx's yellow plastic Play-Doh knife; anything divisive by nature could slowly, effectively separate something that was pliable enough. Why hadn't she admitted it earlier?

What did he mean, something was wrong with him? What was that supposed to mean?

Staring at her phone, still silent and dark, she willed it to ring, light up, buzz—anything.

She went back to looking down the street, left and then right, again and again, not wanting to miss the moment the next person rounded the corner, walking in her direction. As she waited, she came up with a list of reasons for not having called out the growing distance between them. It felt too big, too nebulous, like too much work to name it. Maybe one of them had just been having a bad day. Did every feeling, mood, and thought really need to be talked about? Everything was okay, wasn't it? Was it really that bad?

She wasn't ready to answer any of it, not even to herself.

Oh Ben …

She hit redial. If she kept calling, eventually he would pick up. He wouldn't keep ignoring her calls. He wouldn't do that to her.

But with every second that passed, it became harder to deny what was happening. Ben wasn't just rocking the boat. He had stopped playing by the one rule she was sure they had silently agreed upon at some point—that neither of them was allowed to sink the boat and see where it left them.

11:39 a.m.

Ben walked with no destination in mind. He only knew he wasn't turning around. No matter what. No matter how irresponsible it was. No matter how much it undid him every time he imagined Ella trying to explain to Daxx and Izzy where he was, doing her best to answer all the questions they'd come up with.

Keep going.

No matter what thoughts Ella was sure to be thinking about him as she sat alone on the couch that night. From the tone of her first word or two, he could always tell what kind of conversation they were about to have—playful, clarifying, pressing. He liked to name them. There were so many versions of his Ella.

One foot in front of the other. Look ahead.

No matter what.

Pick up your foot. Put it down.

Again.

No matter what. Because this … this was at least so much better than what it was like before he left. Even though this meant not tucking in Izzy and Daxx tonight, not listening to them make their lists of the *best, best, best ever* things that happened today. Even if it meant not hearing Daxx say the goodnight rhyme he had made up to tell his goldfish every night, which he could never quite remember, which meant it changed just a little each time.

Go.

No matter what. Even if this was how it started. No matter where this was going to take him. No matter who he became because of each step he was taking right now. The people he'd seen in tattered clothes with deep wrinkles and hard skin, wearing life's harshness, in tight, animated conversations with themselves, the ones who made him shift from his left foot to his right and look around, the ones he'd handed money to—quickly—not making eye contact, mumbling something like sorry, thank you, have a good day, sorry … it didn't matter. Even if he was becoming them. Even if that's where he was headed.

"Geez!"

Ben jumped as a car sped by. He moved off the shoulder, onto the sidewalk, then kept walking, trying to focus on the concrete and cracks in front of him.

He would not turn around.

No matter how unstable the ground felt beneath his feet.

No matter how sharp the pain in his throat grew each time he swallowed hard, holding everything in.

Because this … it was better than—

He looked at his phone. It was Ella calling again.

It kept ringing.

It wasn't going to stop.

Ever.

Finally, he made a promise to himself, took a deep breath, and then answered, saying, "I can't do this."

"Oh thank God. You said you never want to feel this way again. Ben, *please*—tell me how you feel, what you're feeling."

A probing conversation, he noted. Or was it pretending, preferring, paving, peeking—*Stop. Damn it. Stop.*

He took a few steps from the sidewalk and leaned back against a tree, falling into its support. "Like I'm losing my mind and I can't get grounded. I can't—I can't get firmly here."

She didn't respond. Maybe she understood. He went on. "There's a part of me that's rejecting it, that's saying no to where I am and what I'm doing. And it's getting stronger than me, and I feel like it's taking over. And I kind of—I want it to … I need to let it. Or I'll lose me. It's already happening. I can feel it."

In the silence that followed, it hit him that he had no idea what she was going to say next, and in too many ways, it didn't matter.

"Oh, Ben. I'm not sure what's happening right now. I don't understand any of this, but … come home. This is crazy, and you're scaring me. Whatever it is, whatever's happened, we'll figure it out together."

It wasn't her words; it was her tone. He heard the fear. *Of course* she would have checked the Where Are You app by now; he knew how much comfort it gave her, especially after Andy died.

"I'm sorry I turned it off. I really am. I needed to though."

He closed his eyes as Ella said something about a promise he had made, that he would *never, never*, a pact they had made together … It didn't matter that her words weren't in order, that she wasn't making sense. He knew what she was trying to say. He had taken away their safety net, the guarantee that they would always know where the other person was. It was never a question of trust; it was a way to prevent worrying, reassurance that the other person was on their way home and not in a car accident. It hadn't been about making sure one of them wasn't going in the wrong direction; they hadn't planned for this.

"Ben, please. *Please turn it back on.*"

He couldn't remember the last time anything about him—any word or action, silence or inaction—had elicited such a response from her, or even a tenth of the emotion coming through the phone now.

"I can't. I'm sorry. Until I can find me, I don't want anyone else to." He hung up before he could say anything else.

12:05 p.m.

As Ella looked at her to-do list and considered ripping it up, a sudden burst of anger surged through her, its force surprising her. How was she supposed to work? How was she supposed to get anything done?

Ben's phone was going straight to voicemail now, and she had gotten a text from Thea, the owner of a high-end clothing boutique, asking if she could come a little early to pick up the necklace because—Ella looked at the time and didn't bother reading the rest.

How was she possibly going to do this?

Normally, being in the room she and Ben had converted to her home studio felt good. She loved the fountain, the plants, the lighting—and the space: aside from the chest of square drawers that helped her keep everything organized, the only furniture was a distressed wooden table and a comfortable chair.

But now, it felt so wrong to be there.

Maybe she could just give Thea the necklace as it was.

Unfinished.

Shit. Ella tried to will herself to focus.

The necklace was for one of Thea's VIP customers. Thea would be giving it to her at a birthday party that evening, a small gathering of some of the town's most influential members—according to Thea—being held at the wine bar down the street from the boutique.

Knowing that everyone else's life was going on as normal brought back a long-ago but familiar feeling, the deep loneliness Ella felt after Andy's funeral. Ben had been there for her then; she had talked to him about it, and he understood, even felt the same way. They had felt the loneliness together.

Ella unwrapped the tissue surrounding the necklace. She at least needed to check all the cradles, prongs, and clasps to make sure everything was tight and secure.

Where are you?

This was also her last opportunity to make final tweaks to the design itself—nothing too dramatic, because the majority had been agreed upon and had taken days to assemble, but final tweaks that usually ended up making all the difference. A delicate twist. One more tiny stone.

She looked down the hallway to the front door—again, hoping it would open, hoping Ben would walk in.

She picked up the necklace, put it back down, and took off her thin gloves. She pulled the magnifying lamp closer, lifted the necklace, and examined the yellow bowenite, the delicate feathers, the hard chalcopyrite with its iridescence, and her favorite, amber.

Nothing looked right anymore.

She left her office, went to the front door, and opened it, just leaving the screen door shut. It was more welcoming, and Ben would know she was home … if somehow he didn't notice the car in the driveway.

After double-checking her phone again, she went back to the necklace. She didn't know the significance of yellow for the client, only that it was important that the necklace be exceptionally sunny. Ella had made it light, long, and shimmering, based on how Thea had answered the personality survey about the soon-to-be wearer.

She stared at the necklace, then looked down the hall to the screen door.

Yesterday, the necklace was one of her favorite pieces. It had come together with a powerful momentum and fluidity, piece by piece, day after day.

She turned off the music that had been softly playing since early that morning. It didn't feel right to have it on anymore.

She brought her focus back to the necklace.

As much as she wanted to, she couldn't get the pinchers she was squeezing to tighten around the gemstone they cradled; instead, as if with a mind of their own, they kept digging between the prongs and gemstones, carelessly and destructively pushing up and away—scratching, interrupting, and interfering. Soon after, the silver clasps came apart, and the thin strands unbraided quickly between her fingers. She unfolded, ripped apart, unclasped, unwound, bent, and let fall until it was undone—all of it—and it lay in nearly a hundred pieces, scattered on the table, on the floor, on her lap.

Looking at the mess, she couldn't wrap her mind around ever having been able to create a piece of jewelry, let alone one she was satisfied with.

She went back to the front stoop. She would wait. He was going to come home.

12:32 p.m.

Ben's steps couldn't keep pace with his thoughts. Why did he tell Ella he was hitchhiking? Where did that come from? That was the last thing he wanted to do. See anyone. Talk to anyone. Let alone a stranger. *And to have to make small talk?* He walked faster, pushing down harder on the pavement, as if he knew exactly where he was going.

12:58 p.m.

"You've got to have *some* idea, Ella. What happened this morning before he left for work?"

At two o'clock, as Charlotte had explained to Ella, she would be showing her favorite clients a house; she was sure she had found the perfect one for them, quirks and all. Before that, though, she had time. She insisted Ella meet her at their go-to spot, the Blue Express, an old train car turned into a coffee shop. Charlotte assured her it was a better idea than sitting on the front stoop, waiting.

Ella had driven to the café slowly, looking for Ben the whole way, fighting a knowing that told her she wouldn't find him.

The Blue Express wasn't crowded during the lunch hour because they didn't serve any food other than a few baked breakfast specialties, and those were always sold out within an hour or two of opening, so it was easy to find an empty table among the six.

"Nothing happened. That's the thing," Ella said, following Charlotte to a table. "I can't think of what would upset him so much."

"Maybe it was something at work," Charlotte suggested as she sat down.

Ella took the chair opposite her. "Well, that's the other part of this. Danny and Jules might be the coolest bosses ever, but from everything Ben's told me, they're also really serious when it comes to personal issues interfering with work."

How many parts of Starfish did Ben refer to as *cool* three years ago when calling Ella, ecstatic after his interview? It wasn't just a cool company. It had a cool game room for de-stressing, two cool masseuses on call, and a cool koi pond. All to keep cool people like Ben focused on being the marketing and advertising geniuses they were. How proud and excited Ben had been—*beaming* actually. But wait—they had talked on the phone. Maybe he was beaming when he came home. Anyway, he had been ecstatic. Hadn't he? Why was a nagging part of her remembering him saying "cool" with a light, carefree laugh ... maybe even sarcasm? *That wasn't how it happened.*

Ella refocused on Charlotte, who was saying, "... so my guess is he'll be back at work by the end of the day. Just a mini breakdown—crisis averted."

"I don't know ... I've never heard him like this."

"Like what?"

"He wasn't talking about a walk around the block to clear his mind." Ella looked out the window, noticing each person who walked by. She turned back to Charlotte. "What am I going to say to the kids?"

Charlotte shook her head. "I don't know. I don't know because I don't even understand what's going on. Can you help me here? Fill me in? It's Tuesday. I saw Ben Friday—the three of us played cards, competitive and fun as always, he went to bed after the game, pretended to be tired, but it was really to give you and me time together. Blah, blah, blah. You and I stayed up and drank wine longer than we should have. Typical Friday, and he was typical Ben. Right? Am I missing something? What happened since then?"

"Nothing I know of," Ella said. "I've gone over it a hundred times in my mind. Saturday, he was busy with work, and so was I ... until I noticed the plants. They were dying."

"The plants? Which plants? And what does that have to do with Ben?"

"The ones in the house. And I don't know. It's just every time I replay the weekend, this part of it just stands out, and I don't know if it means something, if there's a clue there."

"Okay. Good," Charlotte said. "Tell me. Maybe another perspective would help."

"I thought the ones in the living room just needed a little attention, but then once I took off the brown leaves, there was so little left, and the plants looked so bare, and so I—" Her heart skipped a beat when her phone buzzed. She quickly checked, then shook her head, looking at Charlotte. It was just a client.

Ella went on. "At one point, I turned, and Ben was smiling, watching me. He had been working at the kitchen table. He had just stopped and looked up and—"

"Adored you. He does that. Yes." Charlotte smiled. "I've been around you guys enough to see that many times."

Ella was so grateful to Charlotte for that reassurance. She went on, "Something told me I should stop, go to Ben, but I didn't. I went back to what I was doing, and the more I looked at the other plants and took off the dead leaves, leaving such bare stems, the uglier our house was becoming. I felt horrible about getting rid of them—"

"You threw them out?" Charlotte said.

"I put them outside … with the other plants that haven't made it. And then I felt this strong need to replace them—right away. The house just felt so empty with no plants. So I took the kids to the nursery while Ben stayed home and worked." She felt her face turning red. "I sound crazy … When I just said that out loud …"

"You're doing fine. Keep going," Charlotte said, giving Ella's hand a squeeze.

Ella took her through the rest of the weekend and all the way through Monday, and Charlotte said she had to agree—nothing out of the ordinary happened.

"But you said you thought this was coming, right? Isn't that what you said?"

"I did." Ella nodded, trying to remember what she'd been feeling lately—before Ben called. "It was like something was pulling at my attention, and I just ... I guess I've been ignoring it." With tears threatening, she rubbed her eyes, then went to finish the last of her coffee, but it was already gone. "When I got the call this morning and heard his voice, something told me—I just knew that's what the constant buzzing in the back of my mind has been about. It's been about him ... I think." She put her elbow on the table and rested her trembling chin on her hand, a wave of sadness overwhelming her. "I don't think he told Starfish when he'd be back. I think he might have just walked out."

"Jesus. That's not good. Okay, let's think this through. What can we do? What can *I* do? Should we drive around and look for him? I mean, he can't be far. You said he's walking ... somewhere. Right?"

Ella shook her head. "I looked again on the way over here. I have no idea where he is." She thought again about their conversation. "He was *so* adamant about needing space."

"You can find him and *then* give him space." Charlotte looked at her phone. "Shoot. The Dowlands are on their way." She started getting ready to go, then abruptly stopped. "Hey, I can cancel. I can reschedule and look for

Ben with you. It's way more important. You need to find him before this gets bigger."

Ella insisted Charlotte keep her meeting, placating her by saying they could look later if Ben hadn't returned yet. She had no desire to say out loud how big it already was.

2:15 p.m.

Ben found himself—purposely, he decided—on the edge of town, at the end of the sprawl of houses and developments, nearly six miles inland from the Pacific Ocean, standing in front of the bench of the final bus stop. From there, the buses drove into the large circle just beyond, where the road and pavement ended. After turning around there, they then headed back into the small coastal town. Ben looked out at the rolling hills and valley that lay beyond the bus stop, covered mostly in wild grasses.

He sat down on the bench and leaned forward, his elbows on his knees, his hands together. Staring at the parade of ants circumventing his shoes, he wondered where they were going, if they always traveled in groups like that, and why they stayed in line. Did no ant ever say, "Let's go this way instead"? Did no ant ever just suddenly stop, letting the next few ants behind him pile up like falling dominoes? And, damn, they were small little guys.

He reached down to the sidewalk, letting the tip of his index finger linger, touching the pavement only a centimeter or so from the line of ants. *Come on.* One of them had to veer, had to be curious. *Come on.* One of them had to have it in him to do its own thing. *Get out of the goddamn line.* A sign. It would be a sign. If an ant ventured out of the line and up his finger, across his … He lifted his hand, looked at his sweaty palms, then peered more closely. He traced the lines in his palms. Nothing. He felt nothing. Not a good sign, not a bad sign.

What kind of sign was he looking for again?

Whatever it was, that was it—he needed a sign.

He looked up to the sky. *Anybody?* He wouldn't say more than that. What else could he say? What did he even believe?

Time to get real. Practical. *Think. No, don't—yes, now's a good time to think.* He could wait for a bus, board it, let it take him to the other end of the line, wherever that was. He could sit and wait. For … anything that would tell him what to do. He looked up at the buzzing telephone wires. At the clouds above them, shifting, the space between them— closing, opening, morphing. Back down to the sidewalk, at the cracks, ants carrying ants, the single blade of grass pushing through the pavement.

He stared at the blade of grass. It didn't belong. What was it doing there? Why was it even trying?

He could cry. It would be okay to. No one was around.

His foot started jiggling. What was he going to do for food? Stupid question, he decided. He had his wallet. He could go to a store, pick something up. He wasn't far. Maybe a mile. *Stop being dramatic.* Was he hungry? No, he wasn't.

Okay, that was good. Some clarity.

Maybe this is stupid, he decided. Maybe he should go back. He absolutely should not let himself think about—too late. Daxx's squinty eyes looking up at him, his full little cheeks and curious smile. That kid was always smiling, like he knew something everyone else didn't—or maybe he didn't know what everyone else knew. His probing eyes and constant smile anchored Ben. And Izzy, so serious, so gentle, wanting to understand, to make sense of things, always—such a gentle teacher to her brother, passing everything on as if she was translating this life for him, helping him understand the language neither of them spoke but were adapting to out of necessity. Ben, more than anyone, could make Izzy laugh; he could make her laugh so hard her little body would shake as she stared at him, smiling, her eyes so filled with laughter they spilled tears. And Ella. Beautiful Ella. Why had Ben stopped talking to her—*really* talking to her? He couldn't remember.

There was so much he couldn't remember anymore.

2:35 p.m.

After leaving the Blue Express, Ella slowly drove up one street and down the next, looking for Ben, still fighting the knowing that she wasn't going to find him. After stopping home twice to see if he was there, she drove to the grocery store and parked. Izzy's class was having a celebration the next day, and though Ella couldn't for the life of her remember what it was for, she did remember her promise to Izzy. They were supposed to make cookies together after school for Izzy to bring the next day. Afraid that might not happen, Ella wanted to have a backup.

Before going in, Ella sat in the car and tried calling Ben again. After the fourth try, she was surprised to be able to leave a voicemail. She wondered if he had listened to her earlier messages or just deleted them. The Ben she knew would have listened closely, but she was becoming less sure of everything. "Please come home. It doesn't matter what it is, what happened. It'll be okay, Ben. Just please call me back. Not knowing where you are ... it's ..." She swallowed back the tears, trying to sound clear and strong. "Please call me."

She got out of the car and crossed the parking lot to the grocery store, her mind spinning, wondering what she should say to the kids when she picked them up from school.

In the bakery aisle, she stood staring at all the choices, trying to figure out which one Izzy would be excited about bringing in case it didn't work out for them to make the cookies.

"Ella?"

She looked up and froze. It was Asher from Ben's work. He seemed surprised to see her. And uncomfortable. Why was he so uncomfortable?

She tried to smile. "Hi, Asher." Did he know something about Ben? What did he know?

"So ... how are you?"

"I'm good," she said, feeling like her world had cracked open. "How are you? How's Teagen?"

"She's great, just opened another studio, so she's busy, got her hands full. But you know, that's how she is—go, go, go."

"That's good," Ella said, trying to be present, trying to mean what she was saying. "Tell her I said congratulations."

"I will. Thanks, Ella." He paused, hesitating like he was weighing something. "Hey. How's Ben doing?"

What did he mean? In what way? And why did he say it so carefully? "He's okay," she said, trying to sound convincing.

He seemed genuinely relieved. Too relieved. "Tell him I said hello, will you? We miss him. It's not the same without him."

Unable to translate her thoughts to words, to jump the gap between what he just said and what she knew—or thought she knew—she just nodded and tried to smile and not cry.

"Okay, well, I've got to get this back to the office," he said, holding up a bag of organic coffee beans.

Using all her strength, Ella just continued her forced smile until he finally said goodbye and hurried off.

She was relieved there was no basket to leave sitting in the aisle, nothing to put back on the shelves before she walked out of the store with a singular goal—to get to the car.

By the time she closed the door and laid her head back against the seat, the tears were falling quickly, and questions were coming so fast she couldn't grasp one without the next one tumbling right into it.

Ben had only been gone a few hours. *They missed him after a few hours?* It wasn't the same after *a few hours?*

It didn't make sense.

She looked at her phone. She had checked the texts as they came in but hadn't bothered reading them till now because they weren't from Ben. Ella wiped her eyes and started skimming the texts. The first was from Charlotte, asking if she had heard anything. The other two were from Thea, the boutique owner.

Shit.

She took a deep breath. Her mind raced with excuses and explanations. Which one would she—

Now her phone was ringing. Thea was getting impatient. Of course she was. Ella couldn't blame her. What should she say? Should she—

Just answer it.

"Hi, Ella. It's Thea. You got my texts?"

"I did. Yes. And … I'm so sorry, but something's happened, something personal, and I can't do it," she found herself saying, her honesty a surprise and a relief. "I'm so sorry."

"I don't understand. You need more time? I could *maybe* push it back a half hour, but that's it. I have a lot to do before tonight."

"No, I mean I can't have the necklace ready. There … won't be a necklace."

"I ordered it a *month* ago, Ella, and the party's tonight. You know that. What do you need? An hour?"

"I don't have a necklace to give you, Thea. I wish I could be saying something else to you right now. I'm so sorry." And then it came to her. "I have an idea. I can give you a gift certificate to give her … for twice the amount you paid for the necklace. She can choose her own stones and style … I'll make it according to her wishes directly."

When Thea didn't say anything, Ella continued to fill the silence. "Will that work? I wish I could explain. I know you deserve an explanation, but … I'm so sorry. Is there any way that'll work, Thea?"

She was about to start filling in another silence with whatever words came next when Thea finally said, "No, Ella, that won't work. Not at all. I'd like my money refunded in cash, delivered to my boutique before it closes today." She hung up before Ella could respond.

She had no time to dwell on Thea's response. Hopefully other clients would accept gift certificates or give her more time. She was clearly incapable of completing any of the orders due in the next few days. She was an entire day behind, never mind where her head was.

Ella got out of the car and walked to the ATM a block away. Her stomach turned as she depleted the majority of what was in their checking account. Just wanting to get it over with, she walked the few blocks to the boutique. She was relieved Thea wasn't there and that she could leave the money with the saleswoman, who had obviously been expecting Ella and now felt the same way about her as Thea did.

Walking back to the car, she focused on where her attention should be going next—getting safely to the kids' school to pick them up.

She turned on the car, put it in reverse, and backed out.

Maybe Ben would surprise her and be at the school.

7:17 p.m.

Three buses had come and gone, as had a handful of people. Ben was still on the bench, wondering who those people were, curious if he'd ever see any of them again: An old man, dressed formally, or at least not casually, in clothes from decades ago, unshaven. A teen with his hood up, over a baseball hat. Earplugs in. No way in, no way out. A man and a boy. Did they see him? he wondered. Did they wonder why he was sitting there taking up space on the bench before they got there—and why he was still sitting there taking up space after the bus pulled up, people got off, and everyone else got on?

And why was he seeing the two of them through a different lens than he saw the little girl and the mom whose hand she was holding? Why was it so close up? He couldn't back up—mentally or emotionally. Why were that man and that boy tugging at him, at his attention? What did they want from him?

And why were his legs so heavy? Why did they feel like they were two sizes too big for the rest of his body, like they were carrying something belonging to the boy with the hood and the man with the scruff?

He could call Ella. He *should* call Ella. Maybe it would take his mind off the heaviness in his legs that kept him on the bench, unable to stand.

He made a promise and then took out his phone. He had missed eleven calls from her. He hit send, and she picked up on the first ring.

"Something's wrong with my legs," he said. "It's like … they're so heavy." *What are you doing? Get a grip.* "I'm sorry. How are you? How are the kids?"

There was a long pause before she said, "We're okay. What do you mean they're heavy? Where are you?"

He looked to his right, then his left. *Who said that?* "They're sad … no, that's not right." He stopped. Listened. "The sadness is filling—it's so damn heavy and not just—"

"I'm going to come get you. Please tell me where you are, Ben, so I don't have to call the police or Jules or—"

"Why won't you believe me—that I just need space?"

"I believe you, but you need help, Ben. I'm not sure what's going on with you, but we'll figure it out. Please tell me where you are so I can come get you." He heard her calling to Izzy and Daxx, sounding distant, like she was covering the speaker on the phone. She was telling them they needed to go, to leave it, whatever it was, just to leave it and—she was hurrying them—*"Right now ... good. Good job, thank you."* She was talking to Ben now, clear, not muffled. "Okay. I'm in the car. I just need to know where to go. Where are you?"

Ben drummed his free hand on his knee, his leg jiggling—movement. *Fight or flight. Fly. Fight. Flap your wings.* He looked around for the source of the voice.

Ella's voice was muffled; she was talking to the children again.

His leg stopped bouncing. His body went still. He could see it, them pulling up, the kids waving through the window before they had even pulled to a stop, eager to get out of their seat belts and scamper out of the car, running to him, him holding his arms out to them and gathering them in a hug.

And then he would have to face Ella. *Oh, Ella ...*

And then what?

He maneuvered his focus and reminded himself of his promise.

He took a deep breath and slowly exhaled. "I quit working at Starfish almost a month ago," he said. "Well ... okay ... no, I didn't technically quit. That's not true. I left after a meeting and never went back—or ... I guess I haven't been back since. I'm sorry I didn't tell you."

He pushed through the guilt he felt for taking advantage of her shocked silence and added one more thing: "You said you'd call people. I hope you don't. It's not like that. Please, Ella. I just need time."

He turned off his phone and stood up.

8:32 p.m.

After grounding herself with a mantra—*I'm here, and it's where I need to be right now*—Ella closed the curtains and switched on the circular rotating lamp that projected stars across Izzy and Daxx's room as they slept. She had read to them and had brushed Izzy's hair for her, way longer than normal because of how calming it was for both of them. As they had gone through their nightly routine, she felt keenly aware of Daxx and Izzy, of their presence, of them being there, almost as if she was watching herself interact with them.

"Good night, sweet pea," she said to Izzy, kissing her on the forehead and tucking her in, trying to pretend this was just a normal night and their father wasn't gone and hadn't lied to her for the past month—maybe longer. She did her best to genuinely smile and ignore the fact that Ben had quit his job and taken off, walking or hitchhiking, somewhere on some road, sounding so off ... really off ... like ...

Turning to the other bed, she kissed Daxx and said, "Sweet dreams, little one."

"Is Dad home yet?" Izzy said.

Daxx pulled his covers off and jumped out of bed. "Dad!" he said.

There was no question in his statement, and his excitement was so palpable Ella's stomach flipped. She turned around, sure she'd see Ben in the doorway, hoping, realizing in that moment—but no. Just the mention of his dad had triggered the excited response from Daxx; there was simply no containing his emotions, especially when he felt the strong ones.

Ella knelt down, fighting back tears, and said, "Come here, my little artichoke," pulling Daxx into a tight hug. She rested her head against his brown curls. Then, positioning him in the crook of her left arm, she motioned for Izzy to join them. But of course—Izzy didn't mess with tuck-ins, even now at the age of seven. She barely moved once the tuck-in was done, not wanting to "break it." Izzy seemed to be looking right through Ella, patient and waiting, as if she already knew how this was all going to play out.

Ella forced a smile. "You know how Dad sometimes goes away for work?"

Daxx put his head on Ella's shoulder.

Izzy nodded.

"Well," Ella said, "he's on another trip. A different kind this time. And it's a big one, so he's going to let us know when he's on his way back."

"Can we meet him there?" Izzy asked. They had once met Ben after a conference he had in San Francisco, making a family trip out of it.

Ella shook her head. "No ... you know how when you play with your pet dragon, you like to be left alone because if we try to play, we don't hear things right or see things right, and we mess it up? That's kind of what it's like. Dad needs to do this alone."

As Ella finished tucking them in and saying good night, she couldn't ignore the growing discomfort inside her. Why had she made that analogy?

10:16 p.m.

Ben wasn't expecting any cars on the dirt road that began where the pavement ended, so when a yellow pickup truck approached from behind him an hour or so after he started walking and then slowed to a stop, he cautiously approached the open passenger window.

"Are you lost?" the driver asked.

Ben guessed she was in her seventies. But her eyes. There was something about them. It was like her eyes were laughing at him.

"I'm ..." Ben looked around. "I'm just—I'm good, thank you." He started backing away, giving a wave.

She seemed to hesitate, watching him closely. "You don't look so good ... pardon my saying, of course."

He winced from the sudden throbbing in his head, and as the pain moved into his ears, it sharpened.

"Okay then, friend," she finally said before slowly driving off.

Ben resumed walking, his steps a little slower, a little less sure.

"Why can't people just mind their own business," he mumbled, turning his focus back to the dirt road, the desert and hills, the dusty greens and browns and grays.

Day 2, Wednesday

1:24 a.m.

E lla sat up in bed. Ben was having an affair. There was no other explanation. She threw the covers off, turned on the light, and went over to the dresser.

Go on.

Pulling out each of his three drawers, one after the other, she rummaged through, lifting folded T-shirts, pushing around rolled-up socks, and fighting the nausea that was rising. Even though she was terrified of the evidence she might find, she pushed on, needing to know.

She shoved aside the fact that they never snuck a peek at each other's phones or computers or journals. That was before. That was when they were both playing by the rules.

Go get his journal.

Ignoring the nudge that kept getting louder, she moved from the dresser to the closet, checking pockets, sniffing shirts, doing what she had seen people do in the movies, feeling nothing like herself and finding nothing that meant anything.

That's where it'll be.

Ella closed the closet.

You need answers. You have every right to know what's going on.

Ben liked to write in the backyard, so he kept his journal on the shelf in the kitchen, next to his favorite mug, the one Izzy had made for him.

Ella walked slowly down the hall, pausing and looking in as she passed Daxx and Izzy's room, then through the living room, reminding herself she wasn't sneaking around—she lived here—into the kitchen. The light of the moon was enough. She leaned over the counter and took down his journal. The last time she held it was when she gave it to him.

She sat at the table, the journal in front of her. Turning and looking at the door, panic rose at the thought of him walking in right then.

And then a wave of relief came over her.

There was still time.

Come back, Ben. Come back so I don't have to do this. She looked down at the worn cover and traced the leather edges.

There's no turning back if you do this, you have no other way of knowing, don't do it, he left you with no choice …

She turned the journal over, then set it right again.

The ticking of the second hand on the clock merged with her pounding heartbeat, and her memory whisked her back to when they were dating. She was at the apartment he had just moved into, sitting on the living room floor; he had hardly any furniture yet. As she texted Andy, giving him advice about how to make up with his girlfriend, she noticed a heavily used, thick spiral notebook a few feet away, next to the piles of books and open but unpacked boxes. She glanced down the hall to the closed bathroom door. The shower was still running. Without thinking much about it, she leaned over and picked up the notebook. Then opened it. Time blurred as she flipped to a random page, saw her name, and stepped into his version of a night two weeks before. It felt terribly unsettling and chaotic, falling into his perception, exploring his frustration with her, and discovering the comparisons that came from the deepest recesses of his mind. It was like looking at herself in a carnival mirror. It was all wrong. It was bent and skewed. She glanced up from the journal. Outside the open bathroom, Ben stood there looking at her in a way she'd never forget.

Thinking of it now made her shudder. Ella looked at the front door, willing it to open, begging Ben to walk in *then*, right then, before she had no choice but to open his journal.

She unwound the leather strap that held the book tightly closed, her palms sweating.

"If you ever do anything like that again, there's no us— we're over," he had said to her. This came days after distance, apologies, and explanations about how her parents had always read her diaries and used what she wrote against her, and still she kept writing in them. She knew no other way. It was her normal. Ben finally got through to her how messed up that was and guaranteed her, "I'll never do that to you. *Never*. And you can't do it to anyone else ever again—*anyone*, Ella." It wasn't hard for her to make that promise. Once was enough. It had been a sickening feeling reading those sentences in his journal. It wasn't just the distortion of what he had written about her in comparison to her self-perception; it was also the act of trespassing into someone's mind, a place that—she had always known on some level—should be free from outside judgment. In the years that followed, she and Ben made sure their home was a place where no one had to worry about privacy. Izzy could leave her diary on the floor; she didn't need to bother locking it. Daxx could leave his feelings coloring book on his bed; no one would open it. And Ben and Ella could leave their journals anywhere. No one would even think of touching them.

This is different.

She took a long, deep breath, then slowly let it out. She closed her eyes and felt the weight of his journal in her hands. All those words. All those answers.

Turning toward the door again, she imagined it opening, him standing there. She saw the confusion in his face—then the realization. She heard the weakness in the justifications she would use. She heard herself trying to convince herself as much as she would be trying to convince him.

Deciding she'd rather sit with the havoc-wreaking unknowns than feel what it was like to trespass into his mind again, she refastened the strap and put the book back on the shelf. For now—just for now.

As she took the car keys from the counter, she began rationalizing leaving Izzy and Daxx at home while she drove around looking for Ben. She could make a list of hotels and motels within walking distance, go to each one until she found him. One by one, she'd stop in, have a look for herself, then ask someone who worked there … What would she ask? Had a man with Ben's description checked in? Would they even tell her? What if he hadn't checked in anywhere because he had somewhere to go? Someone's house. Someone's apartment.

It was all wrong. It was all *so* wrong.

Maybe he felt guilty. Maybe he realized what a huge mistake he had made and ended the … whatever it was. Where would he go? Would he sleep on a park bench? What about the beach?

The truth was she couldn't even guess where he might have gone. That bothered her more than the thought of leaving the children at home while she went to look for him, which she found disturbing—but so much was disturbing right then that she couldn't place where on the spectrum of disturbing it went.

She put the keys in her pocket. She would wake up the children and get them in the car. They'd go right back to sleep. Why hadn't she thought of that before?

She hurried to her room, put shoes on, pulled a sweater over her pajamas, and started back down the hallway.

She stopped.

Come on! What's wrong with you?

She pushed Izzy and Daxx's door open a little wider, still not stepping in their room. It was back again—that knowing that she wouldn't find him.

Why did it feel so wrong to wake up the children, to leave the house?

Was it because Ben was about to come home? Was he about to walk in the door? And if she left, she would miss him?

Ella stayed in the hallway, watching Daxx and Izzy sleep, waiting for the front door to open, and as fatigue set in, her thoughts drifted from questions about Ben and when he would walk in to the costume she needed to make for the play Izzy was in. As an animated tree, she'd need a trunk and branches that allowed easy, free movements of her arms and legs. Ella considered the options. Thinking about which material she could use to give the costume a shimmering, magical feel made her wonder how expensive the costume was going to end up being, which led her directly to *What was he doing all those hours he wasn't working? A mistress. Who calls them that? A whore. Stop it. You don't know. You don't know anything—clearly. Calm down.* If he hadn't worked this past month, what did that mean? Was he on leave? *Don't you get it?* Would there be a paycheck? If not, how would she pay the mortgage?

Ella closed her eyes and swallowed tears, holding her emotions tightly inside. *This is* not *happening. How could he do that!*

He wouldn't.

Nothing made sense.

Nothing felt right.

Finally, she continued down the hall, opened the front door, and checked outside. Stillness. He hadn't come home. He wasn't sitting there on the step in the moonlight, thinking of ways to apologize before coming in.

She went back to bed, staring at Ben's empty pillow, tears pooling until her eyelids were too heavy to keep open.

3:06 a.m.

Ben had no idea how long he had been walking through the desert toward the foothills. When sleep beckoned, he moved a good twenty steps off the unpaved road into an open space between the wild brush and lay down right there on the ground. He wasn't worried about scorpions or snakes or coyotes because he felt toxic, and he had a comforting feeling that any creature would sense that and stay far away. Not all of him felt toxic—approximately half. A month ago, he would have said 80 percent of him. Now his toxicity level was closer to 50 percent. He could feel it. It was progress, and he was glad for it. Still, this fifty-fifty, this standoff between the two sides of him had deepened. Neither side was budging. Ben felt stuck in the middle— and on both sides. At least when he slept, there seemed to be a temporary truce.

Sometimes after he fell asleep, the sensation of something crawling over his hand woke him, and his eyes opened to the stars straight above, everything around him cloaked in darkness. Whatever had been on his hand continued on its way. The desert was so quiet and cold, so still now. It was perfect. Finally he was far enough. Finally he was alone enough. And most importantly, finally it wouldn't matter. He could say anything. No one would hear. Both sides of him could say anything they wanted to the massive night sky. It would be as if none of it was ever said, any of it. It would just get absorbed into the dirt beneath him or carried away on the wind. He wouldn't have to worry about how it sounded, how it was heard, or what he actually meant to say.

He would get it all out. *Finally.* And then maybe he'd know what to do next.

But as soon as he gave himself permission to let it out, to speak to the night, he felt overwhelmingly tired, and the last thought that went through his head before he fell asleep again was a fear just then being realized: he had nothing to say—not a single word worth listening to, because everything he said could be canceled out by another part of him.

5:55 a.m.

Ella picked up the framed photo from her dresser—the one of the four of them at Sand Dollar, their favorite beach. Ben was on his knees, leaning forward, carefully placing seaweed in the sand dragon's mouth. Ella was laughing in the picture, taken by Charlotte right when Izzy and Daxx were trying to convince her that the dragon was spitting fire, not eating. The more she stared at the picture, the more she missed everyone in it. She put it down.

Last night felt like a blur, but even just two hours of sleep had brought some clarity: First, there was a reason why—up until last night—she had never once worried about Ben having an affair. He wouldn't do that. And if he proved her wrong, she wouldn't even know where to begin to collect her shattered sense of knowing again. So she decided to take the chance of believing what she was pretty sure she knew, at least about that. Second, one of the best decisions she had ever made was to not open his journal.

Lifting the shade all the way to let in the rising sun, she felt confident everything would be okay. Ben would come back this morning, and she'd finally get answers. Everything would make sense, their world would be right again, and she would never again take for granted Ben being there. She would talk to him for real—find out what was really going on. They'd work through it—whatever it was—together.

Until then, she would start researching counselors. Ben might try to convince her it was unnecessary, but she would put her foot down, assuring him he *did* need someone to help him get things back under control. Of course, he'd need to get in touch with Starfish right away too, get that whole mess figured out, apologize, do whatever was necessary for them to take him back. Immediately. They had a little savings she could use to pay the bills stacking up in her inbox, but losing another paycheck was not an option.

It took no time to make the bed. She had forgotten how little it got messed up when just one person slept there. What next? was the question. Should she take a shower? Or should she get to work finding that counselor? She looked at the time. She had an hour and a half before she needed to wake up the kids. Just as she went to grab her phone, it rang. It was Ben. She had been right; today was going to be way better than yesterday.

She had barely said hello before he cut in with "Listen, I'm sorry. I'm calling to apologize and because my phone's running out of battery, and of all the things I need to tell you, this one's actually important. I wasn't thinking. Or I was trying not to. I didn't realize I kept you waiting. I'm so sorry. If I had thought about it, I wouldn't have done it, but I just wasn't thinking. It's just that I've made this promise— No. *Shoot.* Sorry. Okay …"

"Ben—"

"Okay, so as I was saying, I was calling to apologize for being rude. I just have to take it one step at a time, not to play games or make you crazy—*shit.* Shit. Sorry. That's not what I wanted to say. Not at all what I meant by—"

"Ben," she said calmly but determined to have her say, "take your time. I'm here. I'm not going anywhere. Just take your time." She took a deep breath, hoping he would do the same.

"I just need to stay clear," he said, "to keep everything clear in my head because things aren't so clear anymore, and so I need to tell you that I've been at a bike shop for the past few weeks when I said I was at work. I'm sorry." Suddenly sounding more like himself, he said, "Please give the kids a hug from me. Tell them I miss them. And I miss their mom. And I love her. And you—you three—you're everything, all that matters to me." And then just as quickly, "It's just that there are so many other hearts, and I can hear them. And I know that doesn't make sense to you. I *know* it. I can hear my words as I say them, and they're so far from what I mean. This is why—shit, shit, shit. This isn't working. I have to go."

He disconnected the call.

Ella put the phone on the dresser and slowly stepped back. Turning to the bed, she pulled the covers back, climbed in, and curled up deep under them. Her head on his pillow, her quick, cut-off breaths were unable to catch up with the blinding tears that came easily now.

7:05 a.m.

Fast asleep, Ben's eyes flickered, and his body involuntarily jerked. A blurry circle filled his field of vision, surrounded on the edges by a mess of faces showing exaggerated emotions, all kinds of emotions—not really believable, his dream self decided—until he was jolted away from that judgment as if slapped.

Look.

He tried to ignore the emotional faces and focus on the blurry center, but he could only look closer at them. Their heartbeats grew louder, merging into a chaotic mix of offbeat bongo drums—until it was suddenly punctuated by a loud ringing, the blurry center now gone, a vibrating gong in its place.

Ben jolted awake in a cold sweat. There was no escape. Asleep, awake, it was all the same now.

7:30 a.m.

Ella's timer went off. She put away the pens, wax, and stamps and placed the four gift certificates in a pile. They weren't made out to anyone yet. They were just in case. She would get it together. She'd be able to put things together rather than rip them apart—soon. Very soon. This was just in case, she reminded herself again. She left her studio and went down the hall to the children's room.

"Good morning, my little sunshine," she said quietly, kneeling next to Daxx's bed. He opened his eyes right away, as if he'd been waiting for her, and smiled like it was going to be the best day ever. When he reached over and pulled her in for a hug, which he did not only every morning but also every time he said hi or goodbye, she marveled at the love that was always bubbling up and spilling from him. He didn't use a lot of words, but his eyes and his smile and his body language spoke so loudly. She knew his voice just hadn't caught up yet.

"Hi, Mom."

She turned around. Izzy was sitting on the edge of her bed, looking wide awake and eager to start her day.

"Hi, my angel," Ella said, giving her a hug. "Ready to get up and have a great day?"

Izzy nodded. "Miss Janet's bringing her guitar, and she's going to teach us a new song. After that, we're going to paint the …"

Ella didn't mean to tune her out; she just couldn't stop wondering when either one of them was going to remember that their dad wasn't home. Would it be during breakfast when they noticed he hadn't left a joke on the table for them? Maybe she had been more convincing than she thought last night; maybe, for them, this was no different from Ben being away on a work trip.

Going through the morning routine, it struck Ella how much there was to absorb, all that took place in this room every morning when Izzy and Daxx woke up to their world. Time was going so quickly; they were babies just yesterday.

Their enthusiasm was so pure and so innocent, and they were so vulnerable, and it was her job to take care of them and protect them—and fiercely love them.

And they needed their dad. Maybe not today. Or even tomorrow. But they needed their dad. *Ben.* Not just any dad. Because he was the perfect dad for both of them. Ben had told Ella hundreds of times that he was born to find and spend the rest of his life with her, and she almost always believed that. But what she never questioned, what she knew without a doubt was that he had been born to be Izzy and Daxx's father.

Who else would have known how to comfort Daxx when he was inconsolable after his turtle died? While Ella had tried making his favorite food, macaroni and cheese, reading his favorite book at the time, *Moosey Moose*, and taking him to the park, all those attempts were just flimsy Band-Aids. It was Ben who came up with the idea of making a "Tribute to Timmy the Turtle" scrapbook. So they all sat around the kitchen table drawing pictures of their favorite memories of Timmy. Slowly, Daxx relaxed into it. A little more than an hour later, Daxx questioned Ben's last few pictures; he had just noticed them. Daxx said he didn't remember Timmy flying a kite or going down a water slide or eating popcorn.

"Well, of course you don't remember," Ben had said. "It's happening *right now*. I think we're coming to the end of the pages for the scrapbook, so I figured we should draw some pictures of what Timmy's doing now in Turtletopia." He'd said it with such a serious face.

And then Ben had asked Daxx, "What else do you think Timmy's doing there? I hear it's a pretty awesome place." And that was that. By the time the scrapbook was stapled together, Daxx was clapping his hands, so excited for Timmy's new adventures and all the turtle friends he was meeting in Turtletopia.

And when Izzy didn't want to go back to school because of the boy who was mean, nothing Ella or Ben said gave her any confidence in herself or in the situation getting better—until Ben suddenly shared something, a trick he claimed he used all the time, one that always worked. After he explained, Izzy, clearly not convinced, said, "That's *all*? Just picture him with an ice-cream cone?"

"Well no, of course not," Ben had said. "You have to really use your imagination. Sometimes he goes to lick it, and the ice cream falls off, slides down his favorite shirt, and lands right on the ground, and now he's just got a cone. Oh! I forgot to tell you! And you have a banana split." Izzy smiled. "And his cone is *really* soggy." Daxx giggled. "But that's not all. Sometimes when you see him at school and picture him with a cone, you'll imagine that the ice cream was dipped in chocolate and sprinkles. On those days, it might feel good just to picture him smiling. And other times, you might just picture him holding an ice-cream cone and leave it at that, moving on to other things ... *really important things* ... like figuring out what one ocean said to the other ocean ..."

"Nothing!" Izzy and Daxx said together, having already memorized that morning's joke. "It just waved!"

"Exactly!" Ben said. Then he looked at Izzy for a long moment and smiled. "You get to decide, Izzy. It's your world; he's just a part of it."

Izzy was actually excited to go to school the next day—and every day after that.

And Ella had fallen deeper in love.

8:10 a.m.

Ben made a decision. It was now or never.

He stood up and started pacing. *Just let it out, whatever you're thinking, no one's here, just let it out, and it'll get sorted out ...*

Silence.

Damn it. Why was he so scared? It made no sense.

Kneeling down, he wanted so badly to be someone else, someone bold and stupid enough to bang his head against the ground to dislodge the warring thoughts and stubborn refusal to speak them. Someone brave enough to spit the words out. Instead, he looked up and watched a hawk fly over him. His eyes were so heavy, just like his legs had been.

9:15 a.m.

Charlotte had sent a text insisting Ella stop by the real estate office, whatever time worked for her. Ella finally agreed to, realizing she needed to talk to someone instead of keeping everything jumbled inside.

The receptionist greeted Ella, and before she could even direct her to Charlotte, she came around the corner. After hugging Ella and relieving her of one of the coffees she was carrying, Charlotte led her through the office, out the back door to the patio. They sat on a bench in the sun.

"Thanks for bringing these," Charlotte said with a nod to the coffee and croissant. "You're a good friend. And I'm going to be straight with you because I'm a good friend too. The best. Ready?"

"Okay," Ella said.

"How are you not freaking out? I don't understand. We're going on twenty-four hours since Ben waltzed out of work, announcing to you that he's going on some sort of walkabout, and look at you! You're bringing *me* coffee and breakfast. I think you might be in denial about—"

"He didn't leave work yesterday."

"What?"

"It's been a month. Or it might be three weeks."

"Wait …"

"I know. It's hard to keep the details straight. Between things that don't make sense, and trying to get a word in before he hangs up, and listening for clues of where he might be, it all kind of blurs, and I wonder if what I heard is what he actually said. But this one I'm pretty sure about— that he hasn't been going to work."

"A month? He stopped going to work *a month* ago?"

"Apparently. He's been going to a bike shop instead."

Charlotte took a napkin from the bag and wiped her mouth. *"What?"*

"I can't figure it out. Why would someone who's never shown any interest in riding a bike—"

"Not only that," Charlotte cut in. "I don't know anyone who gets more heated talking about bikes and cars sharing the same road space. Bikes and Ben don't go together. Why would he hang out at a bike shop?"

Ella shook her head. "I have no idea." She sat back and took a deep breath.

"I can't wrap my head around this, so I can't even imagine what it's like for you," Charlotte said. She put her coffee on the ground and turned so she was facing Ella. "You don't have to be so strong. I know you need to keep your shit together for the kids—in front of them—but with me, you don't have to do that. It's safe. You can lean on me. I want you to know that. You're not alone. You don't have to do this alone."

"I just can't stop thinking about … Ben doesn't lie. But he *did*. I can't even …"

Charlotte's face confirmed Ella's concern—it was so un-Ben.

"For the past month, he's *pretended* to go to work. What was he doing at a bike shop? Why didn't he tell me that he—" Swallowing a sudden torrent of tears, she took a moment.

Charlotte was quiet.

"Why would he lie to me?" Ella said, wiping her eyes. "What was so …" She turned to Charlotte. "What would make him do that?"

"I know. It doesn't sound like him—at all." Charlotte stood up and started pacing. "Are you sure he lied though? Did you guys talk about work? Like when he came home, did he tell you about his day?"

Ella's mind started spinning.

"Because I'm thinking back, thinking about the conversations between the three of us the last few Friday nights. Okay, not that I can remember everything, but he laughed off a lot … and spent plenty of time focusing on me having had the shortest marriage ever and telling me I had better things to do than hang out with the two of you—were you in the room when he said that? I was like, 'Do you not know me at all?' And then the other thing is he went to bed early *a lot*. More than he used to, I think."

When Charlotte finally stopped pacing, Ella looked at her. "He said that? That you had better things to do than to hang out with us?"

Charlotte's eyes softened as she sat back down. "It was probably his way of trying to get rid of me. He's *crazy* about you, Ella."

"I know he is, but …" She pushed past the strong feeling she should change the direction of the conversation and instead went on with "I'm so embarrassed. I kind of had a breakdown last night, thinking maybe Ben was having an affair, that that's what this was all about, what he can't tell me. It was horrible. For so long before finally getting out of bed, I just lay there thinking, *What are the chances this has something to do with someone else?*"

It was something about how Charlotte said, "Zero. The chances are *zero*," that gave Ella pause and made her forget what she was about to say.

She tried to think of what to say to continue the conversation, but her mind had gone blank, and her stomach was suddenly in knots.

Unable to think of an excuse for leaving, Ella just said, "Sorry, I have to go"—so quickly there was only time for a one-armed hug and a half-hearted promise to call later.

For the second time in twenty-four hours, Ella had one goal: get to the car, open the door, get inside, and close the door.

10:09 a.m.

Ben was confident the hawk looked like a hawk, whatever a hawk was supposed to look like. He, on the other hand, had looked less like himself with every day that passed; he was certain. Didn't anyone notice? Were Ella and the kids just being nice?

He made a circle in the dirt with the toe of his shoe, round and round like the hawk's path above.

Who did he look like? he wondered. *Someone.* Someone he knew. Someone he was familiar with.

No name or face came to mind—just vagueness. A blur. It felt accurate.

He picked up a rock and tried to skip it across the ground. It didn't work.

One thing was for sure. He was *not* going to go back to confiding in the hawk. In fact, he decided, he was glad the hawk wasn't talking back to him. "I don't want you to anyway!" he yelled up to it. "You just ... just keep going around and around ... and around." He sat down, his thirst deepening. "I do it all the goddamn time."

As he watched the hawk dip and swerve, a thought occurred to him. He pulled his wallet from his back pocket, opened it, and took out a handful of bills. He lifted his arm as high as he could reach it, straining, pushing his hand, waving the money. The hawk seemed to come closer, inspecting. "Come on! Take it!"

When the hawk seemed uninterested, Ben went to put the money back but then let it go, not caring where the wind took it.

"You don't give a flying fuck," he said to the hawk. He slapped the ground. "Ha! Did you hear that?"

He looked down and quietly explained, "A flying ... and you're up there flying ..." The hawk wouldn't get it.

He watched the hawk change directions and circle back around. He wondered what it was like, how the hawk made its decisions.

The hawk flapped its massive wings, then soared a ways before flapping them again. Were the hawk and the winds on the same team? Did they want the same thing?

Was the hawk's motivation anything but survival?

Ben stood up and started walking in circles again, one foot over the other, tight ones first, then wider and bigger.

Shit. How could he be losing himself even more than he already had? What was he doing wrong?

He was so bad at this—whatever this was. Anyone— *anyone in the entire world*—could do it better than he was.

He stopped and looked around, wondering which direction the road was in, which direction he had come from. Turning all the way around, a hill in the distance caught his attention. He turned away from it but quickly felt pulled to look back in its direction. What was it? Why was it tugging at him?

He began walking again, not in circles now but toward the hill, one foot in front of the other ...

Is smart still called smart if it becomes manipulative? Or is it something else then? Does it get a different name?

Deliberately zigzagging from side to side ...

"Oh, that's not really a lie ... I just left a few things out."

Just tell the truth. Tell the goddamn truth.

Fine. You want to know? Okay. Here you go.

I love what it's like.

Know what else? I want to punch myself.

Do it then.

Ben stopped. He hit his cheek. Then he did it again, a little more accurately this time, more aware of the angle needed.

Do it again.

No.

I was talking. I was talking, and you ...

I was saying something. I was saying I can't stand being so arrogant, but still ... being the one, the one they rely on ...

Walking from side to side, letting each opposing thought turn him and pull him in the opposite direction, he kept going.

I love my reputation. Okay? I love it, and at the same time, it's not the one I want—not even close.

"Do you see?" he yelled up to the hawk, who seemed to be keeping its distance. "Do you *see?*"

Ben kept going. One direction, then abruptly the next. Finally. Finally something was matching his thoughts. His movement. It matched. And he wasn't going in circles.

"Ha!" he yelled.

They're great, I love 'em all, every one of them—okay, you're right. Honesty. Okay, most of them. And I despise them as much as I despise myself. Yes, that's true.

Good.

And I love doing what I'm good at, and I hate not doing anything I feel like I'm supposed to be doing, and I love the security, and I hate how confined I actually am, truly, truly, truly, if anyone actually wants to know, and I love the freedom, but I know I'm only pretending to use it. Freaking pretender. And the prestige. Of course I love it. Of course I want to gobble it up. I'd eat it right now. Then spit it out. I hate how it makes me feel when no one's looking but me. And I love that they ask me, it's me they ask—and I hate how easy it is to shut myself up and not tell them anything and ... I ... I ...

He ran out of words.

It was a start. He knew he wasn't getting down to what it was all about—he understood he wasn't ready to go there yet—but at least he was telling the truth. At least he was keeping that promise to himself.

And even if the hawk knew what he was thinking, there were no repercussions.

10:22 a.m.

A half hour after closing the door, Ella was still sitting in her car down the street from Charlotte's office. She was still going over her options. All she had decided was she would not go back and ask Charlotte why she said what she said the way she did. Ella didn't care. She didn't even want to know. So what if Charlotte had been texting her the past half hour, encouraging her to come back and talk, then pleading, then apologizing for upsetting her however she might have upset her—because clearly she did. Ella had enough to deal with.

She needed to figure out what to do about Ben. She could go to the school, pull the kids out—no, go home first, pack a few things, *then* go to the school, pull the kids out, and follow through with what she had planned to do last night: drive around till they found Ben. He couldn't have gone far. Unless he had ... Either way, they didn't need to stay there and wait for him to come back. There had to be a way to find him. Because certainly she wasn't the first person whose husband just walked away one day and then kept on walking. She could go to the police, get their input. Get some direction. She could find him—she would find him—and then, yes, she decided, she and Ben and Izzy and Daxx—they didn't even have to come back to this town. The four of them could start driving to who knew where and just keep going. Together. As long as they were together.

But first, there was one question she needed answered.

She turned the key in the ignition, her next destination finally clear.

10:42 a.m.

The hawk had flown off, and a fly had taken its place. It kept circling Ben, buzzing like it was trying to get his attention, as if it didn't already have it.

The fly hovered in front of him now.

Ben had no idea what to think. His mind wasn't nearly as loud now.

Clearly not content with something, the fly started zipping around him again.

Ben had let both sides have their say. One zigzag after another. There was no winner. But at least now it was better than what it felt like in those terrifying seconds right before voicing some of the truths he had been so scared to admit.

The chaos was still alive in him though, his fear begging him not to get *too* clear.

Where would it leave him if he gave in to what the moment called for? *This moment.*

The question lingered.

He had dipped his toe in.

It had taken courage. He felt it as it was happening, as he was telling himself the truth—he felt in-the-moment courage.

There was something about the way the fly kept dive-bombing at him and around him, with such an annoying urgency. It wouldn't let up even as Ben repeatedly swatted at it and tried to move away.

Finally, Ben stopped. He stood still. He put his hands down by his sides.

The fly slowed down.

It was time, Ben realized. He had to decide what to do with this moment. To back up, jump over the edge, or purposely fall in.

10:59 a.m.

It was now or never. Ella had sat in the parked car long enough, and she had already driven by the two other bike shops, several times. Something kept bringing her back to this one.

Something.

Something had made her offer Thea the gift certificate for twice the amount she paid for the necklace.

Something was telling her she wouldn't find Ben, no matter where she looked for him.

Something had told her to get up and leave the conversation with Charlotte—right then.

Something in Ella was speaking loud and clear, and following its lead was the only thing that felt right.

The bell chimed as Ella opened the door. She tried to appear patient as she surveyed the shop filled with old bikes and new ones. She perused slowly, brushing her hand against the handlebars of one bike, the seat of the next one. The guy who worked there was taking his time with the only other customer in the store.

Ella listened as the woman went back and forth, trying to decide between the yellow beach cruiser with the basket and the refurbished bike with the blue and white flower designs. She began listing the pros and cons, wondering which one her daughter would like more. The guy who worked there followed up with questions, helping her navigate the choice.

"I'll be with you in a minute," he said to Ella.

A good seven minutes later, Ella's nervousness intensified when the woman left, having decided she couldn't decide; she needed to bring her daughter in rather than getting the bike as a surprise. Finally, the man turned his attention to Ella.

"Hi." Ella tried to smile.

"Sorry about the wait," he said, his tone genuine. "How can I help you?"

She realized she should have spent every second since she walked in figuring out what she was going to say. "I ..." She looked away and swallowed hard as tears suddenly spilled. Where could she possibly begin? "Sorry," she said, putting a finger up to ask for a moment.

"That's okay," he said, the concern in his voice obvious. He went over to the water cooler, filled a paper cup, then came back and handed it to Ella. "This might help."

She thanked him and drank the water. When she was finished, he took the empty cup and tossed in the garbage next to the counter, then turned back to her, the concern still evident in his face.

"It's my husband—" she started.

After another bout of tears she couldn't hold in, Ella apologized again, then said, her voice shaky, "I'm pretty sure he's been coming here ... for the past few weeks." She cleared her throat and took a deep breath. "I was wondering if you know him, if you've seen him here."

"What did you say your name was?"

"I'm sorry. Ella. I'm Ella." She put her hand out, and he shook it.

"I'm Ethan. Nice to meet you, Ella. So, your husband?"

"Yes ... I guess I'm wondering if you noticed a guy showing up here about a month ago and then coming back a lot, maybe every day—I don't know. I'm not sure. Maybe hanging out, looking at bikes or ... or sitting on the ground outside your shop or ... just ... acting strangely."

She was about to describe what Ben looked like when Ethan said, "No, he wasn't doing any of that."

"He was here then. So you know him? You know Ben?"

"Yeah, I know him," he said.

"And ... how do you know him? How ... what was he doing here?"

Ethan was looking at Ella, clearly weighing his options and deciding something.

"I've got some work to do," he finally said, "but come on back." He headed toward the back of the one-room shop and got settled on a crate in front of a bike frame, pieces and parts scattered around him. He gestured to another crate. "Pull up a seat."

Her heart beating hard, she made her way to the turned-over crate and sat down.

11:07 a.m.

It didn't take long. Ben decided to fall into the moment, directly into it, wherever it took him. That way, he wouldn't have to go back—because he couldn't, there was no way— and he didn't have to figure out how to go forward.

He didn't care about getting it right anymore.

He was done trying to force things.

He gave himself to the moment, handing all control over to it, surrendering to it.

He stopped pacing and lay down on the dirt, facing the sky. He moved his palms back and forth over the earth, feeling it, clumping handfuls and then releasing it. He noticed the sharpness and bumps of the uneven ground under his back. He didn't fight it; he felt no need to fix it or change it.

The heaviness began to dissipate, and the words in his head got quieter and fewer.

Everything he had been holding onto fell off of him, piece by unnamed piece, seeping down into the ground underneath him, deeper and deeper.

It felt good lying there, suspended in the moment of now, between the earth below, grounding him and supporting him, and the sky above him, calming and mesmerizing as the wispy clouds slowly changed shape and position, moving into and out of the sky they were a part of.

Relaxed now, on the brink of sleep, he suddenly felt a strong nudge. Something inside him was offering him direction. It was a new moment. He could feel it.

Again he gave into it, letting go of reason or needing to understand, following the nudge and nothing else.

He stood up, found the road, and started walking in a direction he gave no thought to, focusing only on the moment of now and how to give into it, whatever it asked for.

11:12 a.m.

As Ethan sanded down the bike frame, he said, "Ben came in a few weeks ago. I could tell right away he wasn't here for a bike. After running this place as long as I have, I've gotten pretty good at reading the people who come through that door. We got to talking, and I could tell he didn't know a thing about bikes." He laughed, shaking his head. "But he said he wanted to learn about them, how they worked. He wanted to watch them being taken apart and put back together. At first, I thought he wanted a job, but he said no, he'd be happy to help and didn't want to get paid."

All Ella wanted was for him to keep talking, to tell her anything and everything. "So he came back?"

"Every day since—except weekends." He leaned forward, blew the dust off the frame, and gently wiped it with a cloth. He looked closer, rubbed his fingers over a small section, and then replaced the worn sandpaper with a new piece and continued sanding. "Until yesterday and now today. I was wondering where he was. I'm glad you came in because we never did get around to talking money, but I have a check for him." His face serious, he said, "He's been a huge help; there's no way I'm not paying him."

Ella was trying to figure out which of her questions she should ask next when her phone rang. Seeing it was the kids' school, she excused herself, standing up and moving a few feet away.

After a quick greeting, Mrs. Parker said, "Ella, I just wanted to let you know that—out of nowhere—Daxx seems to have developed a stutter, a pretty intense one. It just started in class this morning, and I was wondering if you noticed it at home before he came to school."

When Ella said no, she had never heard him stutter— ever—Mrs. Parker reassured her that it was going to be fine, she was sure, but she wanted to know, had anything stressful happened at home for Daxx?

"Uh ..." *Tell the truth.* "Yes ... things have been a little rough the past day or so, not before that though ... I don't think." She turned, gave a half wave to Ethan, and made her way outside.

"Just a day or so ... oh my," Mrs. Parker said. "Whatever it is must be very big in Daxx's little world."

When Ella didn't say anything, Mrs. Parker continued, "Let's keep an eye on this. Not to worry. It'll likely pass once he's adjusted to whatever's causing the stutter. My advice, if you'll have it, is just to be extremely patient with him. Assure him he can take whatever time he needs to get his words out. And I'll let you know if I notice anything else."

"Have you ever seen this before? Is it normal?"

"I haven't, not a sudden onset like this ... and so severe. But Daxx has always struck me as a particularly sensitive child. Last week, in fact, I had a student teacher for a few days," Mrs. Parker said. "As she was sitting there cutting paper for their art project, Daxx went up to her and hugged her tight, which I'm used to, of course, but she wasn't. She smiled and said hello to him, and then he asked, with such curiosity, 'Why are you so sad?' Well, there was no stopping the tears that came from that girl. I don't know what Daxx picked up on, but it was something all right." She paused and said, "Daxx is gonna be fine. He just feels a lot."

Ella's throat hurt from trying so hard to hold back her tears. She was barely off the phone before there was no stopping them.

1:59 p.m.

The sudden ringing jolted Ben. He stopped walking and looked at the phone to see who was calling. The red battery indicator was blinking. "Hello?" he answered after renewing his promise to himself.

"I'm sorry I wasn't paying attention," Ella said. "I'm sorry I didn't see that something was wrong. I knew something was wrong, but I didn't know what it was. I should have said something. I should have—"

"No, no, no, this isn't your fault." Ben felt dizzy. "Please don't do that; please don't take this on and make it your fault. Then you add on so much, and it's already—there's already enough. Take care of you, take care of the children, and—"

"You can't do this." Gone was the calm, kind Ella. It wasn't sad Ella either. "You need to think about the children. The *children*, Ben. They need you."

He started pacing. "I know. You're right. And I have—I *have* thought about them. Do you know how often they're all I think about? Can you hear their heartbeats, Ella?"

"No, no, no. Do *not* start talking crazy on me again. Do you understand? Do you understand, Ben? Because I can't have that. This isn't all about you. I've been patient, but enough's enough. You can't do this. If not for me, at least for the kids. Where are you? I'm coming to get you. It's not an option anymore. *Where are you, Ben?*"

"Haven't I told you, Ella? Haven't I told you already?" He wondered. Had he? "I thought I did." Gearing up for a conversation he felt he'd already had, he was distracted by a plume of dust in the distance, coming from the direction of town. "I have to do this. It's not an option anymore. Is that what you just said?" He watched the yellow pickup approaching, the same one from yesterday.

His phone started beeping, the red light blinking faster.

"No, that's not—you need help, Ben."

He stared at the woman in the pickup who had come to a stop, smiling at him again through the open passenger window.

Trying to figure out what she wanted, he said to Ella, "I'm so sorry, I don't know how to do this, and my phone is going to—"

"Ben! Come back! Please! You can't just leave me like this!"

He looked curiously at the smiling woman. Why was she holding up two fingers? Was she giving him the peace sign? *Odd*, he thought. Ben gave into the last thing on his mind and said, "I think I—" His phone went dead.

He slipped it into his pocket, not taking his eyes off the woman as she gestured for him to come closer.

"I'm gonna say you need to come with me, my friend. Call it a hunch. I'm not sure when I'll be coming back this way, and it's twice now you've crossed my path. It's good to meet you." She stuck her hand out. "I'm August."

It was her eyes again. The laughter in them … it was nice, the nice kind of laughter, he realized. He reached in through the open window and shook her hand. "I'm Ben."

"Ben, you look like you're in need of a good meal and maybe even a good listening ear or two. I have the food, two ears, and just the place to go along with it all. Will you come with me?"

He looked around at the never-ending land, the open space, and it felt so vast, like it could swallow him. When he looked back at her, her eyes anchored him the way Daxx's laugh did. That's when he knew what to do.

He opened the door, climbed in, and as the pickup began moving, Ben looked in the side mirror, his life growing smaller and smaller behind him.

2:09 p.m.

The police, though sympathetic, didn't have much to offer Ella other than statistics about affairs and other likely causes for Ben "not wanting to come home," as they put it. He was an adult, left of his own volition, and had no history of mental illness. They were sorry, but there wasn't much they could do.

Ella had no idea what to do next. There were errands to run, emails to answer, calls to make, meals to be made, laundry to be put away, bills to pay, and jobs that needed to get done in order to make the money to pay those bills. Ella couldn't bring herself to do any of it. Nor could she answer any of the texts still coming from Charlotte.

Nothing that mattered before mattered anymore.

Standing by the kitchen door, she looked out at their yard. She had always loved that it was small enough to easily maintain but big enough for the children to run around. She and Ben had talked about planting herbs and vegetables but were concerned with how much it would cut down on the run-around space for the children—unless they could come up with a creative way to set up the beds, maybe in a leaning ladder style, a conversation they never got back to.

A swing dangled from the branches of the only tree, a hearty jacaranda that was just starting to do its thing, going from bare, gnarled branches to an explosion of the most intoxicating shade of purple. It did it once a year, only in May. The rest of the year, it was just those bare branches.

She let the screen door close behind her and sat on the step. Ben had told her that in Australia, Queensland to be exact, the jacaranda was nicknamed the Exam Tree. It bloomed in October, right before the end of the school year and final exams, and apparently the students there believed that if they hadn't started studying by the first bloom on the jacaranda, it was too late. Further, if a bloom landed on their head during exam time, they were destined to fail—with only one way out of the curse, if they caught a second bloom before it hit the ground. Ben had told her all that on the day they hung the swing. She had no idea how he knew about Australian folklore. She wished she had asked him.

She stared at the Exam Tree. Her life felt a lot like a test right now. And the fear of having already failed—terribly—weighed heavily as she watched a too-early bloom falling.

Andy.

It was right on that same back step that she had sat into the night, a week or so after the call, after the wake and funeral, after her parents had gone back to their lives and everyone else's lives had gone back to normal. Still unable to wrap her mind around how things could change in an instant, she had sat there trying to run calculations in her head. It had little to do with the math, which she was barely attempting, and more to do with the what-ifs. A truck was carrying bales of hay. That she could understand. But what were the chances of one bale on the top not being secure enough when it had never happened before according to the driver's meticulous records? What were the chances of the twine splitting exactly when it did, leaving the bale to catapult off the truck, bouncing hard on the highway and exploding into a storm of hay? What were the chances of one car swerving to avoid the straw cloud and the exact number of compensating twists of steering wheels, at those precise angles, leaving one dead and two people injured? What were the chances of him being in that lane on the highway at that exact time on a Wednesday afternoon? What were the chances of his pregnant fiancée calling him exactly when she did, telling him to hurry home because something was wrong, she was bleeding? What if he had taken the side roads instead of the highway? What if he had gone a little slower, missed a light, gone a little faster, passed one more car, and been ahead of the collision?

Ben had come out to the step and joined Ella. He had put his arm around her and listened while she said all the what-ifs and chances-were out loud, heartbroken sadness fueling the words, pushing them out one after another, no matter how crazy any of it sounded. He listened to all of it. He let her just keep talking while he held her and looked beyond them, into the yard, past it, and gently nodded, urging her to go on, to let it all out. When she had nothing left to say or wonder about, she put her head on his shoulder and cried. Her guttural wail shocked her, but it didn't seem to make Ben at all uncomfortable.

She turned something off after Andy's death, she realized now. It was the first time she had experienced the death of anyone close to her, and she felt changed by it in ways she was just now seeing, more than three years later. Even so, her mind still reverted to questions she had no answers to and calculations that were pointless.

What if Ben had come home instead of walking away?

What if three years ago she hadn't—

That topic was still off-limits.

2:16 p.m.

August shifted into fourth gear. Why did she *still* look like she was on the verge of laughing? While it had anchored Ben before, he now found it unsettling again.

Even more unsettling though was that she would pick up a complete stranger. A part of him wanted to warn her that giving him a ride to wherever she was taking him probably wasn't a good idea. Not that *he* wasn't safe. It was just that …

Never mind, he thought. It would be too hard to explain.

It kept bothering him though. He glanced at her again. There was nothing frail about her, but she was definitely in her seventies, or at least around there. What if she had picked up a serial killer? What then? Before they parted ways, he'd mention it to her. Just tell her to be careful—or better yet, not to pick up any more strangers at all.

August had switched on the radio and was slowly turning the dial until the antenna finally picked up something other than static. Ben couldn't remember the last time he had listened to music. It was an old song he recognized and obviously one August did too, because she was humming along. After cranking her window down, with one arm out the window, her hand playing against the wind and her other on the wheel, August seemed to fall so deeply into the music that Ben wondered if she forgot he was there. She looked lost in the best of ways.

Ben slowly lowered his window and tried to feel the music, to get into it. As nonchalantly as he could, he put his arm out to play in the breeze they were slowly sailing through, but the wind felt like slaps against his hand, stinging and sharp. He brought his arm back in the truck, hoping she hadn't noticed.

"Ben," August said with a glance toward him, "something just occurred to me."

She seemed to be on the verge of sharing what it was, but then something else must have occurred to her, because she said, "We're going about ten minutes or so down the road. It won't be long now." She looked over at him and smiled. There was that almost-laugh again.

And then it came. She laughed as if she'd been holding it in for years.

And she laughed … and laughed … and laughed …

For the first time in a long time, Ben felt like the sane one, and with that, the tension from trying to hold it together slowly left him. There was a definite possibility that August, the one at the wheel right now, was certifiably crazy. And to Ben's surprise, that felt good. In fact, it felt *really* good.

"I'm sorry," she said, shaking her head, her eyes on the road, one hand on the wheel and the other back on the gear shift. "I just … well, I'm tickled to meet you. I don't know how else to say it. It's just *very*, very good to meet you, Ben. Have you ever felt that way about someone?"

"I …" The answer was suddenly so obvious. Ben looked at the desert landscape that was beginning to green. He felt the need to share, uncensored and without thinking, the way Daxx and Izzy did every single day. "My kids. That's how I felt when they were born, the first time I saw them and held them. It was overwhelming … how good it was to finally meet them for the first time." He hadn't heard himself sound that normal since he started walking.

"There's nothing like firsts," August said. "You can never recapture it or replay it just the same." She sounded nostalgic, and he wondered what first she was remembering.

"I wanted to be there when they sang for the first time," Ben said, surprised at how easily the words were coming now. "I don't know why. I just did."

"And were you?"

"I don't think so. But there's a first I'm pretty sure I didn't miss, the first time Izzy—that's my daughter— laughed so hard she cried. She wasn't even two. It was the simplest game of *now you see me, now you don't*, and I did it over and over, and she just couldn't stop laughing, and these big, beautiful tears were rolling down her cheeks."

"Oh my," August said. "Well, I'll be!" She hit the steering wheel. "Maybe that was the first time she sang!"

"Maybe," Ben said, swallowing back tears of his own that suddenly threatened.

Even though there were no cars in sight, she flicked on her blinker and then slowed and turned left onto an unmarked road. Ben didn't care where she was taking him. It felt so good to be in the passenger seat.

2:48 p.m.

Ella sat at the kitchen table with her laptop, answering emails that couldn't be ignored anymore and figuring out how to pay bills that wouldn't otherwise go away, her frustration at its peak. So when a bee came through the loose screen door, buzzed around the room, and then landed on the table, frantically fluttering its wings, all abuzz with its nonstop movement, she slowly leaned down and, keeping her eye on the now jumping bee, lifted her flip-flop off her foot.

She raised it slowly.

Despite her intention to whack the bee as hard as she could, she paused in midair, something stopping her.

It was *that* something—again; she recognized it.

Out of nowhere, an idea came to her.

She got an empty cup from the sink and, after a few tries, successfully used her flip-flop to scoot the bee into the cup and then cover it.

She took it outside, set it free, and then watched it fly away until she couldn't see it anymore.

As she came back in and sat down, she felt a little lighter. A miniscule amount but still noticeably so.

All she knew was that it had something to do with that something. For the moment, that was enough.

4:01 p.m.

August parked in front of a small house that looked like it had seen better days, nestled among nature's wildness.

"Welcome, Ben," she said, her voice spilling excitement as she got out of the truck. "Let's get you something to eat. Then I'll show you around. Come on."

As they walked around the house to the field behind it, following a worn path surrounded by wildflowers, August gave Ben a friendly pat on the back and said, "Get ready for this."

He looked at her, unsure.

She stopped, looked up at the sky, put her palms together, and said, "Comb honey."

They walked a little farther, and then she stopped. "You stay here, Ben. You're not ready yet. And that's perfectly okay." She patted his arm. "You *will* be. I'll be back." She headed toward a stand of trees about fifteen yards away. About halfway there, she turned and called out, "The wait you've had—it'll be worth it! I promise!"

Then she continued walking over to four white wooden boxes stacked on one another. She lifted a flat board off the top box and put it on the grass.

When the huge swarm of bees surrounded her, Ben quickly took a few steps back. He kept waiting for her to react, but she just continued to stay calm. He wondered how in the world she wasn't getting stung.

August continued taking rectangular panels out of the box; they looked a lot like the air-conditioner filters Ben changed at home on a mostly regular basis. But the frames of these appeared to be wood, not cardboard, and spread from side to side were tons of bees. August was singing now as she gently brushed the bees off and into the box. Then, after inspecting closely, she pulled off a piece of what Ben guessed was hard honey. For the next several minutes, August continued singing while slowly guiding the bees back into the box. She had that old-lady singing voice, Ben decided, one devoid of hesitation and ego, filled only with determination.

She came back to Ben with a huge smile on her face. "You're about to taste the best thing you've ever tasted," she said.

She led him back to the house where two rockers sat on the front porch. Gesturing for Ben to take one, she sat in the other and then scooted hers so it was close to his. "Now then," she said, handing the wax slab to Ben, "this is comb honey. Eat it slowly, one cell at a time. You need to *taste* it. You need to really *taste* it." She pointed to a hexagon in the honeycomb that appeared darker than the others. "Who knows what's in this one? Which flower, which honeybee, what set of circumstances came together for this cell of honey that'll never be matched and has never before been tasted. Never before, Ben. Go on. You do the honors."

He looked at the comb honey, not sure how to proceed.

"You can't do it wrong," she said.

Ben used his finger to scoop out the honey from an individual cell and then ate it. "Holy ..." August was right; he had never tasted anything like it.

"So, tell me," she said. "What does it taste like to you?"

Ben tried to think of the right description. *Salty? No, it's more sweet than salty.* "There are so many flavors ... I guess it's sweet and a little ..."

"Oh, it's so much more than that, isn't it? Free yourself! What do you *taste*?"

Ben scooped honey out of another cell and closed his eyes, letting go of descriptive constraints, focusing on the taste.

"The sun," he said. He could taste its nurturing heat, its warmth.

"Yes, Ben. What else?"

"The dance of the bee ... a darting bee ... a flower ... I can picture it—it's yellow and buttery, gentle ... silky—I don't know its name ... dew in the morning, it's that light ... the flutter of the bee's wing ... crisp and clear air." He opened his eyes.

August smiled. "That's it. That's what it's all about. My abide-by number one. I'm not a fan of rules, you see. Abide-bys, they're a different story." She raised her comb honey in a toast to Ben's. "My new friend, allow me to introduce you to abide-by number one: you've got to taste what you're doing."

6:03 p.m.

Ella had been nervous on her way to pick up the children from school, afraid of how bad Daxx's stutter might be and how Izzy might react to it. So she was shocked when the afternoon unfolded as normally as could be expected, minus the awareness that Ben probably wouldn't be coming home. As Daxx answered questions about who he sat next to during lunch and who he played with at recess, there was no sign of a stutter. Ella's relief continued as the two of them played Legos and then found a few more pieces of the hundred-piece puzzle they were working on. When Izzy told Daxx it was time for her to do her homework, because if she wanted to be a good reader, she had to practice every night, and reading made you smart—there wasn't even a pause as Daxx said, with a gentle tone and soft look, that playing I Spy with him would also make her smart and was also very important and that she had to really practice at looking to see. She was convinced. Her homework could wait until after dinner, she decided.

All of that, all those little interactions … Ella couldn't think of the last time she just sat there watching them, taking it all in. Normally she was in her studio, working, coming out to check on them, sometimes hanging out for a little bit, but then getting back to getting things done. She was so absorbed in the way they were interacting she forgot she had been listening for Daxx's stutter.

It was when they sat down to a dinner of spaghetti that Izzy turned her attention to Ella and said, "When's Dad coming back? It's almost my turn to bring Kirk home." She had been counting down the weeks until it was her turn to bring the class teddy bear home for a three-day visit, which would be documented with drawings, photos, and a Kirk journal, then shared with the class upon Kirk's return.

"It's next week, right?" Ella said, having lost her appetite.

Izzy nodded. Ella kept looking at her, waiting for her to say more—but the silence only grew.

"How-how-how-how-how-how-how long …" Daxx stopped, and Ella felt paralyzed, unable to do what she wanted to do—lift him into her arms and cradle him. She knew what he was trying to ask, the question on everyone's mind. She knew that in his generous way, he had also been trying to fill the uncomfortable silence. It was excruciating, more painful than seeing him physically hurt and needing stitches after landing on a branch the time he jumped from the swing in midair.

Determined, he tried again. "How-how-how-how-how-how-how-how-how-how-how …"

Shit. Do something. She swallowed tears that felt like a knife in her throat and scooted her chair beside him so she was facing him. Trying to remember what Mrs. Parker told her, she held his hands and said, "It's okay, honey. Take your time. You're doing great."

The deep breath he took seemed so filled with calm that it jolted her when it was followed with "I-I-I-I-I …" He looked in a panic at his sister, who was looking at him with as much confidence as Ella was trying to muster. Izzy moved her chair back from the table, came around, and said, "Mom, can we play?"

In a moment more surreal than any she had ever experienced, Ella said, "Sure, of course. Go ahead." Izzy took Daxx's hand and led him outside to the backyard. Not even thirty seconds after kicking the ball around in another of their made-up games, he was smiling. Ella stayed at the table watching them through the screen door, her trembling chin resting in her hands, the tears running.

A few minutes later, a knock came at the front door.

6:20 p.m.

When August opened the door, Ben tried to remember the last time he and Ella had left the house without locking it. On the other hand, there was no one around for miles, so he could see how it wasn't really an issue.

The house was basic, the main room serving as both the kitchen and the living area. It felt comfortable, even before August said, "My house is your house. Why don't you go freshen up, maybe splash some water on your face, soak your feet in the tub. Whatever you need." She pointed to the partially open door next to the bedroom. "Go on, Ben. Make yourself at home."

Standing in the tiny bathroom, Ben stared at himself in the mirror over the sink. The guilt was building, the fact that he was still there, as if each minute he stayed, he was taking another step away from Ella, Daxx, and Izzy. But as wrong as being away from them felt, as much as he missed them and wanted to go home, he knew he might never leave again if he did—not like this. And then he'd be right back where he started, and everything would have been for nothing.

Just a little longer, he thought. "See it through," he said quietly to his reflection. He had made the promise to be honest, first with himself and then with other people. So as he continued looking at his reflection, surprised at not needing to look away, he admitted the truth: it felt like he was walking a fine line between taking care of himself and hurting Ella. He needed to call her, to let her know where he was and that … He couldn't say he was okay. He didn't know if that would be a lie.

When he came out, August set a plate on the table with a chunk of bread, a pile of salami, an assortment of olives, and miniature pickles. "Have at it, Ben. That honey was just an appetizer."

"That looks great. Thank you. I hate to bother you for anything else, but do you have a charger? My phone is dead, and I need to call Ella—my wife—and let her know where I am."

"Oh, Ben," she said, "this place has been off the grid for a long, long time. There aren't even any plugs."

For the first time, Ben noticed the worn-down candles and absence of overhead lights and lamps. He realized the refrigerator and stove probably ran off propane.

He put his hand in his pocket, feeling his phone, wondering what to do.

"I can drive you back to town if you'd like," August said. "I'd be happy to. The nice boys at the fire department always let me use one of their desk phones when it would be really helpful for me to talk to Heather. She's my daughter. She always drops off honey and other things from my garden for them, so we have a nice setup. I'm sure they'll let you use their phone."

Why was it so hard to say that was a good idea and thank August and start walking outside to the truck? Why was he still standing there, silent, not saying anything?

August finally took charge, grabbing her keys from the hook. "It's no problem at all. Come on, Ben."

"Wait," he said. August turned around. "I'm … I'm not sure what I'm doing here. Things haven't been … This has been really good, and I just …"

Her face lined with concern, she said, "Okay, Ben. That's okay." She got quiet and looked away, thinking. Then she said, "Do you *want* to be here right now? How does it taste?"

She caught him off guard; it wasn't the response he was expecting. He did his best to follow her line of questioning. Did he want to be standing where he was or holding a phone, Ella on the other end? He pictured getting back in the truck, heading back to town, calling … It tasted metallic. He thought of not calling, just staying where he was, and while it didn't bring relief, it felt better, at least neutral.

Ben shook his head. "I don't know why, but it doesn't feel right to call her right now, even though I think I should." He looked down. His shoes were filthy. "It doesn't make sense, and I'm not sure it's right, but … I like being here right now. The idea of leaving feels … just *not* right."

"Well, sometimes that's all you need to know. You'll figure out the rest when you need to. Does that sit well with you?"

"Yes," he said, feeling a little less heavy.

"You have a *wonderful* presence in the moment. Just wonderful, Ben. What a gift."

Ben swallowed hard. It had been a long time, longer than he could remember, since someone complimented who he was. He had received awards for what he did at work, but this … what she just said. "Thank you," he finally said. "I like your place. It feels good to be here. Thank you for having me—for picking me up and bringing me here."

"Oh, it was my pleasure. It's so good to be in your company. Not that my bees aren't good company, because they sure are, but you're you, and that feels good and true." She squeezed her hands together, beaming. "I *love* when I rhyme by accident." After putting her keys back on the hook, she picked up the plate and said, "Let's sit," leading him out to the rockers on the porch. "And by the way, this is all for you. I had more than my share earlier."

Sitting in the rocker next to August's, Ben dug in and realized how hungry he was.

After Ben raved about how good the food was and they talked about the history of the house and the land, she said, "I like the way you talk and ask questions. The bees don't do much of that—at least not with me. With each other though, that's a whole different story."

"How long have you … Are you actually a beekeeper?" Ben asked.

"Well, I've never really thought of it like that. It's just kind of my thing, what I like to do." She pushed her feet to get her rocker gliding back and forth again. "First thing when I wake up, it's usually Heather I think about. But pretty soon, my bees come to mind. I like thinking about them, and it's good to have a reason to get up and start the day. What about you? What do you think about when you wake up?"

Ben felt like he had just walked out of a movie theater, his senses suddenly having to adjust to harsh lights and a starkly different reality. He was having trouble making the transition. "I ..." He didn't want to think about it. "I guess ..." He *really* didn't want to think about it.

August patted his hand. "That's quite all right. You don't need to tell me. I'm like that sometimes. I just stay there in bed, wondering and wondering. And then, like I said, I get to thinking about my bees. They just come buzzing in. Do you know, Ben, that they wake up each day knowing exactly what their role is? Imagine that. There are tens of thousands of bees in those hives back there, and each of them, *every single one*, knows why they're there. Some are circling the queen, taking care of her and such, and some are construction workers, building the honeycomb. Every single one of those worker bees, which are all female by the way—not everyone knows that—they each wake up knowing *exactly* why they're there and what they're supposed to do that day."

"What about the males?" Ben asked.

Her enthusiasm only increasing, August seemed thrilled to continue. "Well, the drones—they're the males—there are just a few hundred of them, if that. Some people like to think of them as lazy because supposedly work isn't high on their list of like-to-dos. Well, I don't know about that. They do none of the work all those female worker bees do—building, keeping up, and protecting the hive. And they can't sting; they don't have stingers like the females do. They fly around, lazily—okay, I'll admit that—and they have their purpose too. And if they have their purpose, then what's work? What does it mean? Why is it more important?"

Trying to follow, Ben said, "What's their purpose?"

"To mate with the queen bee. That's it." She shrugged. "And then they *die*. Just like that. Can you imagine?" She started laughing. "Aren't you glad you're not a bee?"

Ben smiled. "That I am."

"I don't know why they're set up like that, but I do believe it works, for all of us. What they do, what they contribute … they're *amazing*, Ben. That's why I try really hard not to let even *one* slip between the cracks when I'm opening and closing the hive."

"I noticed," Ben said. "You're so good with them."

"I really try my best. It's *very* important that I do. They're the only insects that produce food eaten by human beings. Want to know something else that might blow your socks off?"

Ben smiled. "I do."

"Real, true, raw honey has everything you need to sustain your life—enzymes, vitamins, minerals, and water— to *stay alive*, that is." She looked at him. "*Feeling* alive, *being* alive, that's a whole other story. Isn't it, Ben?"

Ben agreed with her, doing his best to ignore the overwhelming fatigue he suddenly felt.

August, on the other hand, seemed nowhere near ready to wind down. "Yes, Ben, honey is a miracle. On top of that, bees are also responsible for propolis, an antiviral, antifungal, antibacterial goodness that works more miracles. How's that for a mouthful! Oh, and did I tell you honey contains an antioxidant that improves brain function? Bees' brains, even though they're the size of sesame seeds, are capable of complex calculations, and they do them all the time, figuring out distances and speeds and trajectories. They really—I'm losing you … Where are you, Ben?"

"I'm sorry," he said. "I just ... I keep wondering, did Ella send you to get me?"

"Oh, Ben," she said, the way he would say it to the children when he wanted to scoop them up in his arms and hold them tight. "No one sent me anywhere. You're here because the timing is perfect, just *perfect*."

She looked at him and held his eyes for a long moment. "Do you know that I had a feeling a visitor was coming my way? I could just feel it. Maybe it's been a few days now. I think it has. And that feeling just kept stronger and stronger. It's why I got in my truck and just started driving. I didn't even have anything I needed in town. Not a thing! I just had a feeling. And then when I saw you the *second* time, I knew. And it made me really, really happy. Thank you, Ben, for being here."

Ben shook his head, trying to wrap his mind around it all. "I'm sorry. I didn't mean to ... my mind's been in overdrive. I've heard of people 'just knowing' things. Do you have ESP or one of those things?"

August started laughing and slapped her knee. "Lord, no! I've never been particularly gifted in any sense of the word." She wagged her finger at him. "Now, don't you look at me like that, Ben. I'm not saying that in a sad way, not at all. I'm one of the luckiest people I know. I've just done a lot of things and really enjoyed them, and I've had talents here and there, things I'm good at, but *gifts*, those talents that can just ... hmmm ... jump out of you and be really big, so big it becomes who you are. I've never had one of those. I just knew someone was coming this way because, well, I suppose I'm good at getting quiet and hearing what there is to hear. But that's something anyone can do."

Ben wondered if it really was something anyone could do or if it was so natural to August she couldn't imagine it any other way. He remembered one of the speakers who came to Starfish's Wellness Week; he had talked about meditating as if it was as easy as turning off one light and turning on another—so convincing Ben was confident he might be able to do it. He just never got around to trying. "Do you meditate?" he asked. "Is that how you do it?"

"Ha! I might be the worst meditator I know," she said. "Now, Heather, she's very good at it. Oh, she just looks so beautiful when sits there like that, so serene. Like a gentle butterfly. She tried to get me to do it once, but I just didn't understand how—no matter how sweet she was about trying to explain it to me. Finally, she said to me, 'Mama, I think trying to meditate might be taking you out of the meditation you're already in.' And then she just let it go and let that be that."

"What do you think?" Ben asked. "Do you think she was right?"

"I don't know. I guess meditation is about getting quiet and listening, and I suppose I get quiet and listen a lot— whenever I get the feeling it would be a good idea." She started counting on her fingers ... "Well, I'll be darned. I suppose that happens thirty or so times a day."

"Seriously?" Ben said. "How long do you get quiet when it happens? Do you just stop what you're doing?"

"Pretty much ... I don't even know actually. Now you've really got me thinking, my new friend, Ben! Let me see ... I hear this feeling, and the feeling says, 'Now, August, shhh ... listen,' and so I do, and then I know or feel something I didn't know or feel before I got quiet.

Goodness. Do I sound like a crazy old lady who's ..." she started laughing and laughing, "who's ..." she could barely get the words out, "... off her rocker! That one just came to me!"

Ben had no words for her right then. He just wanted to hug her because he was laughing, and he couldn't stop.

7:02 p.m.

Charlotte started talking as soon as Ella opened the door. "I tried to time this right. I know you eat early when it's just you and the kids. I tried to give you some time—you know, time with them. But not too much time—like time to be left alone, well, not alone but on your own. Wow. You'd never know I practiced this a hundred times on the way over, would you?"

"Do you want to come in?" Ella said. It was so awkward. Charlotte never knocked.

Handing Ella a bottle of wine, she said, "Yes. Yes, I do. I hope this is a good time."

"It's fine," Ella said, steeling herself for a conversation she'd have to have eventually. "Come in." They went into the kitchen, where Ella cleared the table and Charlotte struggled to get the wine opener to work as they made small talk.

After pulling out two glasses and handing one to Charlotte, Ella sat down across from her and said, "You wanted to talk to me?"

"Yes. Because this," she motioned back and forth between the two of them, "this is not us. What happened this morning?"

Ever since Charlotte had texted to say she was going to come by, Ella had changed her mind many times about what to say. Now that the moment was here, Ella forgot which approach she had settled on. Her eyes were on Daxx and Izzy, still playing outside. "I don't have time for … whatever you're doing right now—or the energy. You tell me, Charlotte. *What happened this morning?*"

Charlotte nodded. "You're right. I know. I came over here planning to talk to you, and then I—whatever. It doesn't matter. Here I am, and here we are." She sat up straight. "So, I need to tell you something."

Ella resisted the urge to look away from Charlotte, to look back at the children, who had been on their hands and knees, peering at something in the grass, or to look at the picture of her and Ben. They were laughing, such a candid shot, and if she turned even slightly, she could see it on the table next to the couch. Anything to anchor her. But she didn't. She kept her eyes on Charlotte as Charlotte said, "It was about a year ago …"

And that was when Ella knew. So she purposely tuned out most of what came next, listening for only one thing, not wanting to hear any details except what really mattered to her. She finally cut Charlotte off and said, "I have to ask you something. Please answer me with as few words as possible. Okay?"

Charlotte nodded.

"Did you hit on him, or did he hit on you?"

Charlotte cleared her throat. "I did. I'm—"

"Did he go along with it?"

"No. Jesus. I think he hates me now …"

And as Charlotte went on and on about how drunk she was and how she admired both of them so much and she was so sorry and would never have hit on him sober, Ella was beginning to realize why Charlotte suggested what she did earlier that day, that Ben's leaving had nothing to do with another woman—Charlotte was positively sure. Because he had turned *her* down.

Ella stared at Charlotte. "Why are you telling me this now?"

"I don't know. There's something about Ben just going off the way he has, everything just coming undone. It feels like it's really important to be real and get down to what's really going on, because that's the only way we can help each other."

"Who needs help, Charlotte? Is it you? And what's coming undone for you that you didn't break already? Is this drama a little boring without you in it? Is that why you decided to tell me now—" she looked outside, registering the children's proximity, and lowered her voice—"instead of a goddamn year ago? Because now—now is a great time, because the focus can shift to you and why you hit on my husband, all so that you could have a few more minutes as the center of attention. I suppose it's thoughtful of you to divert the attention, to turn it away from all the pain and confusion I'm feeling so we can talk about *you*."

"You don't understand—"

"Oh, I do. I understand the fact that you're lonely because you're needy, and so you do really stupid things. Don't you see? The only reason you can't last with anyone is because you know you'll eventually stop being the center of their attention, so you get out before that happens. And you wanted to bring that poison into my marriage. Get out."

"Ella, I—"

"Get out—now." Ella stood up, walked to the front door, and opened it. She didn't say another word as Charlotte left.

Ella closed the door, her hands shaking, her insides in turmoil. Her mind was going in circles, and most disturbing was the dizzying thought that was so much louder than the rest: she felt as poisonous as she had accused Charlotte of being.

She was a terrible person. How could she have said such awful, hurtful things?

7:32 p.m.

August showed Ben around the property, which included touring the chicken coop and meeting Betsy, her hen. Then they headed to her garden, where they picked zucchini and green tomatoes from raised beds, then thyme, oregano, and Italian parsley. Now August and Ben stood in the kitchen, making dinner, listening to the only radio station August could tune into.

Ben felt like he had known August his whole life, and it seemed odd he knew almost nothing about her. He had a growing list of questions, but it wasn't until after she finished teaching him how to coat the tomatoes that Ben had the opportunity to ask one. "You mentioned your daughter," he said. "Does she live close to you?"

"Heather? She lives about an hour up the coast, but she's on the road a lot, like a feather. Not fast, just slowly making her way from here to there." August smiled. "Heather, my feather. She comes and visits when she can, just shows up and makes my day. And she goes ahead and helps with all the honey, taking it from here and then doing what she does to get it into people's hands." August started flipping the tomatoes, perfectly timed, as the topsides were now a golden brown. "And not just the firemen. She goes to all the markets up and down the coast, sometimes selling the produce from here too. Nothing ever goes to waste. She makes sure of that."

"Sounds like it works for everyone. What a great setup," Ben said as he finished cutting the zucchini. He then followed directions as August explained why the thyme should sit on the zucchini with a little olive oil before adding the salt and the oregano.

"Have you two always been close?" he asked.

"Oh, yes. I suppose we've just never had any reason not to be. She and I can sit in those rockers out there and talk until the sun comes up. And every time I'm with her, I just feel so lucky ... so lucky that I know her and get to hear her thoughts and what she's excited about, because it sure can be unpredictable from time to time." She twisted the grinder, adding more pepper to the tomatoes. "She knows how to work with wood, how to make flutes and other wind instruments, how to play them too, and she's really into gardening. And she's always volunteering at animal shelters wherever she goes. She's a good soul. A kind, gentle soul. Just like her dad."

"Is he … What happened? Do you mind me asking?"

"Oh, there's no sense in having questions you can't ask. Don't you think, Ben? Because the way I see it, if there's a question you can't ask, there's an answer you can't hear, and that doesn't say much about either person in the conversation. You can ask me anything."

He held the plate as she tipped the pan and slid the fried tomatoes onto it.

"Go ahead and set that on the table," she said. "I'll cook up the zucchini, and in a jiffy, they'll all be at the perfect temperature together."

"This looks amazing," he said, his mouth watering.

"Well, thank you, Ben. To answer your question, it's been sixteen months now since Henry died, and oh, do I miss him. We were married fifty-three years. I don't even remember *not* knowing him, not having him in my life. We had so much fun together." She smiled, turning up the flame and then rearranging the zucchini.

"Fifty-three years? That's amazing," Ben said.

"I've had a lot of time to think about those years these past sixteen months, and you know what I came up with? I think we lived about seven lifetimes together in this life, about seven years long each, give or take. We didn't plan it that way; it just kind of happened. All of a sudden, it would be time to make a big change, and we'd do it. And then we were off on another adventure—sometimes without even leaving home."

"How would you know it was time for a change? Would you *both* know?"

"Rarely. No, usually, one of us would feel it, we would just know, and then we would tell the other person. We got good at trusting that when it happened. It was always right—well, as far as we knew, I suppose." August moved the zucchini to the plate and turned off the burner. Then she put the bread and cheese on the table, and they sat down to eat.

Ben ran out of compliments to give about the food. He was sure August had secret ingredients she put in when his back was turned, and when he told her so, she laughed and said, "My love for this food. I think you can taste it."

"I have no doubt," Ben said.

"When it comes to that, the honeybee is a pro," August gushed. "A single hive of bees—just one, mind you—will fly what's equal to three times around this beautiful planet in order to make—are you ready?—*two pounds* of honey. That's honey love if I ever knew it. Now, keeping that in mind, think of this: your typical worker bee, those females flying around that hive getting the job done, day to night, they—one of them—will make about just one-twelfth a teaspoon of honey in her lifetime. All of that work for *one-twelfth of a teaspoon* of honey."

Ben tried to imagine that kind of dedication in a person's life. What would that look like? What would be the equivalent? "How long do they live?" he asked.

"Well, it depends on what time of year they're born and what role they play in the hive, and also what their job is. Most of the worker bees live six or seven weeks. And I'll tell you something. Sing to them, and it'll calm them and lower their stress, and you just might give them a little more time." She stood up, got a jar out of the kitchen cabinet, and set it on the table. "I almost forgot!"

The sides of the jar were caked with something clumped and whitish. When Ben seemed hesitant about accepting a heaping spoonful, August said, "Those are crystals, honey crystals, a sign of the purest, best honey around—after the comb honey, that is." Laughing and shaking her head, she ate the spoonful herself. She closed her eyes, clearly savoring the taste. Then she reached over to the drawer under the counter, pulled out a new spoon, and gave it to Ben along with the entire jar.

After trying the second-best honey he had ever tasted, Ben's taste buds felt like they were on high alert, actively anticipating what might come next. As dinner went on and August talked more about one of the loves of her life, *every bee in every hive*, Ben realized he was eating one of the best meals he had ever tasted. Certainly one of the top five. Fried tomatoes and zucchini, hard-boiled eggs from Betsy, fresh bread, herbs, cheese, and honey. The combination made it seem as though he was trying an entirely new food group.

As they were cleaning up, August adjusted the radio. Ben did the dishes with the slowest trickle of water he could use, just enough pressure to be effective. During dinner, August had explained the importance of conserving water, especially there at the house. He felt himself slip into a slow, methodical zone of wiping the dishes, feeling the water, and listening to the music. There was a certain twang to the song playing, not quite regret, but it seemed the singer was wondering about how the past dipped into today. There was lilting hope in his tone. He sounded sad but okay, as if he'd come to terms with something from the past and simply needed to express it. Ben felt sure that if he was back in the truck, sailing down the road with August driving and this song playing, his hand would know how to play in the wind.

As Ben was wiping down the sink, August started talking about her bees again, about how they communicated by dancing, and Ben realized she had been moving around to the music the entire time.

Seeing her twirl, in her own world, made his heart hurt. He missed Izzy, Ella, and Daxx.

August suddenly stopped and looked at Ben. Her eyes were so gentle and always seemed to be looking, observing, never anything more and never with judgment. "What do you need, Ben?" she asked.

He realized he could have answered anything— anything in the entire world—and she would have believed him and trusted him and helped him. He wondered if he had ever asked Ella or Izzy or Daxx that same question, not needing their answer to be anything other than what it was. Standing there then, he wanted to. He wanted to ask them—right then.

When he still hadn't answered, she said, "Let's go sit outside." So they went back out to the porch and took their places on the rockers. The air was warm and still.

"Let it out, Ben," she said.

It felt like an invitation he would regret turning down, so he went with it. "I feel so guilty. I feel so bad being here when my kids and wife are home with no idea where I am. I want to do the right thing, but I don't know what that is anymore. I love them so much, but I ..." The slight look of alarm on her face gave him pause. "What?"

"Oh, Ben, I feel confident saying you love them *so* much more than that. It's that *but*. It goes and messes with things. It subtracts—every time, Ben. It never adds. What you're saying here, telling me, these are things from the *heart*, how you feel—how you *feel*, Ben. And that makes each of them big, important words. And every time you say 'but,' you're saying 'not really' or 'forget that' about the words that came before it. And those were big, important words. Try this: 'I love them, *and* I ...'"

Ben nodded. "Okay. I love them so much ... *and* I don't know what to do." It felt good. It felt different. Something inside him was opening wider, and he wanted it to keep going. "I'm happy being here ... *and* I don't want them to worry." How could one word make such a difference? Of course it could, he realized. How many times had changing one word at Starfish changed the entire meaning of the question, the message, or the directive?

"Wow," August said. "By the light of the moon and with all the power of the stars twinkling right there above you, I have to tell you that was beautiful. It sounded like music, Ben. Please keep going."

"Okay ... It feels good to be sitting here. And I'm afraid I'll never be ready to leave. I'm grateful to be here, *and* I really miss my family."

"You can stay here as long as you'd like. You know I love your company. I suspect you'll be ready to go back home as soon as you're ready, and that'll be just the right time. Don't you think, Ben?"

He sure hoped so. "I can't argue with that," he said.

"In the meantime, you miss them, and you're worried they're worried, which doesn't leave you feeling how you want to feel. Is that about right?"

"Exactly," Ben said. "In my head ... I just keep hearing these things like ..."

"Like what?"

"Like I'm crazy and a *really* bad dad and a worse husband and I'm selfish and losing it and going off the deep end ..." He looked over at August. "It kind of just keeps going."

"Well, then, never mind your mind. What would make you feel good right now?"

"If I could let them know I'm okay, if I could let them know ..." He wanted to say he'd be back soon, but it didn't feel like a promise he could make, and it didn't feel right to be anything but totally honest. "I guess I just want to let them know I'm okay and tell them not to worry."

August nodded. "As I was telling you earlier, the bees, those wondrous creatures, they communicate by hipping, hopping, and dancing. That's how they let each other know what's going on, where to go, and who's doing what. Now, I'm not telling you what to do, Ben, just to take some advice from certain yellow-and-black-striped friends of mine, numbering in the tens of thousands, who are millions of years old as a species and just as wise."

Ben smiled. "And what advice might that be?"

"Dance it to them. Send your thoughts, that picture in your head I just know you're seeing right now, maybe of your wife, maybe of the kids, probably you hugging them, reassuring them, smiling with them, telling them it's all okay, it's all good—dance it to them, from here to there, through the wind, the stars, the flying leaves. Don't you see? It'll get to there from here. Always does. I'd bet a comb of honey on it. And you know that's no small bet."

August stood up, stretched, and said, "You'll stay here then. Until it's time to go. As I'm sure you saw, there's a couch in there. Make yourself comfortable."

He thanked August, leaned back in his rocking chair, and began counting the stars that were continuing to sparkle their way into the night sky, picturing each of them as messengers showing up in Ella's and Daxx's and Izzy's dreams that night, carrying messages filled with love and as much promise as he could honestly offer.

Day 3, Thursday

7:18 a.m.

As Ella sat, unable to coax an appetite, her focus was on Izzy. She had brought a stuffed animal to breakfast, a floppy elephant. Normally, it was situated in her room with things to do—something to guard, something to play with, or a window seat if the weather had caught Izzy's attention. This morning, she sat the elephant on her lap and then gave it a few bites of pancake, which made Daxx smile bigger than he had all morning.

When Izzy reached toward the center of the table, toward the small mason jar holding the chamomile flowers, Ella knew what was going to happen next, and an irritation she had been fighting all morning suddenly had its way with her. Why would Izzy bother checking for the joke of the day? It wouldn't be there. *Of course* it wouldn't be—because Ben wasn't home yet. Izzy *knew* that. So why did she keep looking for the stupid Post-it Note that wasn't there? What was she *doing*? Obviously it wasn't going to be under Izzy's glass of juice ... or there under Daxx's ... or there under the syrup bottle. Why wasn't she stopping? Why was she getting Daxx's hopes up like that?

When Izzy's voice cracked as she asked when they would be getting another joke of the day, it took all Ella's willpower not to burst into tears.

She avoided committing to a time frame and assured Izzy and Daxx that Ben loved them and would be back as soon as his trip was over.

Ella's mind started racing. Should *she* have found a joke, written it down, and hidden it for them to find the way Ben did every morning?

No. No way. That strategy never worked.

Only Ben could be Ben.

How could he take that away from them? How could he do that to them?

7:55 a.m.

Before Ben opened his eyes, he remembered where he was—and that Ella wouldn't be lying next to him.

As he lay on the couch, his focus shifted from the old wood beams across the ceiling to August, who had her back to Ben and was busy cooking, moving her head to the softly playing music. She seemed to love that battery-powered radio as much as she loved her bees.

He sat up and said, "Good morning, August."

She turned around. "You're awake! How'd you sleep?"

"Great. I don't even know the last time I slept through the night." He looked at his watch. "Shoot. I'm sorry. I had no idea it was so late. I ..." He got up and started folding the blanket.

She shook her head. "No apologizing—not to me and not for that. A good night's sleep is no small feat." She turned back to the stove, adjusted the flame, then said, "I know it's first thing in the morning, but I'd like to introduce you to my abide-by number two. Ready?"

He had a feeling that August was coming up with these abide-bys as she went along, that there was no real order to the rules she lived by. Maybe she was trying to make them orderly for him. Maybe she understood the way his mind worked better than he did.

Ben placed the pillow on top of the folded blanket. "I'm ready," he said.

"Pause when you need to."

He waited for more, then said, "That's it?"

"It's plenty. Believe me. Now, I put some fresh towels and a few things in the bathroom for you. I just need a few more minutes here, and then breakfast will be ready. Go on now," she said, shooing him away from the kitchen. "You take your time."

When Ben joined August at the table a little while later, she was reading *Bee Culture* and hadn't yet touched the food—slices of bread, combs of honey, a plate of eggs, melon quarters, and a bowl of sliced cucumbers. She put down the magazine. "Now don't you look all cleaned up. Here, have some of these to start," she said, removing the lid covering the eggs and then passing the plate. "There's some goat cheese and fresh thyme and oregano in there. And salt and pepper of course. They're still warm."

"Thank you so much." He was famished. "This is amazing, August. You must have been up early."

"Oh, I *was*. And that's the way I like it. Sometimes I like to sleep when it's dark and the whole world is quiet, except where it isn't. And sometimes I prefer to rest right in the middle of the day, when the world is as busy as a bee around me. I just need to stop, get quiet, and relax."

"You mean a nap?" He and Ella used to love taking naps. And then it became something just the children did. Now, none of them took naps.

"Maybe but not necessarily," August said, covering her bread with a thick layer of honey. "I mean just being myself for a few minutes and sitting down and doing nothing, right in the middle of everything. I do it ... well, a lot, I suppose. It's a great way not to forget the things it's important for me to remember."

The teapot whistled, and August got up and turned off the flame. Placing what looked like a sock attached to a metal handle in a pewter pitcher, she said, "Can you pour some of those coffee grounds into this sock? It's so much easier with two people."

"Sure," he said, smiling, amused that it actually was called a sock. As he spooned some of the grounds from the tin canister into the sock, August slowly poured the boiling water from the teapot, and what made its way through the sock into the pewter pitcher was coffee with a noticeable hint of cinnamon. August poured them each a cup. After they sat down to breakfast again, August picked up right where she had left off.

"It's the same with the bees, you know. Some people think bees don't sleep. I don't buy it. Maybe it's not sleep like we know it. They're busy, that's for sure, and then you can spot one with its antennae drooping down, and it's sort of just hanging out in one of the cells, looking like it's working." She leaned forward and smiled. "The thing is it's actually taking a nap, using that cell as the perfect hammock. I'm just sure of it, Ben."

"I wouldn't be a bit surprised," he said, raising his coffee to toast hers. "You seem to know a thing or two about bees."

Ben took another piece of cucumber, and it surprised him with a minty taste, different from the lemony taste of the last one. "Yesterday when you were getting the comb honey, how did you not get stung? Do you always do that? Not wear gloves or a helmet or anything?"

August dabbed at her mouth with her napkin. "How does it go? As so you thinketh, so you be-ith—or it be? It's something like that. Anyway, I *know* I'm not going to get stung. I just know it, Ben. It's not something I can fake knowing or pretend to know. If doubt's there, I can assure you—from plenty of past experience, mind you—it's enough to change the entire equation. With about 32,000 bees in that hive ... well, you do the math of trying to fake that knowing." She smiled and passed him more eggs, which he gladly accepted. "I'll tell you what. I know you're not going to be here for longer than you are, so after breakfast, come with me as I tend to the bees. You just might be interested in my third abide-by."

"I'd love to," Ben said. "Did Henry work with the bees too?"

"Oh goodness no. He left them to me, said they were my thing."

Ben was surprised; it was hard to think of August doing something Henry had no part of. "How did you two meet?"

August took a long sip of coffee. "We were both in the Peace Corps." She smiled. "I fell in love in about two seconds. Oh, Henry. He just had this way about him, and I knew the sun would always shine when we were together, no matter what the weather was. You know what I mean by that, Ben. I'm sure you do."

Ben smiled. "I do." Listening to her gave him a new appreciation for why Izzy and Daxx loved when he read to them and why they always wanted him to keep going, just a little longer. It was such a good feeling to be swept away by August's words, to step into her story for a while. "Where were you in the Peace Corps?"

"In a tiny corner of the world. Of all the places, that's where we found each other. St. Vincent—officially St. Vincent and the Grenadines." She laughed. "Now don't you worry; most people have never heard of it. New to you?"

"Never heard of it," Ben confirmed.

"It's in the eastern Caribbean. Henry was there as a music teacher, and I got to teach English. I remember … oh, those sweet boys." August closed her eyes and shook her head. "We saw a lot of pain, not at all the kind of pain we went there to alleviate, and we found ourselves trying to be gentle advocates while being careful not to rustle too many feathers. In the end, I don't know how much good we did, but we were both so grateful for the chance to live there and get to know those beautiful people."

Ben offered August the last of the honey, and when she declined, assuring him she was full, he finished it off. "You know, August, I'm finding more and more that I have *no* idea what I'm doing when I try to lessen other people's pain. I don't think I really know what kind of pain anyone else is in."

August nodded. "It's a tricky thing. That's for sure. Whenever I look closely, I can see that fine line between recognizing pain and, well, recklessly just assuming that what I see is pain, instead of something else. I know reckless is a strong word, but that line is so very fine, Ben."

"Yeah … I can see that. Lately, I've also started to see the difference between coming from a place of humility and one of arrogance." It felt good to acknowledge it.

"Ah, yes. Humility. What a gift. I have to say, Henry was humble to the bone, even with all his talents. He's the one who taught me how to just *love* being me while not making myself better than anyone else. Not by trying, mind you. No … he did it just by being Henry."

"I really wish I could have met him."

"Oh, me too. I wish you could have heard him play the oboe. Remind me later, and I'll show you his wood shop. He's the one who taught Heather how to make—I think it was the flute he started with. Anyway, he played all the wood instruments, but the oboe was by far his favorite. He just loved what he could do with those notes. And so did I, Ben. I really did."

Ben loved the picture in his mind of Henry and August on the porch, sitting in their rockers, Henry playing the oboe for her. "After the Peace Corps, what did you do? Did you come back here?"

"Oh no. It was a little while before we showed up here. Before that, we lived on the outskirts of San Francisco … let me see. Then that tiny town in Colorado … and then just outside Portland. We spent some time going from here to there, not sure where next was. Henry would start as a substitute teacher, and that sometimes led to full-time positions. When we were really lucky, I'd find some position or other in the school too. Henry also had a good business making wood instruments, and it wasn't hard to get set up wherever we were." August laughed. "He really was like the Pied Piper. He could just start playing a note or two, and people would come to him, and once they met him, well, there was no turning back. People loved him." She paused and took a deep breath, smiling. "Of course they did. There was nothing not to love." August started to get up, but Ben jumped up and told her to stay put, insisting that he would clear the table and clean up. He asked her to tell him more about her and Henry—anything she wanted to.

"Well. Let's see. You name it, Henry was so supportive. I worked for a while at a nonprofit. I just *loved* it there. We provided eyeglasses to children whose families couldn't afford it. I was mostly behind the scenes, writing grants and petitions, that sort of thing. But when I got to be there when a little one could see clearly for the first time … oh, it took my breath away. Oh! It's been years since I thought about this … Ha! At one point, Henry set aside the woodworking and teaching and tried to put pen to paper and figure out the different inventions he had in his head. Oh, there were so many of them. When we go to his wood shop, I'm sure I can dig up some of them to show you. I think, in the end, he had so many places to start, he could never finish any of them. But he had fun, and so did I."

"Your life with him sounds amazing. Did you always get along so well?" Ben said, drying the dishes.

"Not in the beginning. We *thought* we did, but over the years, as we learned from our mistakes, we really worked on being good to each other, and that brought us closer and closer. It goes fast, Ben. So fast ..."

He turned to her and smiled, his feelings conflicted.

August stood up, took a deep breath, and clapped her hands together. "Look what a nice job you've done sprucing this place up. Thank you, Ben. Thank you *very* much. Now let's get you outside. The bees are calling."

She was already on her way, and Ben was more than happy to follow, wherever she wanted to lead him.

9:07 a.m.

After dropping off the kids at school, Ella parked down the block from the bike shop. A little before nine o'clock, Ethan flipped the sign to Open and turned on the rest of the lights.

As Ella was about to get out of the car, her phone rang. It was Charlotte. She let it go to voicemail and then listened to the message.

"Okay, Ella, I'm sorry. I think I said I was sorry like a hundred times last night, but I'll say it again. *I'm sorry.* I'm a shitty friend—well, not always, almost never, but I've had my moments, and now you know the one I'm most embarrassed about. My horrible secret is out. And I'm sorry for it. I really am. You're like my sister, Ella, and we need to be there for each other. Jesus. See? This is what happens when you don't pick up. I go on blabbing away. Anyway, let's make things right. Let *me* make things right. I want to be there for you. This is a shitty time for everything to be falling apart—all of it, all at once. Okay. Call me. I miss my best friend."

Ella did her best to shake off the turbulent mixed feelings before going into the bike shop. She wanted to focus.

Ethan looked up from behind the counter when the bell chimed. "Welcome back, Ella." He didn't seem surprised.

"Hey, I'm sorry about leaving so abruptly and not coming back yesterday. There's just a lot … well, it doesn't matter. It's not why I'm here and—"

"Why *are* you here?" he said, though not in an unfriendly way. "I'm not sure I helped with anything yesterday. I thought about it after you left. Ben—is he okay?"

"I'm not sure. See … he's … he's taking some time for himself, I guess, but he's not really talking to anyone and …" The tears were back, so she just nodded, hoping that was enough of an answer.

Ethan looked pensive, then said, "I'm glad to know he's okay—relatively anyway." He stapled a thin pile of papers together, then put it on top of a stack of other papers. "Sometimes space is a good thing. It can be hard for the ones not taking it though. I think we've all been there."

"Yes," Ella said, more composed now.

"Listen, it could get busy in here soon, so if you don't mind, can we continue this conversation in my office?" he said, heading over to his workspace.

"Of course," she said, following behind him and then sitting on the same crate as yesterday. She watched him set up. There was something comforting about being there, about the bike shop itself, with its newness and possibility right when she walked in, and then the old, tried, and tested in the second half, his office as he referred to it, the space so evenly split, no divider other than the peninsula-shaped counter jutting into the middle.

Ethan pointed. "That wheel's an old one but a good one. Ben was working on restoring it for me. When he started here, he didn't even know what this was called."

Ella looked at him blankly, and he smiled, then said, "A truing stand." He clicked the wheel into place and spun it. "Have to make sure it's free to move. This morning, the plan is to re-tension the spokes. Ben's getting good at that." As he flicked his finger against the different spokes, he said, "Can you hear that?"

"I'm not sure …"

"The different tings?" He did it again. "The looser ones have longer tings, bigger vibrations. That lets me know they need tightening. But first, you have to relax the whole wheel."

She watched as he slowly spun the wheel and carefully sprayed a small amount of liquid from what appeared to be a homemade concoction—given the old, well-used spray bottle—on the concave rim where the spokes met the circular frame.

"What else did Ben do when he was here? Did he … did you talk to him much?"

Without breaking his focus on the wheel he was still turning, Ethan said, "Yeah, we talked. I like him. He's a good guy. He was really respectful and interested in all this." He motioned around him. "He *got* it—that it's what I love to do, and he seemed as interested in that as anything else. Wanted to know about every little piece and then the smaller pieces that made up those pieces. He asked so many questions, he had me thinking of things I'd never considered—and I've been doing this since I was little. I used to help my dad here."

"This place has such a great feel to it," Ella said.

Ethan smiled as he slowly turned the wheel again. "Yep, my home away from home. Anyway, Ben ended up being so helpful. He didn't want to have anything to do with talking to customers, but while I was doing that, he'd continue working on whatever I had been doing. He paid such close attention, and you know, now that I think of it, I never had to explain anything to him twice. He's a quick learner."

She nodded, trying to digest everything. It was mesmerizing watching him work.

Reaching into his toolbox, he pulled out a thick, notched metal ring, hollow on the inside, about the size of a quarter. "This is a Japanese spoke wrench. Ben was fascinated by it." He fitted the notched ring against one of the spokes, close to where the spoke met the rim. "You just give the wrench a half a turn. That's all it needs."

He counted to three and did the same half turn of the wrench around the third spoke over. And then the next third one over, counting each time.

Watching, she silently counted along, *One, two, three, half a turn … One, two, three, half a turn …* "Why do you do every third spoke?"

"That way I don't get any flat spots, and the wheel stays even and balanced the whole time. Takes three times around to get all the spokes, and then—it's like magic. It's beautiful. Perfect tension—not too little, not too much. Sometimes I need to do another round, but always, always, just half a turn of the wrench at a time. Want to try?"

"Oh … no … I wouldn't trust myself not to do a full turn right now. But thank you," she said.

He stopped and twirled the wrench in the palm of his hand. "My dad taught me the half turn. When he wasn't looking, I decided to speed things up, get my work done in half the time with a full turn." He shook his head, smiling. "I sure was stubborn. Didn't make that mistake again though, and I started to trust my dad. It was a lesson I needed to learn: if there's too much tension, it'll snap. Everything has its breaking point."

"Are you talking about Ben?" It just came out, and right away, she knew he hadn't been. "I'm sorry." She shook her head. "I think I have a one-track mind right now." The smile he gave her was tinged with sadness, and she wondered at the empathy he seemed able to feel, considering she had just met him.

The bell dinged as a customer came in, and Ella reluctantly took it as her cue to leave. Standing up, she said, "Thanks for talking to me. You're very kind."

"My pleasure. Ben'll be okay. I know a solid soul when I meet them. Ben's one of them. You too, Ella. It'll be okay."

She thanked him again, so appreciative of his perspective.

Sitting in her car, she checked her phone—just a text from Charlotte: "Blue Express? Please? My treat."

She hesitated and then finally wrote back: "ok."

It was time.

9:41 a.m.

August had suggested taking the long way to the beehives. She was excited to show Ben the path through the fields of wildflowers. Ben understood why; it looked straight out of the storybook he had read to Izzy and Daxx hundreds of times. Along the narrow, worn path, strategically placed, years and years ago according to August, were clusters of trees that provided shaded areas. Standing under a huge ficus, August instructed Ben to crouch down just like she was, facing the next field beyond them. "Look at the air between the tops of the flowers and about one foot above that," she said. At first, it was hard to focus on the air, but finally Ben saw what August wanted him to see—the activity of the bees, flitting and flying, nose-diving into flowers, coming up for air, then zipping to another landing. The more he watched, the more choreographed it appeared.

"Oh!" August whispered, clasping her hands. "They're just so amazing. Look how they *feel* their way. Oh, Ben, I imagine being like that sometimes." She smiled. "I suppose

I try to mimic them. It's just that the more I get to know them, the more I'm convinced they never stop hearing the music ... ever."

Yes, Ben thought. *That's it.* She was putting words to what he was feeling. "Do *you* hear music, August?"

"I do right now." She inhaled deeply. "Oh, yes." She patted his arm, and they continued walking. "And you? Without my radio, can you hear it?"

Ben felt deeply present in the moment, each sense fully aware of his surroundings. "I do. I hear it too ... at least here, now."

After a comfortable silence, August said, "Ben, I'm wondering something. It didn't look like you were hearing the music yesterday when you got in my truck. And thank you, by the way, for not giving me a hard time and just getting in. That was good of you. I've been meaning to tell you that. Back to the music though. Are there times you can't hear it at all? Or does it just get quieter?"

August's first abide-by came to him. Talking about it was exactly what he had a taste for. "It's when I think. Or think too much. I can't hear anything else." He stopped himself from explaining more, not wanting to dilute the truth. It felt so safe talking to August.

She nodded, saying, "Hmmmmmm," as if she understood precisely.

"It's caused ... some problems for me," he said. "The past couple of months, especially the past few weeks ... the problem's been getting bigger."

"Yes. That certainly happens. Yes, indeed, Ben. And what's the problem?"

"I honestly don't know, and that's what's … Well, August, it's a little terrifying. There was something at work, something … I just can't figure out … I guess I think a lot at work. It's … it's what I'm paid to do." He ignored the feeling he got from talking about work in the present tense.

"You're paid to think? Of all the pickles. Tell me what that looks like, Ben. I can hardly imagine."

Considering a typical day, Ben said, "Well, I'm given problems to solve and—"

"What kind of problems?"

"It's usually related to how to raise sales when they're not on the climb already, how to get them even higher, how to keep our niche in the market when it's threatened, how to keep our target market's attention …" He stopped.

"Okay then, maybe I can see that," August said, nodding as if she was trying to picture it. "And then what are you in charge of thinking about?"

Ben wanted to talk about August's bees and comb honey and which spices to plant in the shade and which thrived in full sun, and which weeds were actually edible and important. He wanted her to tell him more about Henry and Heather and everything she was excited about. "Well … we have brainstorming sessions … we talk about ways to … I'm sorry, August." He held his hand to the side of his head, pushing against the sudden sharp pain with as much pressure as he could. "Can we talk about something else?"

She patted him on the back. "Sure thing, Ben. No problem at all. You know what? The bees can wait. Let's invoke my abide-by number two, pause when you need to. I have the perfect spot, a little surprise I was holding onto for the perfect timing—and it just showed up out of the blue when I least expected it. Don't you love when that happens?" She started walking and said, "Follow me. Not much farther. I promise."

Ben felt foggy and heavy as she led him to a gathering of eucalyptus trees. Even distracted by the pain in his head, he felt a deep appreciation for the beauty of such raw nature and the strong aroma of the eucalyptus. August pointed to the hammock strung between two trees and told him to get comfortable and rest, assuring him she'd be back later, when it was time.

Cradled in the hammock, staring at the leaves in the canopy of branches above him, Ben felt the tension in his head slowly release.

10:11 a.m.

After sitting down with their coffees, Charlotte looked like she was about to continue with her apology, so Ella jumped in and said, "First, I'm glad you told me. I realize you didn't have to, and I appreciate that you did."

Not hiding her surprise, Charlotte sat back and just looked at her.

Ella went on. "Second, I judged you." She took a deep breath and slowly let it out. "I just kept thinking I would never do ... what you did, and maybe I wouldn't, not exactly that, but I ..." With a quick swipe of her hand, she stopped a tear from leaving her eye. "I'm sorry for the things I said about you. I know it was bad. Really bad. You didn't deserve that. No one does."

Charlotte squeezed her hand. "Apology accepted. You're such a good person, Ella. I mean, if there's anyone I look up to and try to emulate, it's you. You know that."

"Well, that's one of the reasons I thought it was a good idea for us to talk. You might want to think twice about that. I get why you had to tell me about … you …" She couldn't bring herself to say *you and Ben*. "There comes a point when a secret—it's just run its course."

Charlotte leaned forward. "What's going on, Ella?"

An old couple walked into the café, holding hands. Ella looked back at Charlotte and cleared her throat. *Don't.* "When Ben and I decided to have kids, we had this vision of sharing all the responsibilities equally—work, parenting, the house, finances, all of it. Not that we'd both do everything, but we'd both have a hand in each part." *Stop. Stop right there.*

"Okay … I can see that with you guys, mostly. Kind of."

"It's okay," Ella said. She cleared her throat. "That plan didn't play out. After Izzy was born, and then especially once Daxx came into the picture, it was pretty obvious our plan wasn't going to work. As our family grew, so did our expenses, way more than we realized they would. Do you remember when Ben and I were both working from home? Or had we not met you yet?" Things were starting to get confusing.

Charlotte looked shocked. "You don't remember? The Christmas party? Ben was new at Starfish. I was with that loser Craig. You saved me, and I decided right there and then to be your best friend."

It wasn't how Ella remembered it, but she let it go. "Of course. Okay, so ..." *Stop. Right now.* "This was before then. Ben was freelancing as a branding consultant, and it just wasn't cutting it, mostly because his clients were start-ups." This she remembered clearly. "There was a lot of passion and energy, and Ben was really excited about what those young companies were doing. But there wasn't a lot of money in it yet. And my jewelry wasn't bringing in much either."

The couple had sat down two tables away, the man's hand shaking as he put his cup and saucer down. The woman reached over and helped him open the sugar packet that was escaping his grip. Ella had to make herself look away.

"The thing was, as much as we both loved our work, we loved parenting just as much. We were getting to know a different side of ourselves and each other."

"You've both always been such good parents," Charlotte said. "If I ever have kids, I'm signing up for lessons."

Ella ignored the compliment. If she slowed down now, she might stop. "It came down to money. We wanted to be able to stay here—it's such a good place to raise kids. But we needed more money to do that. So we came up with a new plan that felt right. We gave it a year. Both of us would do everything we could to grow our individual businesses, branch out in our contacts, and see how to leverage our skills in other areas. One of us was bound to raise it up a solid notch; we were confident in that. When that happened, we'd have our moneymaker. Problem solved. If for some reason that didn't happen, we had a backup plan, one we promised each other we wouldn't have to resort to: one of us would set aside our passion and get a regular job with a guaranteed salary." *It's not too late. Take it in another direction. You can easily take it in another direction.*

"And you gave yourself a year for which part of this?"

"If we didn't have a solid, steady income after a year, one of us would close our business." *Don't do it.* Ella's face started itching.

"Okay ... so it didn't work ... Ben closed up shop and ended up working at Starfish. How did you decide it would be him?"

"He volunteered." Now it was the back of her neck itching. *Stop.* "He wanted to be a stay-at-home dad and work from home, continuing his consulting business ... God, he wanted that, and he was *so* good with the kids— not just our little ones, but also the twenty-something ones with big ideas, the owners of the start-ups ..."

"But he did it. Because that's who Ben is," Charlotte said.

Ella nodded. The itching was overwhelming, spreading down her arms. Still she refused to give in to it and scratch. The voice inside her was yelling now. *Shut up—just stop! Not now, it's the wrong time, not to Charlotte, not now, shut up shut up shut up.*

She looked at Charlotte, weighing her options. "I should have stopped him. It might be the worst thing I've ever done ... not stopping him."

And just like that, skimming answers to Charlotte's umpteen questions and inwardly shaking her head at Charlotte's assurances that it wasn't that bad, that she was being overly dramatic, Ella quietly closed the door again to her secret, resolving never to open it again. Not even a crack.

She watched the old couple leave, walking slowly, his arm hooked into hers. Ella imagined following them, wherever they were going, so she could watch them a little longer. But Charlotte had started talking, and she wanted to be a good friend and actually listen.

10:59 a.m.

Ben woke up in the hammock.

August was sitting on a folding chair a few feet away with the radio on. The singer's voice dragged heavily and with determination, as if every word was attached to something big and brave.

August looked comfortable, or at least as if she hadn't been in any hurry for Ben to wake up. She was inspecting a comb of honey with a magnifying glass. Seeing that Ben was awake, she offered him the comb, along with a banana and then a jug of water with sprigs of rosemary and slices of lemon. "Drink and eat," she said. "I've been saving this for you. You look better. Is that how you feel?"

"Yes ..." Ben took a moment to make sure the pain in his head was really gone. He sighed with relief. "So much better."

"Good. That's good, Ben."

He unpeeled the banana. "Thank you so much. This is perfect."

The combination of the honey, banana, and water energized him. He thanked August again, pointing out that she always seemed to know exactly what he needed.

August stopped fiddling with the radio, which had gone to static again, and said, "Oh, I've been getting lucky. Either way, it's important for me to try. I *like* to try. Whenever Henry was teaching a student their first instrument, he'd say, 'Try it out first. See if it makes your fingers sing.' He was a big believer in everyone being able to play *something*, whether it was an oboe or a recorder. Sometimes it just took more than one try to get the right fit, and from the stories he would tell, I knew one thing for sure: everyone had a lot more fun when the learner was playing what they felt matched to." She smiled. "I feel perfectly matched to guessing what my new friend Ben might need. It's a good fit for me."

"Well, you might be one of the nicest people I've ever met," Ben said. "And I really appreciate all you've done for me."

"It makes my heart sing, and that feels good." She smiled as the static cleared and she landed on a station.

Enjoying the gentle sway of the hammock, Ben said, "I bet some of those students took Henry's advice and kept it their entire lives. I had a professor I really liked in a philosophy class in graduate school. He told me it wasn't smarts that were going to make me successful; it was my people skills." Ben laughed. "I thought I understood exactly what he meant. Didn't doubt that for a second. Looking back now, the way he smiled when he said it, it's like he knew I didn't have a clue what he was talking about—but that someday I would."

"And do you?" she asked.

"I don't know. I just know I've started questioning what happy implies, what it means for me." Ben swung slowly back and forth. "All those years in school, and that's the one comment that stuck with me."

"You have beautiful people skills, Ben. That professor was exactly right."

"I haven't used them well, August. I haven't done anything good."

"Well, I don't know about that, not at all. I'll pretend it was true though. Why does it matter? Ha! Why does your face look like that right now? Don't you see? Today's today. This is exciting, Ben. You have wonderful people skills, and you're very smart."

"But—*and* not the good kind, August. That's what I'm trying to tell you." Why wasn't she listening to him? And why was she *always* smiling? And who cared if he said *but*? It was a ridiculous rule. It just made the conversation stilted.

Seemingly oblivious to the sudden turn in his mood, she went on. "I have a feeling it's the perfect time for my abide-by number three: learn more about what you care about. It's the key to so much, Ben." Her words and the way she looked at him—the kindness in her eyes tugged at him and softened his frustration, though it still lingered below the surface.

"You know what you care about, Ben. You know that about yourself better than anyone will ever know it. And it changes. Whatever you care about, keep learning more about it," she said. "Why do you think Henry didn't want anyone trying to learn an instrument that didn't make their fingers sing?"

121

"Was he more concerned with them liking an instrument or being good at it?" Ben asked.

"Well, let me ask you something. Liking it or being good at it—which comes first?"

Ben thought about it. "When ..." He changed his mind. "If you ..." He changed it again, his mind arguing just as persuasively in the other direction again.

"I don't know either!" August said, laughing. "Not a clue. Oh, Ben, I don't have any answers. I just know it's a good idea to spend your energy on the things that actually matter to you."

Ben sank deeper into the hammock and closed his eyes. "I'm so confused. My head is swirling." He looked at August. "I don't know what I'm doing wrong."

August leaned her head back, the sun on her face as it beamed through a break in the branches. "Well, I can tell you that when I try so hard to get things right, I usually end up forgetting what's right for me." She looked at Ben. "I can also tell you that *nothing* will tell you what's right for you more clearly than your heart, but you won't have access to all that clarity unless you're willing to feel what you feel— honey, stingers, and all."

Ben fought the agitation threatening to take over, frustrated that it kept showing up out of nowhere. *Just let it out. Get it all out.* He got out of the hammock and started pacing.

"The company I work for—we're really good at what we do." Why did his voice sound so stiff and formal? Who had he just become?

August nodded. "Which is to be thinkers, from what I understand."

He cleared his throat and tried to relax. "Yes, but—and—it's more than that. Basically, we specialize in how to market to teenagers. So, if you have a new brand of clothing, for example, and your market is teenagers, you would pay us a lot of money to figure out what you need to do in order to guarantee that teenagers will buy your clothes. It's our job, at least the group I work with, to figure out how teenagers think, what they care about—"

"Well, that's something interesting now, what they care about. For a minute there, I thought all you did was try to get into their heads to sell clothes to them."

"That *is* what we do, August." Why was she being so naïve? Had she spent too much of her life talking to bees? And did she need to punctuate *every* sentence with a smile? He shook his head and went on. "We figure out what teenagers care about and why they make the choices they do, why they buy what they buy, what motivates them, the list goes on and on. And in the end, we come up with a branding and marketing plan that'll get teenagers' attention."

"So they'll buy the clothes."

"Or whatever. It's not always clothes. But—and—yes, that's the point."

"And then what?" August said.

Ben started to answer and then stopped.

And then what.

It hit him. No matter what he said, he was going to hate his answer.

11:11 a.m.

Still sitting at the Blue Express, trying to shut the door to … what was no one else's business—Ella didn't like thinking of it as a *secret* anymore—wasn't as easy now. It felt so much bigger, that thing that was no one else's business, and the door, it felt tiny in comparison, and the thing that was no one else's business kept spilling out of the not-quite-closed door, pushing with all its weight. So Ella said as little as possible, letting Charlotte do most of the talking, about whatever she wanted to talk about—her nightmare client and the guy she was thinking about dating and the dry cleaner she would never go back to.

1:48 p.m.

Upset with himself for being anything other than patient and kind with August, even if it was just in his thoughts, Ben looked around for how he might be helpful when they went back to the house. The potbelly stove in the center of the room had only a few pieces of wood in the crate next to it, so he asked where he could get more for her. To his surprise, she led him to another part of the property he hadn't seen, where she handed him an ax and thanked him profusely, promising to have lunch ready when he was done. "Just whatever you can do, Ben." And she headed over in the direction of her gardens. He looked at the pile of logs that just needed to be split and figured he could get a lot done for her in a short time.

It took a while for Ben to get into a rhythm, and it was much harder than he thought it would be to hit the spot he was aiming for. He considered himself to be in good shape, so he was also surprised by how strenuous it felt. Still, with every swing of the ax—even those that felt awkward or landed off target—Ben felt something release, a part of him let go, and before long, his mind was quiet.

By the time he had filled the wheelbarrow and started back to the house, he felt lighter. And hungry.

After a lunch of beans, mozzarella, basil, olive oil, and eggplant, August told Ben she wanted to introduce him to her bees. It was time, she said, though she didn't share with Ben what her timetable was based on. After August assured him he'd be fine, that he wouldn't get stung unless he wanted to—which, Ben reiterated, he did not want to—Ben reluctantly agreed.

They walked a different pathway to the hive. "Now, if you can focus on one—I know it's going to be hard, and just try—you'll see its wings beating very fast, Ben—about 200 beats per second. That's where their music comes from—their buzzing. Try to get very quiet inside so you can hear it. Okay?"

Ben nodded, already trying to get quiet.

August gestured to the field of flowers they were walking through. "Now, consider this. A honeybee will meet and interact with, oh, fifty or even a hundred flowers during its collection-time field trip. Now, remember what I said before? The average bee produces about one-twelfth of a teaspoon of honey over the course of her *extremely* important little life. All that work for those few drops of honey. Do you see it, Ben? Do you see the miracles? Do you see how lucky we are? No wonder they have six legs, five eyes, and two pairs of wings. They have a heck of a lot to get done in a short time."

August stopped and turned to Ben. "I know you're very smart, and do you see it, Ben? If one of these bees can make one-twelfth a teaspoon of honey, which has life-giving and healing properties and is nothing less than magical, and if that same little bee can make music and dance its thoughts, effectively communicating to stranger and fellow beehive cohorts alike, well, Ben, imagine what *you're* capable of."

"You say such nice things, August, and … what?" The way she was suddenly looking at his T-shirt and jeans made him nervous.

"Well," she smiled, "it's a very good thing you're not wearing black. They'd all think you were a bear, their greatest enemy, and well, yup, for sure they'd come after you. All right then, here we are."

Ben's palms started sweating, and he wiped them on his jeans, wishing blue was farther away on the spectrum from black.

They stopped about thirty feet from the hive. "Now, I just gave you plenty to think about, and for the love of bees, that's what I want you focusing on if you're going to think. Think about all those jewels you now know about bees. Wonder about them. Or, even better, don't think at all. Just feel your connection to the bees."

"I think you should know," Ben said, "I don't feel any connection to the bees … not yet anyway."

"It's hard to feel a connection before you think a kind thought and say nice things, which is why I really like saying nice things to you, because feeling the truth of them makes me feel connected to you." She looked at him. "*No* connection to them?"

He shook his head.

"Hmmm … it'll be okay, I reckon. And if not, well … Okay then, I'm going to sing a little something to calm them. I always do. They love it. You—get as close as you can and just observe these lady wonders. Say, 'Hello, pleased to meet your acquaintance.' Just let them know you appreciate them and are happy to know them. And don't open your mouth. Just in case. Whooee! Let's go."

Ben followed slowly behind August, who was singing a song Ben had to admit did have a calming effect, even on him. It was more humming than words, and Ben wondered if that was the key. Maybe the bees mistook the humming for their buzzing, their music as August had said, and they thought she was one of them.

Fifteen feet away, Ben started to feel like everything was happening in slow motion. With a single thought, his focus went from the humming and buzzing to the possibility of getting stung. And as his heart rate increased and he started to sweat, he tried to stop thinking, to feel a connection to the bees instead, but then as August removed the first lid and thousands of bees began swarming, fear took over and grew so loud in his ears, and he felt like he and the bees were on opposing teams, and only one would win, and so resentment crept in fast, and he began to dislike the bees, and anger started to take hold of him as he covered his head, crouched down to the ground, and then instinctively stood up and started running in the other direction, swatting at the bees following him, leaving a trail of dead bees behind him, their stingers embedded in his skin.

3:02 p.m.

When Ella came home with the kids after school, the house felt different. Her studio was more an albatross than a sanctuary, and every time she looked at the door, she felt guilty for not working, despite feeling incapable of it. She had spent time that afternoon delivering gift certificates— or in some cases, trying to—with full apologies to clients whose jewelry was due to be delivered or picked up within the next ten days, a random number she had picked. There was relief in it, in releasing the pressure, but the sadness was cutting; her creativity and drive felt like they had vanished, as if they never belonged to her in the first place.

Ben always said that when the two of them weren't working, nothing worked. And it was true. They had even had electrical issues—sudden computer crashes, lights going out, a toaster not working. Then, once she and Ben were in sync again, the electrical issues would miraculously resolve themselves.

She wondered what it would take for her and Ben to get back in sync now—and, far less important but still on her mind, she wondered if she'd be able to salvage her business. She knew she had entered dangerous territory and might not be able to return from it. A bride had refused the gift certificates, and Ella wasn't at all surprised; she was so embarrassed to be offering them in the first place. Of course the bride wanted to give her bridesmaids an actual piece of jewelry to be worn during the ceremony. Naturally, she wanted her money back. Other clients were more accommodating and understanding, and she wondered if they knew about Ben. Had people from Starfish been talking? Despite those clients' flexibility, she could feel the tarnish spreading itself over the reputation she had built.

Needing to escape it all and wanting to do something the kids would enjoy, Ella decided to take them to the beach. She filled a backpack with snacks, sand toys, and a towel. On their way, while walking the few blocks to the bluff, Izzy and Daxx played tag, not going more than ten seconds without tagging each other and saying, "You're it," which they found hysterical. Their laughter was so contagious Ella couldn't help but smile. The game ended when they reached the top of the 126 stairs that would take them down to the sand. The three of them counted each step and held hands all the way down.

Once they got set up, Izzy and Daxx started digging a hole, using their hands and a bucket.

It was chilly and overcast, but every now and then the sun came through, and the surge of heat on Ella's skin felt like heaven. She loved watching the gentleness of the waves; they were small, which was why no surfers were out. Being outside, with so much breathing room to think, she felt more space than she had in a while.

Ben seemed so far away, and she could feel the distance between them growing, not physically though. Was it emotionally? she wondered. Mentally? Instinctively, she felt Ben was in his own world, removing himself bit by bit from her, though not from Daxx and Izzy. She knew it without a shred of proof. She could feel it, and the awareness and loneliness made her heart hurt so much it took all her willpower not to curl up into a tight ball right there on the towel.

When Daxx stopped what he was doing and looked at Ella, she had a panicked feeling that he knew what she was thinking—and an even bigger fear that he would try to say something and stutter. So, feeling exactly like the mom she was trying not to be, she preempted it all by jumping in with, "Are you hungry?" She made a big deal out of rummaging around the backpack to find the pretzels. Offering him the bag she quickly opened, she said, "Here you go, sweetie. Have some."

"N-n-n-n-n-no … I-I-I-I-I—" He stopped, then came over and took a pretzel. Just one. For her. To please her. And in that moment, she missed Ben even more, because none of this would be happening if he was there. And she wouldn't be flailing so badly and resorting to forcing food on Daxx instead of opening to his feelings, because when Ben was there, his presence somehow brought the best out of Ella so that when they were together, she was more patient and stronger and more like herself, a self that didn't make her cringe.

Izzy was sitting in the hole they had dug. She looked up at Ella and said, "What if Dad gets lost and doesn't remember how to get home?"

Ella's stomach dropped. She stopped herself from saying the first few responses that came to mind. They wouldn't help her or the children. *What would I say if Ben was here?* she wondered, willing herself to take her time. The more she thought about it, the closer she was to being able to offer a reassuring smile as she said, "I think he was already lost. And now he's remembering how to get home."

Izzy seemed okay with that. "He can probably look up at the stars if it's dark. Then he could follow them. He's so good at the stars, Mom. He tells me and Daxx a lot about them."

His face lighting up, Daxx said, "Yeah and when-when-when-when he-he-he …"

Ella leaned forward and cradled Daxx's soft, full cheeks in her hands. She looked him in the eye and then kissed his head. "Daxx, one time before you and Izzy were born, Dad and I went on vacation to a beautiful place with jungles and monkeys and wild birds and such beauty, but it was so hot. I mean *scorching* hot, like if the sun came close and said, 'Hi, Daxx, I'd like to meet you.'"

His eyes got big, and she felt encouraged as she went on. "Suddenly, when I tried to talk, it … thounded like thith becuth my tongue didn't like the heat. It had never happened before, and it's never happened since, but for a little while there, I couldn't talk the way I normally do, and it was a little strange, and it made me want to be very quiet, but Dad told me to talk anyway because he said otherwise he'd get bored if he had to do all the talking." Ella smiled. "So I talked, and eventually I sounded just like me again." Daxx threw his arms around Ella.

"It's gonna be fine, Daxx. Don't worry about a thing. Okay?"

He nodded, still holding on, and then Ella looked at Izzy, who seemed content.

Feeling a rush of happiness, Ella said, "Who wants to race!" And so the three of them raced forward to the big rock down the beach, then backwards to the towel, then side-leaping down the beach to a clump of seaweed, then back, again and again, amidst tumbles and slips and falls and laughter, until no one was thinking about who was missing.

4:40 p.m.

Using what August referred to as tweezers—but which might have been pinchers or pliers, Ben wasn't convinced—she had taken each of the stingers out of his arms, hands, neck, face, and head, at least the ones she could see. Then she had taken a whole basket full of lavender from the garden, pounded it with a mallet, and then rolled it and crushed between her palms. As soon as she placed the lavender on his skin, it immediately lessened the pain. Finally, she had topped each lavender-covered hole off with a few drips of honey. The irony was not lost on Ben.

Since then, August had been back out with the bees. She had some healing and helping to do, she said.

Ben was sitting on the couch, trying to ignore the pain and listening to the radio, which she had thoughtfully left for him. He looked through the old nature magazines and the stack of books, a few of which he had read. In college, he had taken a class on Thoreau, and at nineteen years old, Ben had been able to picture himself going off and living in nature for a while. He smiled at the memory he hadn't thought of in years; this felt a lot like what he had pictured at the time—minus August and the bee stings.

One of the books was falling apart at the threaded seams, the glue old and dry. He carefully opened it, landing on a random page that, once he started reading, felt anything but random. Slowly, line by line, he let the words by T. S. Eliot speak to him: *Let us go then, you and I ...*

At the end of the poem, he put the book back down on the pile and lay back. Soon, he felt himself getting absorbed by the song playing, with no static at all—a first in a while.

The lyrics were a story, the melody dramatic, the singer a man in pain who threw out quick words, snippets that let Ben peer into his mind, revealing what had happened to leave him feeling so melancholy. First, he was telling, *this happened and then this*—just saying it aloud to anyone who would listen, it seemed, and Ben felt the need to hear him well. And as the story went on, everything increased—the tempo, the volume, the intensity. The song seemed to get louder and louder as his emotions built, and he was spilling emotion, pouring out his pain, feeling the vulnerability of having his heart twisted and wrung out, saying how much it hurt without using words, only sounds—

The screen door shut as August came in with a basket full of fresh herbs and vegetables, and Ben realized he was crying.

Not understanding what was happening, fear surged through him. Why was August just standing there staring at him? Unable to catch a full breath, he was scared he might be having a panic attack.

"Okay," August said calmly. "Okay. Let's get some air." She put the basket on the counter, helped Ben up from the couch, and led him to the patio. "Here you go. Sit here," she said, pointing to the closer rocker. "Take some slow, deep breaths. I'll be right back."

As Ben inhaled the fresh air, he started to feel better. August came out a short time later with two jars filled with water and cucumber slices. She handed one to Ben, clinked hers against it, took a sip, and then set it down by the other rocker. Then she went back in and brought out two plates filled with bread, butter, tomato slices, radishes, mint, carrots, honey, and green beans.

As they sat there in the rocking chairs, looking out at all the trees, flowers, chirping and darting birds, and swaying grasses before them, Ben felt a peace enveloping him. Balancing the plate on his lap, he was trying to decide where to start. None of it was food he was used to snacking on, but it all looked so good. He wondered how this batch of honey would taste. "Is the beehive okay? I mean, all the bees that were lost—I'm sorry, August. I'm so sorry. I don't know—"

"No sorry necessary, my friend. Nature is nature. Everything is as it should be, even though it's not always easy. How are you feeling? How are those stinger holes feeling?"

"They're better. The honey and lavender are helping—thank you. But my mind. I'm not sure what ..." Again, he was at a loss for words.

"Ben, if you don't finish your sentences for yourself, you're inviting other people to finish them for you. And I don't think that's doing you or anyone else any favors. You were saying you're not sure what ..."

"I'm not sure what's happening to me." His appetite lost, he set the plate down next to the rocker. "I don't know what's happening to me." With terror creeping in, like he was sinking in quicksand, it felt like trying to throw a rope around a branch when he asked, "Do you know? Do you know what's wrong with me?"

August took a long sip from the jar, shielding her eyes with her hand and squinting up at the sun. "Abide-by number three. We started talking about it earlier and got interrupted by a certain stinging episode." She smiled at him.

"I remember," Ben said. "Learn more about what you care about." He wondered how this was an answer to his question.

"That's right. Never fall into the trap of thinking you know all there is to know about something—or someone."

A sadness he didn't understand surged through him.

"You're doing it," August said. "Do you see? You're learning, Ben. And you're being a humble learner at that. The best kind. You're taking the chance to learn something you didn't know."

"Like what?" Ben said. "I have no idea what you're referring to. It might be obvious to you, but I need specifics right now, August—as specific as you can get, because I feel a little like I'm going crazy—not learning."

She wrapped a small piece of radish in a mint leaf and ate it. "Well, for one thing, even though you know plenty about it, you're learning more about when to stick to your beets."

"My *beets*?"

August looked confused and then started laughing. "My goodness! I'm so used to saying that I forget not everyone uses it. Henry came up with it, just said it by accident one day, trying to express what it's like when your will has real staying power. He went on and on about how the red won't willingly leave your hands or anything else the beet touches. 'You just stick to your beets,' we'd encourage each other after that."

Ben felt himself relax. "I love when you talk about Henry."

"Ha. Me too. He was a big believer that there are *mountains* to learn about who you are, not just who you've been but who you can be. Tell me the third abide-by."

"Learn more about what you care about," he said.

"Exactly. And it's plain to see: among many other things, you care about Ben. You care about the person sitting right there, rocking back and forth in that chair. You care about who you are in this world. Am I right?"

He nodded.

"Yes. Well, a lot of people look backwards to learn about who they are—old things that happened and once-upon-a-time choices. Not Henry. As much he could, Henry stood right where he was, and if he was looking anywhere other than that, it was forward."

Ben liked picturing that.

"You're just learning a lot of things you didn't know before. And a big one—you're learning when to let something other than your mind take over. You have a beautiful mind, Ben. And you also have a beautiful heart." She patted his arm. "I didn't forget your question. You wanted to know what's happening to you. You're *learning.* That's what's happening, Ben. That's all. And you're doing a mighty fine job, if I might say so myself."

"I'm learning ..." He liked the sound of it and how it made him feel.

"Be nice to you. Learning's not easy. Not at all. Well ... except when it is."

"I have a feeling right now might be one of those not-so-easy times," Ben said.

"Well, that's why I'm so proud of you I could pop! It can be so scary to feel, to get in there the way the bees dive in and really commit to the experience. Any time you're afraid to feel, it's safe to bet three cells of honey you're holding something big inside, big feelings, and you're afraid if you let yourself feel what you're feeling, well, a part of you won't survive it. I remember the feeling, Ben. I remember it like it was yesterday. And what *always* proves itself true is that, yes, a part of you doesn't survive feeling those feelings: the pain of holding them in. It's gone, just like that." August held out her finger, and a lime-green bug landed on it. "Now here I've gone and talked your ear off again."

Ben shook his head. "You have a way of getting to the bottom of things. I've been trying to figure everything out for so long, and it's like the harder I try, the more it all falls apart. I'm happy to hear any advice from you. You could talk all night, and it wouldn't be too much for me to hear."

She smiled. "Well, the funny thing is you're the one you really need to hear from. You know that, Ben, don't you?" Before he could answer, August stood up and said, "I'll be right back."

Ben leaned back and stared up at the stars.

When August came back, she was carrying the Maglite he had seen by the door. Considering how heavy and solid the flashlight was, he had assumed it was as much for protection as anything else, a weapon of sorts.

Handing it to him, she said, "Go ahead and stand, Ben. Come on then."

He stood, holding the flashlight at his side, not sure what to do next.

"You know what a flashlight's for, Ben, don't you?"

"To brighten the darkness," he said, knowing it wasn't a trick question.

August smiled and nodded. "Exactly right. To shine light into the darkness. It's been a little dark inside you, but that light, it never goes out. It's always there. Sometimes you just need a reminder, that's all. Now, go on and hold the flashlight like this, right there in front of you—good … but facing up. Face the light up to the sky. Good. Now go ahead and turn it on."

Ben flicked it on, and a bright beam shot up into the night. It felt good holding it, kind of like a *Star Wars* light saber. He smiled, suddenly feeling a connection to Daxx that gave him goose bumps.

"Yes, indeed, Ben. Yes, indeed," August said. "Now, you know my abide-by number two."

"When you need to pause, do it."

"Close enough. The crickets are chirping slower now, so you'll feel a drop in the temperature soon. Stay with it. It's okay; it won't go too low. I'll leave you with this thought for the evening: as you saw today—more than once—a bee dies after stinging, just once. And us, well, Ben, I think a part of us dies a little bit every time we sting someone or something. And sometimes, when there's a whole lot of stinging going on, and it's called something else that makes it sound nice, you can end up with colony collapse disorder, which is what happens when the darn pesticides used on plants affect all those bees who interact with those plants, messing with the bees' nervous systems. It leaves them confused and disoriented and not so sure which way is up or down. And then a terrible thing happens. The worst thing that could happen—to anyone really. They lose any semblance of direction and can't find their way back home."

She patted Ben on the shoulder. "Look at the light you're shining, Ben. Feel your hands *holding* that light. Feel the light coming from inside you, from the center of you, the core of Ben. Hold the space for your light to shine. Just hold it. Hold it until you feel the light warming you, from the inside out. Hold it until you remember that *you're* light, Ben, until that's all you can feel. And then come inside. Come inside and get a good night's sleep."

August went inside, and Ben stood holding the light, feeling the darkness slowly dissolve.

Day 4, Friday

9:20 a.m.

As Ella walked into the bike shop, she realized what kept drawing her back there. It was one of the places where she felt a connection with Ben.

Ethan invited her back to his office and then showed her how he was replacing the chain on a bike, emphasizing that it was important to do it before it had too much stretch.

Looking up from the tool he'd been adjusting, Ethan said, "I've got a question for you. You said Ben's taking some time for himself. Did he leave without telling anyone where he was going? Go missing in a way?"

"Kind of," she said. "Three days ago, on Tuesday. Except he's not exactly missing. I mean, I've talked to him—he's called—well, until his phone died, and now I don't know where he is, but he's not actually missing. He went … walking."

Getting back to work, Ethan said, "That's not all that surprising. I think he was gearing up to go. He tried hard to fall in love with these bikes, to feel the way I do about them, but I'm pretty sure he ended up just understanding them, knowing how they work. But a bike—that wasn't his vehicle."

The idea resonated with Ella. "So, you think walking was?"

"It appears so."

"I hadn't thought about it like that," Ella said. "Did Ben seem okay to you? I mean, I don't know how well you got to know him, but from what you could see, did he seem okay … mentally?"

The way Ethan was looking at her made her think of Andy. That's who he reminded her of, she realized. Like Andy, he was thoughtful with his words, but he also didn't hold back in saying exactly what he thought.

"Mostly, yes," Ethan said. "Have you ever ridden a bike with wobbly handlebars?"

Ella shook her head. "I don't think so. Maybe when I was first learning?"

"Well, if your hands are gripping them and they're wobbling all around—and then say your brakes aren't working. Sooner or later, you're not going to feel like you have much of a choice." Ethan switched tools and started taking the tire off the wheel. "Maybe he just had to jump off the bike."

"Yes … yes, that's exactly what it seems like," Ella said. "On the phone, the past few times we talked, he sounded like he was under so much pressure. I'm just not sure what about." It felt strange to ask, but she pushed ahead anyway, saying, "Do *you* have any idea?"

"I'm really sorry to say I don't. We didn't talk about things like that—personal things. Mostly we just talked about bikes, all these tools and parts." He spun the wheel and watched as it turned. "Everyone knows too much pressure will blow a tire, but another thing I learned early on from my dad is that even a quarter-pound change in the pressure will affect the traction. If Ben was under pressure, I didn't sense it. He didn't show it when he was here."

"No, I guess he wouldn't have," Ella said, her mind spinning. "So, he didn't talk about *anything* going on with him?"

"Honestly, not a thing. I kind of feel bad I never asked. There just never seemed to be a reason to."

The realization of how deeply alone Ben was, no matter who he was with, shook her to the core.

10:15 a.m.

Ben woke up feeling restless. The house was quiet and still, so he wasn't surprised that August's bedroom door was open and the bed was already made. He guessed she was already out with the bees.

He decided to skip coffee, even though August had left the setup ready for him. It didn't feel right to make it without her there.

After considering his options, Ben decided to take a walk. As he made his way along a path he hadn't taken before, he was struck by how different being alone felt now, compared to what it felt like before he met August. He didn't feel like he was running away from anything. Nor did it feel like he was rushing, trying to find something. It felt simpler than that. He was just moving at a pace that felt right. When he surprised himself by ending up at the hammock, he appreciated the awareness that different roads led him to the same place. Though the hammock looked inviting, the ground seemed to beckon, so he sat down and leaned against a huge eucalyptus trunk. Breathing in the misty, heavily scented morning air, Ben started to feel something in him open up.

The more he relaxed, the more he realized how hard he had been trying to stop replaying what August said about people being afraid to feel.

What if he stopped fighting it? What if he just let himself feel?

What was he so afraid of?

Closing his eyes, he sat with the possibility of letting himself feel, open to whatever came next.

A while later, when August walked up, Ben tried to compose himself and smile at her, but tears were running down his cheeks, and he was taking quick breaths, his emotions far from under control.

"I'm losing it," he said.

August took her time getting into a sitting position next to him under the shade of the eucalyptus. "Let it go, Ben," she said after a few moments. "It's safe to just let it all go."

Ben leaned his head back against the tree and said, "I have no idea what I'm doing."

"Good, Ben. That's good to know. Now, what's got you feeling so many stingers this morning?"

He closed his eyes. "I can't stop thinking about work. I keep replaying these interactions, old ones, over and over in my head. I don't know what I've done, and I have to go back, I know I do, but I can't, August. And I can't keep doing *this* either." He put his head in his hands. "This is part of the problem. I can't think straight anymore."

"Don't think, Ben. Just talk."

He took a deep breath, exhaled loudly, and then said, "About three months ago, something happened, and it threw my world off its center—like it tilted it, and things haven't been right since then."

"Good. Okay. Go on …"

With scenes from the past few months flashing in and out of his mind, Ben thought about the ripple effect of how many things got tilted after that, one after another.

"It's going to stay confused in there," August said, pointing to his head. "Say it out loud. Don't worry about getting it right. Out with it now."

Ben rubbed his eyes, then began. "To show we support the community, our company set up these mentoring programs in the high schools. We handpick students and invite them to come intern for us, and then we also go to the high schools once a month to meet with them there. During the focus groups, we basically pick their brains, observing how they think, what matters to them, what's in, what's not, why, and so on." He paused. "You know what's interesting?"

"Tell me," she said.

144

"What's in and not—it changes all the time. But what they care about and how they think—that doesn't change. They're a smart, forward-thinking, *nice* generation. They can do amazing things. They can fix a lot and make things better than they've ever been—they're doing it already. We're just getting in their way. And we're pretending to help them and be there for them. But we're not. We take and take from them, and we don't give them anything. That's the truth, August." He looked at her. "I'm not explaining this very well."

"Oh no, you're doing fine—perfectly fine. It sounds to me like that's all itching your skin, for sure, but what's *stinging* you? I just haven't heard what has you so sad, and I wonder if you even know what it is."

Ben looked down. "I know what it is. It's not going to make sense. It's just … it's personal I guess, just a personal reaction I had to something."

"Well, I would hope so. Go on, Ben."

He rubbed his forehead. "This one day, we were at one of the high schools, and we were sitting around the table with our focus group, asking them questions, and it hit me. The way they were looking at us, looking up to us, as if they should be learning from us so they could become like us."

"And that's a bad thing?" August said. "I just adore you, Ben."

He sighed, starting to feel frustrated. "We were manipulating them."

"I don't understand. I don't feel like I have all the information. How were you manipulating them?"

Ben took a deep breath and fought the desire to end the conversation right there. "Because everything we said was with an agenda. *Every word.* And that agenda never had anything to do with what was good for them. It was about us and *our* power and how the company could make money. I'm good with people, August. I told you that. I know how to get people to listen to me, to trust me and follow my lead. And how do I do that? By pretending to listen to them, pretending to trust them, and pretending to follow their lead." He looked at August. "I know what I'm doing—I've always known. Except maybe now."

He looked at her, waiting for her to say something, to maybe disagree, but she just nodded.

"So, that day, I had to leave the school early. My boss said they needed me back at the office right away—a client crisis, which actually wasn't a crisis at all. It never is. Anyway, all the other students on campus were at lunch as I was leaving. There were kids sitting on the grass in groups, on benches, and then there was this cluster of tables—their outdoor cafeteria—and I was walking by, and all the tables were so packed with kids, probably at least twenty each, ten or twelve students on each side, and they were loud and laughing, and squished together ... all these little groups—except one. This one table."

Ben swallowed hard.

August nodded but didn't say a word.

"At this one table was just this one boy. He was sitting there ... no one on either side of him the whole way down both sides of the bench, and no one across the table from him. He was looking down, eating so slowly, just picking at his food. He was ... how was no one else at that table? I just ..."

"That poor boy," August whispered. And he knew she got it. She understood.

"He was slouched over with an energy that broke my heart. He's one of the saddest people I've ever seen, August. I stopped, maybe twenty feet away. I couldn't help staring at him. I thought of going over to sit with him or asking some of the other kids to. But I didn't. I didn't do anything. I just stood there thinking, *What's wrong with us? How are we letting this happen? How can we just act like it's normal and okay for someone to be sitting right there in the middle of it all— alone and in such obvious pain?* What was he thinking while he was sitting there, August? What's going to happen to him? What if that was one of my kids?"

With tears sliding down his cheeks again, he looked at her and said, "Something broke inside of me then, something happened, and I feel like I haven't gotten over it … because I don't *want* to, and I don't know how to, and I don't think I should. And I feel like I've been losing my mind ever since because—my mind's doing it on purpose, because I'm supposed to *feel* all this. I should be feeling it, but I'm so scared, August. I'm so scared that if I let myself feel the sadness I felt for that boy and everyone else who's so alone, who's sitting in a group but still feels so alone, if I feel how alone *I* feel, I'm afraid so many more feelings will come spilling out, and I won't know how to stop them or what to do with them. So I turned them off. Actually, no that's not true—that's a promise I made to myself—to start telling the truth, no matter what. And the truth is I stopped feeling a while ago. I mean *really* feeling. And when I saw that boy and felt his sadness and aloneness, when I let it in, something unlocked in me, and my mind, it knows what happened."

"Yes, yes, of course it does. And it's fighting for its life. Your mind, your ego, it's never felt so threatened. Of course, yes. Oh, Ben. What happened next?"

"I left, went back to work. Over the next two months, things fell apart. I couldn't stop thinking or talking about that boy. I went back to the school a few times after that, but I never saw him again." Ben shook his head. "Here's the other thing. When I asked the kids in the focus group about him, describing what he looked like and where he was sitting, they didn't know him but said it wasn't that unusual to see. They recognized it as a problem—*theirs*. One of the girls said she was in the Kindness Rocks club—they actually have that as a club—and she said she would bring it up at their next meeting to see what they could do to make sure it didn't happen again."

"Well, did that knock your socks off?" August said. "What goodness."

"Yes. *Exactly*. And it was in such sharp contrast to the reactions I got at work. When I suggested we needed to overhaul what we were doing in the focus groups, the resistance was … there was no breathing room, no space for change—not *that* kind of change. We weren't a charity, I was told. We did a lot of good already. Our company wasn't a division of social services. We were a business, and in any successful business, you always have to ask, does it help the bottom line?"

"Well, what did you want to do? What kind of ideas were they turning down?"

Ben sighed. "I didn't do a good job of offering any ideas." He thought about how strained his interactions had gotten at Starfish, how much tension there was at the end. "That might have been where I went wrong—well, one of the ways. I don't know. I guess my approach wasn't a good one. I was just trying to get them to see we were pretending to be contributing to the community through those internships and focus groups, but we didn't actually care about the kids. We were using them. We were putting ourselves in positions of leadership, but we weren't leading. We were using and manipulating, all for us, for the good of the company. We gave nothing. It looked like we gave a lot. But we didn't. We gave away *nothing.*"

"I see," August said. "Yes."

Ben took a deep breath. "The more I pointed it out, the worse it got. It pushed me to the edge when one of the people I worked with said the boy they wished I would please stop talking about was probably sitting alone for a reason, because he wanted to or had done something to deserve it. *What?* I was told I had to see there's more than one side to every story. That not everyone needs to be liked. That some people purposely push everyone away. *Are you kidding me?* None of it made sense."

"Oh, it does, though, Ben. Look at me. I want you to really hear my words. You are such a good man. Your strength runs deep in your blood. It roars. It won't be quieted. And it detached itself from your ego when you saw that boy, and that's when everything changed. Can you see it? Your strength detached from your ego and has been looking for something else to team up with because it needs balance; it knows that." She smiled and seemed to consider what to say next. "Let's go back though. You weren't finding support at work. Did you find it somewhere else? Did you find it at home or in a friend?"

"No," Ben said. "I couldn't talk to Ella ... I mean, every time I thought about it, something stopped me because ... she just felt like part of the puzzle. I never told her about any of it. I can't explain it. I still don't understand, but I felt like I was on my own with it, like I had to figure it out by myself—that was the only way."

"So, you only talked about it at work?"

"Yes. And then about two months later, when we were in a brainstorming session, I heard this tone in a coworker's voice in response to an idea I threw out, and it hit me what that tone was. It was pity—for me. If I've learned one thing through all this, it's that pitying someone is harmful, because it suggests you've got it better than them, and that's the *last* thing the person needs. Anyway, with everyone at work either exasperated by me or feeling sorry for me, I just ... I don't know. I kind of lost it. I just got up and walked out. At first, it was just to get some fresh air, but then the farther I walked, the more I could breathe, and I never wanted to go back."

"Where did you go?"

"I was just walking. After an hour or so, I ended up in a bike shop. It was the bell on the door that caught my attention. This lady was walking out with a bike, having a hard time getting it through the door, and the bell, it just kept chiming, because the door was partly opening and closing, over and over, and ... I don't know. I just walked in after helping her get the bike out. Then ..." Ben thought back, trying to make sense of it now. "The owner was just a really nice guy. Easy to talk to—about anything. Nothing serious, just interesting things. It took my mind off everything."

August nodded. "So, your mind is being like the male drones. It's being quiet, no stinger, lazily hanging out. It's there for when you absolutely need it—otherwise becoming background noise. *Amazing*."

"Yes, and it's doing it on purpose. I can feel it." It was happening again. His mind was fogging over as he tried to reconstruct his time at the bike shop, and suddenly his thoughts jumped to the morning he didn't go to the bike shop but just kept walking, last Tuesday, and sitting at the bus stop and the ants and the cracks in the sidewalk ... "And it's making me feel crazy. My mind is turning itself off because I can't mesh my awareness with my conscience, around the choices I've made, and I'm aware that it's happening. I'm going crazy, August—I'm *watching* it happen. I'm fully conscious of it happening. I'm in a war against myself, and I don't know whose side I'm on."

"Ben, let me tell you something about those two sides. They're not the problem. They're both important parts of you; they've just been out of balance. I want you to really hear what I'm about to say. Okay? Deal?"

"Yes. I'm listening. I'll take any advice you can offer."

"You need to start *loving* yourself. You need to stop fighting who you are. Let yourself see who you are, *who you really are*. It'll make you happy and free." She smiled. "Only happy and free, Ben. Can you see that possibility?"

Ben tried. "I'm not there yet ... I'm so far from even being able to imagine those feelings, but I believe you. I really do. And I'll work on it."

"That's a start. Good. Because you're *very* lovable, Ben. Now, I'd like to tell you something about that boy sitting alone at the lunch table. Are you ready to hear it?"

Ben nodded.

"Did you know that flowers give off a little electricity, and bees can sense those electric fields? You know how the hair on your arm or neck stands up when you sense something? Well, the hair on the bee's body reacts too. Based on how it bends, they can sense the difference in the electric fields of flowers. They can tell one flower from another. We're not so different, Ben. I'd bet a whole batch of comb honey that that boy felt and sensed someone's concern for him. He may not have known who or where it was coming from, but he received your caring on some level. It reached him. With that intense of an experience, it *had* to. He felt the comfort of someone caring, Ben. I guarantee it."

"Even if he did, I didn't *do* anything. I walked away and just left him there."

August looked at him and smiled. "No, you didn't. You've carried him with you every moment since. He's never been alone—not once since the moment you saw him. In fact, you brought him all the way here with you. Who's to say that's not the most effective thing you could have done? Oh, Ben. There is no *what you should have done.* There's only what you're doing."

Ben felt a sliver of hope wedging itself between regrets.

He never wanted to leave August. Ever.

11:30 a.m.

Ella picked up two salads and brought them to Charlotte's office. All the other agents were out, and the receptionist was sick, so Charlotte needed to be there over the next few hours in case there were any walk-ins.

Sitting on the bench on the back patio, with a view of the entrance, Ella picked at her food while Charlotte told her about the date she went out on the night before, one she hoped never to repeat. The conversation soon turned to Ben, and with the question still nagging, Ella finally asked it out loud. "Do you think it's possible that working at Starfish is what got to Ben? That this has to do with the pressures around money?" *Tell her.* The door was getting pushed open again.

"I don't know. Maybe. It's very possible."

Tell her—now. Before Ella could say anything, Charlotte put her salad down next to her and turned so she was facing Ella, the expression on her face serious.

"Speaking of cracking under pressure, there's something I need to talk to you about. *I'm so worried about you.* Why aren't you more upset? Or angry? You have to feel your feelings, Ella. As your best friend, I'm telling you that you can't shut down. It's not healthy."

Feeling tired and confused suddenly, Ella didn't know how to respond. Was she not feeling her feelings? She was, wasn't she?

Charlotte went on. "Not to lay it on too thick, but it's like you're in denial—this huge … denial about what's actually happening."

"I'm not in denial," Ella said, mostly believing it. "I have a feeling I might know what's happening with Ben. I just ... I can't explain it."

"Oh, Ella," Charlotte said. "Okay, I'm trying to do this gently, I really am, but you're not getting it. This is where it's so hard to be a good friend, but I'm going to do it anyway." She took a deep breath. "You're just so calm about this all, even how you just responded to me. *Ben left*, Ella. And he didn't go to work for a month. And he lied to you about it. And you don't know when he's coming back—*or even if he is*. And—"

"Stop." Ella felt like she couldn't breathe. "Just ... stop." She inhaled deeply and then slowly let it out, grateful that, though Charlotte looked concerned, she stayed quiet. Finally, Ella said, "You're so positive this is bad, and I'm just not sure it is. It's hard, it's terrifying, and I miss him so much it physically hurts. I'm watching Daxx and Izzy hanging on by a thread in moments, and yes ... yes to all the pain involved here. I'm just not positive it's ... wrong."

"You don't think it's wrong? Ben just walking out like that? No explanation?"

"Maybe wrong isn't the right word." Ella looked to the entrance, hoping for a walk-in so she'd have an excuse to leave. "I don't know how to explain it."

"It might be a good idea to try," Charlotte said gently.

Ella felt so tired, but she explained, "So much of this brings me back to when Andy died. When you've gone through all the stages of grief, the thing that brings you out of the depression, that ... that incredible moment where grace touches you, you don't forget that."

"So ... if I haven't gone through grief like that, I can't possibly understand why your husband walking out on you isn't ... *alarming?*"

"I'm not saying ... I'm just trying to explain, Charlotte. When I was at my lowest, out of nowhere, I suddenly had this sense of the big picture—that's the moment of grace I was talking about. I had this new awareness, this knowing that I didn't have all the information, and that if I did, I might understand. It was my lifeline, and I clung to it. I guess that's what I'm doing now."

The look Charlotte was giving Ella spoke loudly.

"Why does this *have* to be so bad, Charlotte? I mean, maybe it is. Maybe. But maybe he just needs a break."

"A break? Oh ... Ella. You need to talk to someone who can get through to you—*really* get through to you. I'll find someone good—someone who knows how to help."

Ella stood up, not knowing what to say, her emotions confusing.

"Did I upset you? I didn't mean to, Ella. It's just that the longer you put off facing this, the harder it's going to be, and I want you to know I'm here for you." Charlotte went to hug her.

Ella took a step back, saying, "No ... just—no," and then left, her sense of self in a thousand pieces.

12:20 p.m.

Ben and August stood a good twenty feet from the hives. "Should I at least wear gloves if I'm gonna be going into the hive?" Ben asked.

"Heck no!" August said. "If you have gloves on, you won't know how much pressure you're putting on a bee when you go to move it. No, this way you can feel it. You can tell. You'll stay gentle. Second, you're not going into the hive. The propolis I want you to get can be scraped off from the edges of the hive. It's the glue the bees make. They mix tree sap and other goodness and use it to seal their hive. That way, no beetles or rain or wind or other bugs can get in there and mess with things—or their queen. Resourceful, aren't they? You've probably had it without knowing it. It's in gum and a lot of other things, including ointments. I was fifty-fifty whether to put it on your stings when you had them, and I followed my instincts with the lavender and honey, and it sure as heck looks like I was right. Don't you just love when that happens?"

Without waiting for an answer, she turned up the volume of the radio in her hand and adjusted the knob till it was playing something classical with distinct piano and strings leading the way. "Let's give them something to dance to," she said.

August faced Ben. "Now, you can do this. Look at what you unburdened from yourself back at the eucalyptus tree. That was something else, no small feat. This? Piece of cake. You're going to do exactly what you've already done, and you're going to get to see it in the physical world, what it does, what it looks like. Are you with me?"

"Yes ... but—and—no. What have I already done that I'm about to do again?"

"Let your guard down. Put down your hackles. Relax. Trust. Let go of what you're used to holding so tightly to. *Do not worry.* Do not worry. You've felt the stingers, lots of them. You know you'll be okay—always. Feel the dancing music in your heart. Get carried away by the music. Let's go."

With a jar hooked into his pocket and a plastic scraper in one hand, Ben walked next to August, and they approached the beehive, August humming along with the music.

Lured by the soothing music, Ben let the slow, rhythmic movement of the notes pull him in, allowing himself to feel the gently building euphoric highs, followed by their gradual descent into deep lows, and then the steady flow of the melody back up and around again. He felt the merging of the instruments and the harmony they were creating. He invited all of it to seep into his being, the lifeblood of the music, wordless expression his heart felt at home in.

He observed the bees he was nearing, and they too, like him, seemed to be absorbed by the music. The louder the music got in his head, the more the bees seemed to slowly bob and weave and dip and twirl right along with the swaying notes.

As August nudged the top open, hundreds of bees swarmed out, buzzing around Ben's head and arms. He focused on the stillness in the center of the music, in the center of the buzzing, in the center of himself. His heart celebrated the presence of the bees, his mind remembering the taste of their honey.

The song on August's radio was louder now but not loud enough to overtake all the buzzing. Instead, they blended together into a new song, one that took Ben back into old memories, and he felt younger, and it reminded him of how things used to be, and it breathed hope and possibility—the music was so harmonious.

As he gently scraped the propolis that August was pointing to from the top and edges of the hive, one bee after another landed on his hands, on his arms, and he silently thanked them for the honey, for their work, for the propolis he was taking, and they lifted off, and new ones landed. Gently, he moved the bee that was sitting on a large chunk of the crusty propolis, and as he felt the bee between his fingers, he could feel its rapid heartbeat, and he gently, gently put the bee down a few inches away.

As the bees continued to land on him and leave him and come back, and the music wrapped itself around him and wove itself between him and the bees and around them, he felt less apart than he had ever felt. He felt like one with something bigger than him, connected instead of isolated, seen and heard instead of alone. He felt joy.

1:15 p.m.

Ella sat on the beach, hugging her legs to keep warm, and imagined how it would feel to talk to Ben right now—her old Ben, Ben in a good place. She could picture his face, see his expressions, and hear his laughter. And she realized something she had forgotten, how often Ben made her laugh. She almost always felt better after talking to him. Maybe that wasn't such a good thing. Maybe she needed Charlotte's directness. Her honesty.

But Ben was honest too. She could hear him as if he was sitting right there next to her, his arm around her. "It's gonna be okay," he would say. And then it would be. Things had a way of working themselves out, especially when Ben believed they would and assured Ella of it.

If Ben was sitting right there next to her, she would look at him now and say, "I'm a mess, Ben."

He wouldn't argue, and he wouldn't agree.

And he definitely wouldn't say he was worried about her.

With plenty of confidence, so much so that she'd believe him, he'd say, "You're *you*, and that's perfect." Then he'd smile and pull her closer into a hug.

And she'd feel so much better.

Ella buried her head in her knees and cried like she did three years ago, the moment it hit her that Andy wasn't coming back.

1:30 p.m.

Back at the house, as they sat down to share a plate of comb honey, almonds, and dried apricots, August said, "So you have little ones."

Ben smiled. "Yes. Izzy is seven. Daxx is five."

"Ah, I see. On the cusp of the age of reason."

"It's interesting you say that. It's been on my mind." Ben laughed at the irony, considering what he was about to say. "They're about to go into their minds. I don't want them to. I don't want them to lose their childlike ways, their curiosity, their ... Izzy has these two imaginary friends. I don't want her to stop being friends with them."

"Mmm, I see," August said, nodding. She swirled an almond in the honey. "You want them to stay out of their minds. To be out of their minds."

"It sounds crazy when you say it like that." Ben sighed. "Maybe it is. I don't know. It just feels like we come into this world so open, and then we get bombarded by all these things that don't matter and some that aren't good, that are outright bad, and they chisel away at the magic and the beauty and the ... the *zip* of life. You know what I mean?"

"I do know what you mean. And they're—tell me their names again?"

Ben smiled. "Izzy and Daxx."

"Yes. *Izzy and Daxx.* They're okay. No matter what it looks like, they'll still be okay."

"I know."

"Do you? Be sure ... be really sure about that." August pointed to the last apricot on the plate. "That one's yours," she said.

"Thank you." Ben took a bite, surprised how much he liked them.

"Did you know that bees see every color except red?" August said. "Sometimes we see *only* red. Your little ones, you want to protect them. Oh, Ben, believe me, I understand." She looked away for a moment and seemed to catch her breath. Before Ben could say anything, she went on. "But all you can do is the best you can do. And that's everything. I'm guessing those little ones will need the green light for some of the things you probably got the red light for. You'll do an outstanding job teaching them about yellow, that sometimes they'll need to yield and sometimes that's the last thing they should do. You'll show them how blue is sadness and it's also as big as the sky, and you'll show them how when yielding yellow gives itself to blue sadness, you get green—growth, new shoots of life. You see, Ben? There's so much more to see than just red because, even without having met them, I have no doubt you're teaching them every color of the rainbow, even the ones they can't see."

"I don't know if I'm ready to go back."

August smiled. "You're ready."

"How do you know?"

"Because you got what you came here to get."

"Which is what?"

"Permission to be you. And that leads me to my last abide-by. Number four. Ready?"

He nodded. "Okay."

She cleared her throat, drummed the tabletop, and leaned back in her chair. She looked at Ben a long time, long enough that he felt the energy in her look, the words she was asking him to hear, and finally she said, "Abide-by number four: only one person can give you the permission you're waiting for."

"Me," he said.

"Bingo, my friend."

1:56 p.m.

Ella wasn't leaving herself a lot of time before she had to go pick up the kids.

When the bell chimed, Ethan looked up from the customers he was talking to and nodded at Ella, letting her know he'd be right there.

She busied herself with looking at all the different bikes, this time really looking, different from the first time she went into the shop, now with a new appreciation. Soon, Ethan was thanking his customers, they were leaving, and it was just the two of them left in the shop.

"Hi," Ella said. "This will be short. I just came by because I want to thank you."

He came around the counter. "What for?"

In her mind, she had gone over what she wanted to say a hundred times. She had convinced herself she could say it without crying. All that was out the window now.

With deep concern showing in his face, Ethan said, "Let's go sit down."

"No," Ella said, shaking her head and wiping the tears. "I don't want to take any more of your time." She took a few deep breaths, collecting herself. "Ethan, you've been a breath of fresh air for me during the past few days ... so kind. Having experienced that, I just, I imagine ... I can understand why Ben came here every day." She took a moment to breathe through the sadness surging through her. "I wanted to thank you. I'm ... I'm just so glad Ben came here. I'm glad he found you and that he spent the past month in a place like this ... happy."

"Ella," he said, gently and quietly, "did you ... get news about Ben?"

She shook her head. "No. I just ... I don't really know anything anymore."

Ethan put his hand on his heart and didn't hide his relief. "Whew … I'll tell you something. My dad always told me I had good judgment, to trust my judgment. Ben is the kind of person … Okay. Before you go on a bike ride, you decide what kind of ride you're up for." He used hand motions to elaborate as he went on, saying, "Are you up for puddles and ruts and sharp curves? Or do you want to sail along on an open country road? Either way is going to land you in the same place, but who you are when you land—it'll be influenced by the path you took to get there. My gut feeling is you can trust Ben's path."

Ella looked around his shop, her focus falling on the area he called his office. Though it was crowded, she saw an order to it all she hadn't noticed before—the neatly marked containers with parts, the open, organized toolbox, the strategically placed crates, the stacks of papers, each with a rock on top. And she realized she was standing in a sacred place and that what made it so was him, Ethan, who he was.

Ella looked him in the eye. "Thank you, Ethan. I don't have words for what you've done for me—and I'm sure for Ben too."

"I'll say this … I can't imagine what this is like for you, Ella. I've only known Ben a month, and the shop doesn't feel the same without him here. I'm hoping when he comes back, he'll stop by once in a while."

She wanted to hug him for saying *when Ben comes back*. But the door chimed, and a man struggled to drag in a bike with two flat tires. Ella hurried and held the door open for him, while Ethan helped with the bike. "Thank you, Ethan," she said and then closed the door behind her.

3:23 p.m.

As August drove Ben back to the spot where she had picked him up—Ben didn't want her to take him all the way back, though he couldn't articulate why—everything looked different.

"You're ready," she assured him again. "Let me leave you with a little something about the queen bee. When a hive gets too crowded in there, there's just too many and too much going on, the queen bee will send out a message to the worker bees. Those bees will get busy making as many as twenty wax cells. Guess what goes in there?"

"Extra honey—to store it for later?"

"Good guess, but no. Those wax cells are special; they're for the new queen. See, the queen bee lays fertilized eggs in those cells, and then the worker bees feed those larvae what's called Royal Jelly. I'm not even kidding, Ben. Gotta plumpen them up with some good food. Then, a week or so later, they cover those cells with wax. In the meantime, the queen bee gets starved on purpose so she's thinner and can fly with her prime swarm to find a new place for a hive. As they go along, they send scouts to check out this place and that. And they communicate, all of them, and finally settle on the best spot for their new colony."

"So what happens with the twenty queens back in the hive?"

"Well, eventually, one of the new queens will make her way out of her cell. Then she has a decision to make. If it's still pretty crowded, she might decide to take a small swarm, fly off with them, and start a new colony elsewhere, just like the original queen did. Or she might decide to stay and be the queen bee right where she is—which means she'll sting each of the other potential queens through the wax covering their cells."

"Killing them?"

"Killing them."

"That's morbid, August."

"That's nature at its best."

"What? How so?"

"Every queen bee, from the first to leave to each one after the other that comes out of the cell has a decision to make. Stay or go. Build a life here or start something elsewhere. Make this their clan or form a tribe somewhere else. These are the decisions that dictate everything else that happens next. And you know what the beauty is? They do what they have to do. They do what they know they must do in order to be the queen bee, because that's *who they are*. You got in my truck because it felt more like you than not."

"And because I might have been kind of messed up in the head."

August laughed. "I suppose so." She put her blinker on even though there were no other cars in sight and pulled over to the spot where she had picked him up. Putting the truck in park, she said, "I'm going to leave you with my final abide-by. Number five."

"I thought the last one was the last one."

"Have you already forgotten number three? Learn more about what you care about. Things don't have to be set in stone. Get flexible, moveable."

"Is that it? The abide-by?"

"No, it's not. And it should be, so we'll make that one number five: get flexible and be moveable. I like it. I like the sound of it."

"I do too," Ben said.

"On to number six then: say and do things that make you feel more like you, not less than you. Always more, Ben. Never less."

"Got it."

"I hope so. Ask yourself again and again. How do you feel after doing something, after talking to someone? Do you feel more like you? Or less like you? It's one or the other. Okay? Don't forget. And don't forget to taste what you're doing, the queen bee of abide-bys, numero uno."

"I won't."

As he started to get out of the truck, the static-filled radio station suddenly turned clear. "Oh shoot," Ben said, a surge of disappointment coursing through him. "I never reminded you to show me Henry's wood shop. I'm sorry, August."

August got out of the truck, went around, and gave Ben a hug. "It's all on time, Ben. All of it. Don't you worry about a thing. Just shine your light. Keep shining that beautiful light of yours."

6:47 p.m.

Ella was glad the watermelon salad turned out and the kids seemed to enjoy it. The grilled cheese sandwiches cut into shapes were always a hit; that was a given. Before dinner, Izzy had dragged a chair over from the living room for her elephant. As they ate, she had shared the elephant's contributions to the conversation whenever it had something to say, which, Ella was realizing, was becoming more and more often.

"C-c-c-c-c-c-can w-w-w-we ..." Daxx stopped and took a deep breath, right along with Izzy and Ella, who were demonstrating, as had become their routine. "Can ... w-we ... have ... ice cream after?"

"Well, I think—" Ella started.

"Dad!"

Ella turned around.

Ben was opening the screen door.

She stood up slowly, keeping her eyes on him, not able to take them off him, the realization sinking in that she could actually do what she'd wanted to do more than anything else for the past four days—wrap her arms around him, inhale his scent, and then whisper in his ear, "Never do that again—never, *please*—I love you, I love you so much—oh thank God you're back, thank God you're back, Ben, I've missed you so much." And then she would help him. Whatever kind of help he needed.

But she just stood there, aware of all the competing sounds. Chairs scraping against the floor as Izzy and Daxx got up from the table. The creak of the screen door as it slowly closed. Shrieks of joy from Daxx.

She couldn't move. She couldn't make herself go to Ben.

Ella just stood there, watching as Ben picked up Daxx and hugged him, saying, "Hey, little guy," looking at Ella though, his eyes bright, adoring. Daxx gently turned Ben's face toward him and started talking nonstop, not a trace of his stutter, telling Ben all about his day.

She couldn't stop staring at Ben. He looked so different.

As Daxx went on, Ben made eye contact with Ella again, smiling, and she knew he was excited about something.

What could he possibly be excited about?

A few seconds later, when he looked at her again—*how was he so happy?*—she held eye contact for a short moment before quickly breaking it and looking down at the floor.

What was happening?

Why wasn't she wrapping her arms around Ben and Daxx, pulling Izzy into the hug too?

Izzy.

Just as Ben put Daxx down and looked past Ella, she turned around.

Izzy was standing next to her chair, trying to smile, biting her lip, tears rolling down her cheeks. Her heart splitting wide open, Ella knelt down, put her arms out to Izzy, and whispered, "Come here, my baby." And as Izzy did, without hesitating, Ella realized how much Izzy had been holding everything together for the three of them.

When Izzy finally let go and walked quickly over to Ben, Ella gave up on trying to feel how she wanted to feel right then, overwhelmed by the screaming thoughts. *You selfish bastard. How could you scare us like that? How could you just leave? You don't get to do that. You don't get to hurt us like that and not have it count. You can't crush our feelings—make us miss you so much it hurts—and then just come back. You can't do that, Ben!* Every unspoken word felt toxic, and soon she was leaning over and coughing so hard she was trying to catch her breath.

Ben hurried over to her, saying, "Are you okay, Ella? Are you all right?" The second she felt his hand on her back, she pulled sharply away while trying not to be too obvious, knowing the children's eyes were on her.

"I'm fine," she said, her voice hoarse, not looking at him, nonchalantly moving farther away. "I just need some water."

Ben turned toward the counter. "Here. I'll—"

"No," she said, more sharply than intended. She tried to soften her voice as she moved around him and said, "I'll get it."

Over the next two hours, Ella successfully evaded every attempt Ben made to communicate with her.

When she was getting the ice cream out of the freezer and he whispered, "We need to talk. Let's go outside while they have dessert," she pretended she didn't hear and asked Daxx and Izzy which one of them wanted to set a place at the table for Ben.

While they all sat eating ice cream, Ella spent the majority of the time swirling hers with her spoon, feeling Ben trying to get her attention, grateful that Izzy and Daxx had so much to say and were directing all of it to Ben.

When that was finally over and Ben started to tell Daxx and Izzy that he needed time with Ella, she cut him off, reminding him that the four of them normally took a walk after dinner on Fridays, before Charlotte came over to play cards, which she wouldn't be doing tonight. In fact, Ella wasn't sure when they'd be doing that again. The sound of her voice was so stiff and awkward, but she couldn't make herself sound any other way.

The only thing she felt control over was not giving into the eye contact Ben kept trying to make with her. It was taking so much energy because he just wouldn't stop. She wanted him to, to please stop, because every time she refused to connect, she felt more disconnected from herself. And the pain searing through her …

It felt like she had sketched all of her plans for Ben coming back on a piece of tissue paper that was now being held under water. She kept reminding herself to breathe.

He was back. Ben was finally back. And now she wouldn't even look at him. It took so much effort to hold back everything good in her, to keep it stuffed deep inside, not letting even the tiniest bit out.

As she continued to go through the motions, she wondered why she was trying to act like it was a normal Friday night. *For the sake of the kids*, she kept telling herself. But she wasn't sure that was a good idea. The charade felt ridiculous. After all, she kept arguing with herself, there was nothing normal about the past few days, and Daxx and Izzy knew that. They had lived it.

Now that he was back, now that she knew he was safe, the questions in her head sounded different. Where was he? Why didn't he find a way to call? What was he doing? Why did he leave in the first place?

And how was he possibly so happy right now? That possibility had never been on her radar. She had only imagined a very sad and troubled Ben coming home, a Ben that needed serious help. The only thing she had been right about was that he would walk in that door.

She was getting to him though. She could tell. Little by little, she watched as her refusal to communicate dimmed his brightness.

When the four of them left to go on a walk, Ella put both hands in her pockets. That way, Ben wouldn't even try to hold her hand like he normally did.

As they walked to the stairs that led down to the beach, she kept her distance from Ben, the tightness of her body and the sharpness in her throat growing stronger, her anger feeling more internally violent than the waves crashing below.

9:00 p.m.

Ben tried to focus on what Izzy was saying as she climbed into bed, but he kept getting distracted by the self-berating thoughts spinning one into the next.

Why hadn't he spent more time during the past four days figuring out this part? Why hadn't he talked to August about how to step back into his life?

"Right, Dad?" Izzy said.

"Sorry, honey. What did you say?"

Why didn't he spend more time during the past four days seeing things from Ella's perspective?

"Yes," he said to Izzy. He would be home next week when she brought the class bear home.

He swallowed hard.

While tucking the kids in, Ben kept waiting for one of them to ask him where he had been or why he left, but neither did. Their focus seemed to be on making sure he continued with the book he had been reading to them—wanting him to start right where he left off.

Afterward, as he kissed them good night, he lingered, wanting to say something, wanting to apologize or to explain, but instead, he found himself just slowing down enough to feel himself present in the room, gratitude filling him. He looked at Daxx, his soft little cheeks, his eyes closed but fluttering; he didn't like opening his eyes after Ben had kissed them closed. He looked at Izzy, her eyes still open, looking at him, smiling. He blew her a kiss and then turned out the light and slowly pulled the door until it was a few inches from shut.

Ella had already given them kisses, tucked them in, and said good night before he started reading to them, the old routine back in order. Ben walked down the hall to the kitchen, where Ella was sitting at the table, not doing anything, just gazing out to the backyard through the open door. Even with her back to him, he could feel that she wanted nothing to do with him right then. How had he thought it would be different? How had he thought that for even a split second? He turned around and went to their room, deciding he'd take a much-needed shower, and then hopefully he and Ella could finally talk.

As he walked into their bedroom, the air was thick, and he felt a heavy awareness. The space felt like Ella's—not theirs. He sat on his side of the bed and put his head in his hands.

What did you do! How could you have—

Ben stopped. It was like August was right there in the room with him—the words were so clearly hers: "That's a rabbit hole. Come on out."

He imagined slowly turning a knob, a dimmer, lowering the volume of his thoughts …

It got quieter.

The physical ache grew stronger. It felt lonely to be alone in their room.

He stood up, forcing himself to move.

In the bathroom, he barely recognized himself in the mirror. It wasn't just that he had been wearing the same clothes for four days between quick showers, trying to use as little as possible of August's limited water supply. There was something else. Leaning toward the mirror to look closer, he felt a gentleness toward himself that was new. He looked into his eyes and felt curious, wondering what he was really looking at—beyond his pupils.

When he shaved and as he showered away the dirt, it felt bittersweet. He was glad to be back but didn't want to lose what he had found when he was with August. All the bee stings had barely left a trace after all of August's potions. He wished at least a few of them had left scars. They could have been like tattoos. He'd be able to look at them and remember to think of his life as a work of art.

Coming home felt like two worlds colliding.

Ella wasn't giving him a chance to explain anything yet, even though she had to have a million questions she deserved answers to. He had some questions too, he realized—though they could wait.

When he went back into the kitchen, Ella was at the sink, cleaning up the ice-cream bowls. He was sure she could see his reflection in the window above the sink, since he could see her, but she wasn't acknowledging him. He stood by the kitchen table and said, "I'm going to start at the end, because that's what I'd want to know. I was with a lady in her seventies. Her name is August. She picked me up and let me stay on her couch for the past few days while I got my mind right." It didn't feel right to say anything else until Ella acknowledged him.

Finally, as she dried the last bowl on the drying rack, she said, "I don't want to talk tonight," still not looking at him. It was resigned Ella, calm and strong but with such sadness in her voice.

"What are we waiting for?" Ben said. "I get that you're angry and—"

She turned sharply. "Don't tell me what I feel. You have *no* idea. I've been alone with my feelings, all of them, for the past four days, and I don't need you to—" She stopped.

He waited, trying to stay open.

She shook her head, swallowing hard, tears streaming down her cheeks. He could feel it, her forcing her words down. His throat hurt watching her. He heard it then, a voice inside him telling to be quiet, to just be quiet. He listened to it.

Standing there, he gave her the space and time to respond, and the longer he waited, the more he understood her silence. It was so clear to him—that for her to say anything right then would only serve him; her venom would relieve him of guilt and leave her feeling horrible. She was being strong in her silence, protecting herself, protecting him. The clarity he felt in that moment—and how quickly it came—was brand-new, and he felt in awe of the gift that came from just slowing down and listening to the voice inside him.

He'd expected Ella to be angry with him, but the amount of distance she was putting between them surprised him, and the fact that he hadn't seen it coming made him realize something. He started to break the silence as they stood staring at each other. "I had no idea—"

"No. You don't," she said, interrupting but so calm. "You have no idea what the past four days were like here. And you never will."

The truth of her words hit him hard. "Ella, I started walking and then—"

She put her hand up and shook her head. "No. I'm not ready to hear why you're so happy right now. I'm not ready for any of this."

What made her think he was so happy?

And then the truth was suddenly so obvious the awareness jolted him. He *was* happy—deeply so. In fact, he was possibly the happiest he'd been in his entire life. Even though he was sad and frustrated and a lot of other things right then, beneath it all, he felt a core happiness.

She folded the kitchen towel, then unfolded and refolded it, finally placing it next to the sink. She turned to him. "There are only two things I want to know right now. Why did you leave us, Ben? And what in the world have I done—or not done—to make you think it would be forgivable to walk out on us like that?"

Ben sat down at the kitchen table, his eyes on Ella. "I couldn't get my mind right. I wasn't thinking about whether you'd forgive me or not. It felt like a matter of survival."

It seemed so far away now. Ben closed his eyes and thought back. When he opened them, they fell on Ella standing there, silent, watching him. "I could have stayed and talked to you. I could have told you what I was doing or tried to articulate it better—I know that—but the thing is …" He took a deep breath. The anger he was starting to feel, the self-defense mechanism kicking in, he had to move through it—quickly. Or he would take the two of them right back to where it all started.

"I know I hurt you," he said, "and I wish I hadn't. I wish I did it better, but I didn't know how to do it better at the time. It felt like I had two choices—keep going or go back. That was it. And I knew if I went back, I'd eventually lose everything—you, Izzy, and Daxx."

"I don't understand," Ella said. "Things weren't *that* bad. Or if they were, why didn't you tell me? What was so wrong? And why didn't you ever say a word about it? What made you lie to me about going to work for the past month? A *month*, Ben! And couldn't you have called me to let me know you were okay? Why didn't you at least call? How could you do that to us?"

"I'm not sure," he said, his stomach tight. "Something's been wrong for a while—well, it *was*. It's not that way anymore. I mean …" His words felt so pointless, so inadequate. He looked at Ella. "This isn't working."

She didn't say anything. He'd seen that expression on her face before; she wasn't going to fill in the silence for him.

Everything he thought of saying next seemed like it would make things worse, expanding the already wide divide between them.

He imagined August standing there in the kitchen. He knew that words weren't working right then with Ella, and August would see that too, but she would take it a step further. She'd convince Ben that it was okay, that it didn't need to be any different.

An idea came to Ben.

"I'll be right back," he said.

He went down the hall to the closet and came back with a few blankets and pillows. "I don't think it's working to talk right now, but I really want to be near you ... just ... I want to be around you. I hope you want to be around me too." He took a deep breath and let it out. "There's just more space outside." He looked at her, waiting, and when she didn't respond, he went out to the backyard. He laid the bigger blanket on the grass and set the two pillows a short distance from each other at the top.

She had moved to the doorway and was watching him; he knew without looking.

He lay down on one side of the blanket, close to the edge, leaving way more than half for her. He pulled one of the other blankets up around him and did his best not to think about Ella, not to pull at her energy, to give her space. He was just grateful that she was still standing in the doorway.

Sometime later, she came and lay down, leaving heavy space between them.

As he opened his eyes and looked up at the stars, another idea came to him, and he decided to try it. Feeling the sadness, he let it grow louder and louder in him until it had its say. Then he pictured it leaving him and shooting up to the star he was staring at. He pictured the star doing its thing, translating the sadness he was feeling into a message that it then directed down to Ella for her to receive. He trusted the star's interpretation and its way with words, far more than he trusted his own ability to translate how he was feeling into words that would help him and Ella instead of work against them.

One after another, he sent messages through the stars to Ella.

So many emotions.

So many stars.

So many translations.

And then when he felt he had no feelings left to process and nothing left to say, though he hadn't said a word, he closed his eyes. He fell asleep picturing the light from his heart shooting up, touching the last star he saw. He wondered how the star would translate it before sending it down to Ella's heart.

11:56 p.m.

Ella was on her back, her eyes wide open. The jacaranda branches framed a portion of the sky, giving it defined edges, bringing it closer and more in focus. She felt like she was part of the picture, absorbed by the night. It calmed her.

She turned and looked at Ben, remembering what it had been like the past few nights, how alone she felt as she cried herself to sleep. And now he was inches away, he was there, *right there*—sleeping next to her.

Did she need to be this angry now that he was home? Was it the only way?

Yes. What kind of message would she be giving him if she wasn't mad?

She watched his eyes, their light flutter. She imagined touching his forehead, tracing the worry lines from left to right and right to left, then slowly exploring the contours of his face and kissing him. She looked at his hand, at the wedding ring he had never taken off, and she thought of touching the tips of her fingers to his.

No. The past four days were some of the worst in her entire life ... and he somehow came home doing better than when he left ... refreshed. How could she be okay with that?

She could just lay her hand on his. Hold it.

No. Absolutely not. Because you know exactly what will happen.

As Ella's mind played out its forecast of all that was bound to happen if she stopped being angry, the anger seemed to collapse on itself, the adamancy finally giving way to sadness, and as that sadness grew and grew, it was so overwhelming it took enormous effort to physically move—to take the blanket off, stand up, and go inside, putting what felt like a necessary, bigger space between her and Ben.

After checking on Izzy and Daxx, Ella climbed into bed, alone again, her heart twisting in pain, her mind refusing to stop—frantically listing off reasons she should never give Ben the chance to tell her about the past four days.

Day 5, Saturday

6:03 a.m.

I t was cold when Ben woke up outside, and before he turned his head to confirm it, he knew Ella wasn't next to him.

His mind started racing, so he slowed it down, trying to focus on what mattered most to him right then. He wanted to feel good, to feel like himself again, like he did at August's. There had to be a better way to do this. The last thing he wanted was a repeat of yesterday, when the majority of his interactions with Ella led to his internal spark fading back to a fraction of itself. He had to constantly check in with himself and use what he learned from August to keep reigniting it.

It felt like he was missing something big, forgetting something. What?

It was up to *him* to make things right with Ella; he knew that.

And it took two to reconnect. She also had to …

No … That wasn't it. That focus would take him in a direction that—even the thought of—left a bitter taste.

He took his phone out of his pocket, which was finally charged again. He had started a list of things to remember two years ago. Flipping through, he read a few of the notes.

It always takes longer to drive to San Francisco than you think.

When Ella's upset, don't tell her not to be upset. It makes her more upset.

Let Izzy and Daxx be in charge sometimes. You won't regret it.

It's worth it to make it from scratch. You're always glad you did.

He scrolled down, stopping only on the ones about Ella.

When Ella's the last person you want to be around (and probably vice versa, don't kid yourself), go out on a date. Have fun being with her even before she's ready to have fun with you.

You're lucky to be with Ella. Act like it.

Ella loves olives and forgets that.

When Ella's in a rut and can't get out, don't treat her like she's in a rut and can't get out. Do the opposite.

Ella—size 7 shoes.

When Ella's mad, don't get mad "with her." It makes her more mad. Then she "feels like she can't get mad without you taking it from her" (still not sure what that means).

He got to his most recent additions: August's abide-bys. As he read them, they sounded so different, their meaning veering in a new direction now that he was home, thinking about them in relation to him and Ella and how to bridge the gap of the past few days and move forward.

He read them again, taking his time.

Abide-by one: taste what you're doing

Abide-by two: pause when you need to

Abide-by three: learn more about what you care about

Abide-by four: only one person can give you the permission you're waiting for—you

Abide-by five: get flexible and be moveable

Abide-by six: say and do things that make you feel
more like you, not less like you

Slowly, a clear picture came into focus about what he
needed to do next—nothing past that, but it was enough
for the moment.

"Hi, Dad!"

The screen door slammed shut, and Izzy and Daxx
came running out.

"Did you sleep here?" Daxx asked. "Can we sleep here
tonight?" He turned to Izzy. "Just like we talked about!
Remember?" Then back to Ben, "Dad, can we?"

Izzy was on board. Ben could see her mind already at
work, planning it out.

"We'll see. Come here, you two." Ben pulled them both
into a hug. "I have some things I have to do this morning.
Want to come with me? We'll let your mom sleep in." They
both nodded, already practicing being quiet, even though
they were outside. Using a serious voice, Ben said, "Okay,
we're on a mission."

"And a mission needs a name," Izzy said, as always.
Then she looked to Daxx, since it was his turn to name it.

"And the name is …" Daxx said, and Ben and Izzy
made their drumroll sounds before Daxx finished with,
"Monkey mission!" which was his go-to name almost every
time.

"Okay." Ben smiled. "That's perfect." He stood up and
gathered the blankets and pillows. "Follow me."

Hope flickered, and he felt happy: he was with two of
his favorite people in the entire world.

8:40 a.m.

Ella woke up to music playing in the kitchen and Ben and the children's voices competing with it.

When she reached over and checked her phone to see what time it was, she saw all the texts from Charlotte and was glad her phone had been on mute. The night before, she had texted Charlotte to let her know Ben was home and to thank her for all her support the past few days. Within seconds, Charlotte had written back: a list of questions. This morning, more texts had come in from her—with more questions. After getting dressed, Ella finally just called her.

After Ella's brief update, Charlotte said, "What? He's been home for twelve hours, and that's all you know?"

"I'm just … there's a lot to process," she said, trying to make the bed with one hand.

"But why haven't you asked him the questions you've been asking *me* for the past few days? You need answers, and you need them *now*."

Ella stood still. "I'm scared of the answers." It was a relief to let it out.

Charlotte sighed. "You're going to be fine. No matter what, you'll be fine. The thing is, if you don't know more about the past four days, you don't know what happens next. What are you so afraid of? He was with an old lady. I don't think you have anything to worry about."

Ella didn't bother saying that wasn't what she meant. "I don't know … anything that would stay between us, like *in between* us, me on one side, him on the other."

"Is that it? That's ... well, it's not what I thought you were going to say."

"What do you mean?"

"Never mind. It doesn't matter."

Ella sat on the bed. "Tell me. What is it?"

"I think you need to look at the possibility that something's off with Ben ... mentally. It's not just about the past four days. How about the fact that he left his job a month ago without telling anyone? That he's been hanging out at a bike shop for a month. And then one day he just started walking and didn't come back for four days—and from what you said, he said some crazy shit over the phone. I guess, if it were me, I'd want to understand what happened so I could know what to do next. You know what I mean? What now? Should he see a doctor? A psychiatrist? That might be a good place to start."

"I don't know ... something being wrong with him ... that's not how I see it. I mean, he hasn't been himself, but ..." Daxx and Izzy peeked their heads in, and she motioned for them to come in, suddenly eager to get off the phone. "I'm just taking it one step at a time. I've gotta go, though. The kids just walked in. I'll talk to you later. Okay?"

"Okay. Give them a hug from me—one for you too."

After hugs and good mornings and an accidental tip-off from Daxx about what to expect in the kitchen, Izzy and Daxx each grabbed one of Ella's hands. They led the way to the table, topped with fresh flowers, homemade quiche and cinnamon rolls, a steaming pot of coffee, freshly squeezed juice, and a plate with slices of kiwi, mango, and pineapple. Ella's first thought was, *Has Ben lost his mind?* It looked like he was throwing himself a welcome-home party.

9:42 a.m.

Thank God for August's abide-bys. They were keeping Ben tethered to the clarity he had found during his time with her.

Ella's refusal to hold eye contact for more than a split second during breakfast was enough to make him lose his appetite and question everything he thought was working. But soon after his thoughts spiraled down into one self-doubt after another, he stopped.

Abide-by one: taste what you're doing.

He knew how to go from the acidic taste to one that was lighter and gentler. August had made him practice over and over. "Find truer, kinder words," she had said again and again.

I screwed up, and I'm learning, he decided while passing the syrup to Izzy. *I'll eventually recover from this. I'm getting better.* He felt the truth in the statements, and the more he repeated those thoughts, the more he believed them.

Still, it didn't take long for old patterns to kick in again. His thoughts were getting loud again, louder than the sound of forks against plates, the conversation between Daxx and Izzy, and glasses being refilled, clanging against the pitcher, then put back down.

Pretty soon, he had convinced himself the day was already ruined and that no matter what he did, it wouldn't make anything better between him and Ella.

But then abide-by four wedged itself into his thoughts: *only one person can give you the permission you're waiting for—you.*

He pictured August with her hands on her hips, smiling, her look telling him all he needed to know right then.

Ella wasn't in charge, he realized. They both were. And he didn't need her approval. He needed his own. If she wanted to be in a bad mood and continue ignoring him, she had every right to do that. And if he wanted to feel the inexplicable joy he was feeling beneath all the other feelings, he had every right to.

It happened the moment he made that decision—one of the most powerful shifts he had ever felt: he needed less from Ella than he ever had, and he had never loved her more.

Right then, she looked at him across the table and held eye contact, for the first time all morning, not looking away.

10:20 a.m.

Ella found out during breakfast that Daxx and Izzy had plans for the day with their favorite babysitter, apparently orchestrated by Ben earlier that morning.

As soon as they left, shortly after breakfast, Ella turned to Ben, her irritation explosive. "Why'd you send them off with the babysitter?"

"We need time together, you and me." He was so calm.

"*They* need time together, with *us*—with *you*!"

He shook his head. "No, Ella. They're okay. You've done a great job with them. You made them feel so safe and so sure everything was going to be okay; they've already moved on. It's us—we're the ones who need time together.

Let's go to the beach. With how overcast is, it'll be empty. We'll go down to the cove and talk there—about everything. I'll clean up the kitchen, you can do whatever you need to do, and then we'll go." He smiled. "Okay?"

What was wrong with him? She put her hands on her hips. "No. Not *okay*. I'm supposed to be happy about this? About having no say about anything—where the kids are and what they're doing, what *I'm* doing? I have no say? Why do you keep smiling?"

"I'm so happy, Ella. I'm so happy to be with you right now and to get to spend the day with you. I know you don't love not being in charge, but I can promise you, I know this from knowing you for fourteen years, if you let go, if you give yourself a break and let me take care of things for a minute … you won't regret it."

"Oh." She felt like she could barely breathe. "I see. *Now* you're ready to take care of things."

"Yes."

"Well, where were you the past few days? What were you doing at a bike shop instead of at work the past month? Have you lost your mind? Who was taking care of things then? What were *you* taking care of? What were you doing, Ben!"

Shit. They were out—the questions.

She didn't need to dread the answers. He wasn't saying anything.

"Say something dammit!"

He quickly said, "I know it was so hurtful of me to leave—it was horrible—and I promise that's the only hurtful thing I did. I spent the majority of the time talking to August and meeting her bees and eating the food she

188

made for me. I can't wait for you to meet her—and for her to meet you. I can't wait to tell you about the past few days and Ethan, the owner of the bike shop. I'll explain it all. I just think we need get out of here, to walk. We always do so well down at the beach. It's a good place to talk. Okay?" He finally took a breath.

Ella felt a calmness come over her. She fought the tears. For the first time in a long time, Ben seemed absolutely sure of something.

"Okay," she finally said.

Ben nodded. "Great. Thank you. I'll have everything ready in about twenty minutes."

Feeling a tiny hint of excitement but not willing to show it, she kept her voice neutral as she said, "What should I bring?"

"Just you," Ben said, as sincerely as he had ever said anything to her.

10:31 a.m.

Just keep being honest—first with yourself, then Ella, Ben reminded himself, over and over.

10:38 a.m.

Ella was walking down the hall from their bedroom to the kitchen, ready to tell Ben she was ready to go, when she heard Charlotte call out, "Knock, knock!"

Her first instinct was to pretend she didn't hear, to pretend they weren't home. There was something new happening between her and Ben, and as she paused quietly in the hallway, Ella realized what that something was: fragile, precarious movement forward to—hopefully—a better place than where they had been. She was starting to understand why he had sent the kids off for the day, why he insisted on the two of them needing time alone.

To cover up her frustration that Charlotte was there, Ella tried to sound especially welcoming as she opened the screen door and said, "Come on in."

Charlotte gave Ella a hug, and then her attention zeroed in on Ben, who was zipping a cooler bag in the kitchen. Charlotte smiled. "Well, look who the cat dragged in." She went and hugged him, saying, "It's good to see you, Ben. Welcome back."

"Thanks, Charlotte. It's good to be home." He said it so casually, giving nothing away, and something about that pleased Ella.

Addressing both of them, Charlotte continued, "I was just at the farmer's market and tried this homemade pesto. It's heavenly. I put it on anything—bread, pasta, a piece of cheese—oh, white cheddar. Do you have any? I should have brought you some. Anyway, I thought you guys might like it. And I figure you probably have your hands full and a lot of catching up to do, so …" She reached into her canvas bag. "I also picked up some pasta, mushrooms, and focaccia."

"That was thoughtful. Thank you," Ella said. "I forgot it was today."

"Me too," Ben said. "Thanks, Charlotte."

"No problem." She looked around. "I *knew* something was missing. Where are the kiddos?"

Ella looked at Ben, and he answered for them, saying, "They're with the babysitter today."

Ella pretended not to notice Charlotte looking at her with questioning eyes.

Finally, after an awkward silence, Ella asked Charlotte if she wanted some coffee, barely trying to cover up her lack of enthusiasm in the offer.

Charlotte, on the other hand, didn't seem to miss a beat. "I wish I could," she said, "but I have an open house, and then I'm showing a new client around. I just wanted to stop by." After giving them each a quick hug, she said, "All right, I gotta go. We'll catch up later." And then she was gone.

The screen door closed, and Ella wasn't the least bit surprised when Ben turned and said, "Whoa. What was that?"

This wasn't the conversation she wanted to have right now, but Ella realized there would never be a good time for it. She sat on the arm of the couch and considered what to say next. Then it just came out. "She told me how she hit on you. We moved past it, at least I thought I did, but seeing her here … with you … I don't know. Maybe I'm not over it." She looked down at her lap and then back up at Ben, her tone sharp as she said, "Why didn't you tell me?"

Ben let out a deep breath and leaned against the counter. "It wasn't an easy decision, and I'm not saying it was the right one—actually, I'm pretty sure it was the wrong one. It was just that her friendship has always meant a lot to you, and I figured as long as I kept refusing and then—"

"Wait. You *kept* refusing? Did it happen more than once?"

"It happened a few times," he said. "Maybe three or four. It was always the same scenario. She had too much wine, you were in the other room or the bathroom, she was flirtatious, and I knew where it was going, so I put as much distance as I could between us without making a scene."

Ella felt nauseous. That was why he had started going to bed early on Fridays. She considered running outside, catching up with Charlotte, and confronting her—but her body felt so heavy, too heavy to move. "Have you been tempted?" she said, her voice a whisper.

"Not at all," he said without hesitation. "I used to really like hanging out with Charlotte. After the first time, I chalked it up as a drunk mistake. We've all done things we wish we hadn't—I get it. But it was doing the same thing *again* ... and then *again*. I just haven't been able to look at her the same."

Ella hadn't noticed him being any different with her, but then again, she realized, her focus was usually on Charlotte when she was around. "But you didn't tell me. Why didn't you tell me?"

"I went back and forth about whether I should or not, and a couple times I almost did. It always came down to worrying about the ramifications—what it would look like for you not to have her in your life. One, this is a small town. Second—"

"You know what? I don't care what your reasons are. You should have told me. I deserved to know. I should have had all the facts so I could decide for myself how to react. I don't need you protecting me from the truth. What's the point, Ben? What's the point of any of this if it's all pretend? I want the *truth*. That's all I've wanted all along."

"That's not true," Ben said. "I tried to tell you the truth about a lot of things, and you didn't want to hear it. I'm all for being honest. I think me lying to myself and you—that's what's gotten us where we are." He paused, then added, "I made a promise on Tuesday. When I started walking, I swore to myself, if nothing else, I would at least commit to being real. To being honest—first with myself and then with anyone who was willing to listen."

His voice calmer, he said, "I'm sorry I didn't tell you about Charlotte. I should have. I think I was conflicted because I didn't want you to lose that friendship. Actually … no, that's not true. I didn't tell you because I didn't have the energy to deal with the fallout. I just didn't want to deal with it. Shit. I'm sorry, Ella."

She shook her head. "I'm not *losing* the friendship. I forgave her. And even knowing that it happened more than once, I'll still forgive her—probably. I get that she's lonely. I don't think she's really trying to be hurtful; she just doesn't always think."

Ben looked out the screen door for what felt like a long time and then turned to Ella. "I'd be careful. I don't think it's a good idea to ignore what Charlotte's tried to do to our marriage—more than once."

Ella felt her face turning red. "So—what—you think I should drop her? Just like that? The relationship hits some bumps, so I should just walk away? Is that what I should do to *you*? And you don't even make sense! You didn't even bother to tell me about it, and now you're giving me advice about how seriously I should take it?"

Is he even listening? He kept looking over at the bee that was hovering right outside the screen door, buzzing.

Finally, Ben was apparently able to pull his attention back to the conversation. He looked at Ella and said, "I don't think you deserve to be stung by anyone. Ever. Including me. And definitely not multiple times."

Ella didn't know what to say. He kept doing that since he got back—saying things she didn't expect him to say. He kept bringing them back, through all the clutter, straight to what mattered—steering them away from a fight and turning them in the direction of healing.

"We had a date," Ben said. "It's not the way I hoped to start it, but will you come with me?"

She looked at him. Twenty-four hours ago, she would have done anything to be with him.

He added a freezer pack to the cooler bag and then put it down, his eyes meeting Ella's. "I'm so sorry for hurting you." After a moment, he said it again: "I'm so sorry, Ella."

"If we're going to go, let's go," she said, breaking eye contact and turning toward the door.

11:41 a.m.

As Ben walked next to Ella on the beach, more than once he stopped himself from reaching for her hand. She had made herself clear.

Nothing was working. The stilted conversation was tense, uncomfortable, and forced. They weren't getting anywhere, so they resorted to silence.

Ben was feeling less and less like himself.

Blue sea glass sparkled on the sand, and he thought about stopping to pick some up, but Ella was walking briskly and seemed intent on just getting where they were going.

A few seconds later, abide-by number two came to mind: *pause when you need to.*

He let Ella get ahead of him as, giving himself permission to fall behind. One step at a time, he focused on his feet sinking in the sand and then lifting out.

Sinking.

Lifting.

Sinking.

Lifting.

And then it was suddenly obvious. There was only one way through the knotted mess he felt himself in with Ella— to admit everything he had done. He had been wrong— period.

He stopped trying to justify any of it.

Abide-by six: say and do things that make you feel more like you, not less than you. It meant something new.

He had tried to justify why he lied about going to work when he was actually going to the bike shop. It felt irrelevant the minute he started trying to explain it. No wonder the conversation wasn't working. He was making it complicated. And he was coming to realize that the truth was simple and that anytime things felt complicated, the truth was hiding under a heap of excuses and dangerous rationalizations.

He hurried to catch up with Ella and said, "Can you stop a second?"

She stopped, and turned to face him, the wind blowing her hair across her face so that she had to tuck it behind her ears and hold it there. He had her full attention.

"I lied. That's the truth. I pretended. I lived a second life you didn't know about. I created a financial mess for us by not working for a month. I left you. I scared you and Daxx and Izzy. I hurt all three of you. And I broke your trust.

"I'm sorry, Ella. I don't ever want to do any of those things again. That's not who I am—or who I want to be. I never want to hurt you again."

Even though his words fell embarrassingly short, he was sure it had been a step toward bridging the gap between them, so he was surprised when nothing budged—not a single bit. Somehow, even though he had taken himself into the space between them, both sides were just as far apart.

12:25 p.m.

Something was off. Ella knew Ben was being sincere in his apologies, but they still sounded hollow, not in their delivery but in her ability to hear and accept them.

Deeply annoyed by something she couldn't put her finger on and not wanting to give it any more attention, she finally changed the direction of the conversation by asking Ben questions. But every time she asked a question, all she could hear was how flat her voice sounded. The spark inside her felt nearly extinguished.

Luckily, she didn't have to prod much; Ben was more than willing to talk about honey and bees and rocking chairs and hammocks and coffee and socks and August.

There was no doubt August had been a life-changing force for Ben, and the more he shared about those four days, the more she wished for her own time-out and someone like August to step in and help her.

They reached the hidden cove that wasn't actually hidden, considering the fact that all the locals knew about it. Today it was empty, as Ben had predicted. They set up the two beach chairs, facing the ocean, and for a while, they just sat there, not talking.

Ella couldn't think of a thing to say or another question to ask. She just felt tired.

Finally, Ben said, "I'm going to hit the reset button. I have to. I don't know how else to move forward. I'll answer any other questions you have. I'll share anything you want me to. But this tension …"

Still, Ella couldn't think of a thing to say.

After another long, uncomfortable silence, Ben said, "August's abide-by three is to learn more about what you care about. I care about *you*. I care about what this has been like for *you*."

Suddenly she knew exactly what she wanted to say. "I met Ethan."

"How?" Ben's surprise was obvious. "You went there?"

"I needed to know why you went there, what the draw was." The words were coming quickly now. "I wanted to know what would hold your attention for a month, so

197

much so that it was entirely yours and you felt no need to share it. I was curious, Ben. I felt like I didn't know you anymore." She looked at him. "I get it. Ethan …" A wave crashed, and the water came up close enough that she thought it might get them wet, but then it receded. "I have no idea what you two talked about, but he seems like an old soul."

"I'll always be grateful to Ethan," Ben said. "He got me thinking. This might not be a good time to talk about it, but I don't think I can go back to Starfish. I'm not sure what I should be doing, and I know I have to figure out the money, especially after the past month, but I can't—"

She put her hand up. "Stop. Please." She couldn't listen to him say another word. Because then she would tell him. She would tell him everything. "I know we need to talk about that. It's just not time yet."

Think, Ella. Think.

She needed to redirect the conversation. "You were saying some things … when you were gone and we talked on the phone, you said some things that sounded … it scared me. I didn't know if you were okay in your head."

Ben ran his hands through his hair. "Oh my God, Ella. I didn't know either. I've never been so scared in my life. Nothing's ever felt like that."

"What do you think happened? Do you know?"

Ben took a deep breath and said, "I have an idea. I think I know. But before I go into that, will you tell me more about what the past four days were like for you? Please, Ella. In the past, when you've kept to yourself like this instead of talking … when you finally opened up, you always felt so much better. Will you talk to me? Tell me where *you're* at?"

Hesitantly, Ella finally said, "Okay." Then she added, "Let's eat, and you can ask me questions."

Ben said that was a great idea and then started setting everything up. He seemed relieved.

As Ella watched him spread the blanket and set out four types of cheese, cashews, almonds, a sliced baguette, honey, and tiny purple champagne grapes, more than anything in that moment, she wanted to meet August, the person who brought Ben back.

2:06 p.m.

It was one of his favorite things about Ella, how she stayed mad as long as she needed to, until she was really done. When it was over, that was it. He knew they weren't there yet, but as they sat there eating and talking, Ella softened a little—he saw it in her face and eyes, and he heard it in her voice. The tightness was gone, and though they were still treading lightly and every movement was still fragile, she seemed to at least feel safe again with Ben.

But she still wouldn't let him touch her. That was the turning point that would tell him more than any words or tone or body language could—if she let him hold her hand or hug her.

He would wait as long as she needed him to.

Whatever it took.

It was hard to hear what it was like for her and Daxx and Izzy while he was gone, but what struck him most was that it wasn't possible for Ella to be any gentler than she was being—her cautious choice of words, her thoughtful tone. She was filling him in, not making accusations.

When they finished cleaning up lunch, he suggested they walk down to the water, far enough so the water could come up, cover their feet, and pull back into the ocean, leaving them a little heavier in the sand, a little deeper. He needed to get grounded. The water was cold, but it felt good. The hypnotic feeling of watching the water sweeping in and rolling back out reminded him of how he had started to feel around August's bees.

It was a relief to stand there next to Ella, letting the pull and release of the waves do the talking until one of them was ready to again.

After a few minutes, he said, "Last Tuesday, I started walking to the bike shop, but I knew I wasn't going there. I had no idea where I was going, but I knew it wasn't there."

"Charlotte thinks you're losing it—mentally." Ella closed her eyes and took a deep breath. "I'm sorry. I don't know why I said that."

He knew Ella wouldn't have said it unless a part of her wondered too. "I'm not losing it, but something's changed. At first, it was terrifying, but I think I get it now. I think I know what's happening."

"Can you explain it to me?" Ella said.

"That morning was so scary, but on some level, I also felt relieved because I knew I was coming face-to-face with it—*it*, whatever it was. I was dizzy, I couldn't think straight—and that had been happening a lot. I was worried because there were things I couldn't remember anymore … but even as I say that, I can't even see it as bad anymore.

It's like for everything that happened that terrified me, I got an explanation for it. From the bees, from August, even from just walking … I'm not even sure where it came from. But it happened over those few days."

"But that morning, Ben, when I talked to you … you didn't seem right. Before you got clarity, before you met August and all that, what happened?"

Ben thought back to that morning. "I was done fighting with myself. The more I fought for my sanity and to keep my mind thinking the same thoughts it had always thought, the deeper and wider I felt the division. Inside me … it was inside me. And I couldn't reconcile it or fight it anymore, so … looking back, I must have let myself wonder for a second what it would be like not to be battling myself anymore, to be at peace, and it was like that hint of a possibility, that single thought, made me take a step— literally. I mean, it actually made me start walking without any destination in mind. And then I took another step and another, and with each step I took, I felt this peace growing inside me … and a quieting. And then I would try to verbalize what was happening by talking to you, and nothing came out right, and it felt like taking a hundred steps backwards, and I knew, I *knew* I had to keep going, Ella. I had to see what would happen if I stopped fighting myself and was totally honest with myself—if I gave into my fear of losing it and just went with it."

"I don't get it," Ella said. "How were you so confused … but so clear about being confused?"

Ben put his foot forward so it would reach the water crawling up the sand. "I didn't understand it at the time. The clarity didn't come until later, at August's."

"Like what? What kind of clarity did you get?"

"When I was walking, it felt like my memory was changing—it had been happening slowly, and then it went into this surge mode—and I was aware of it, and when I was at August's, it went from being scary to a relief because ..." It was hard to articulate it, but he knew it was important to try. "I felt like the things I was forgetting were okay to forget; they didn't matter, and they were opening the space for me to remember important things I had forgotten."

"Like a birthday?" Ella said. "Or what we had for dinner the other night—things like that?"

"No. Maybe ... sometimes. All I know is it was purposeful, like my mind knew what it was doing."

She looked at him and seemed to be searching for something to say. "You mentioned heartbeats—you said it a few times, that you could hear them."

Ben nodded. "Not all the time and not always literally. It started when I was sitting at the bus stop—or at least that was the first time I noticed it. It's hard, Ella. The feelings that come with it ... it's usually sadness, a really painful sadness, and I don't know what to do with it. I haven't figured that part out yet." He shook his head. "I still don't know what to do with it."

It was happening now. He could feel a deep sadness sweeping in, and it took all his self-control to not show it.

2:41 p.m.

Ben suddenly stopped talking and seemed distracted by the music that had been playing from his phone. "Sorry," he said. "I'm just not in the mood for this one." The song stopped abruptly as Ben forwarded to the next one.

Looking out at the water, Ella soon felt herself melting into the song, one of her favorites. She had no idea it was on his playlist.

The highs and lows of the violin breathed through her.

She felt him looking at her, and when she couldn't ignore it anymore and turned to confirm it, she recognized something: *The reset button.* He had hit it, just as he said he would. He hadn't waited for her. Ella was surprised by the relief she felt in that.

Along with the relief came the release of a burden she hadn't been aware she was shouldering. It just fell away, and somehow she knew it was time to move forward. There would be no good time. There would never be enough time or the right amount of time.

It was up to her. She could stay where she was. She could continue in pain.

Or she could let herself reset too.

The piano keys spoke to her, the notes gently pressing on her shoulders, relaxing them.

Her throat tightened at the crescendo … until she finally just let the tears fall.

It was time.

Okay.

She nodded.

Not breaking eye contact, he stepped forward and put his arms around her, pulling her close.

She let him hold her.

Heaving sobs she couldn't contain, she realized how much she had missed him. This Ben.

2:44 p.m.

There in the sand, under the heavy gray sky, Ben held Ella close, heart to heart, and as he knew she was falling into the song she had played hundreds of times, he felt her heartbeat and all of its sadness, and he pictured all of his love for her wrapped around her heart, absorbing its sadness so she wouldn't have to feel it anymore.

Day 6, Sunday

8:55 a.m.

E lla had been awake a lot of the night, unable to stop thinking, so it didn't surprise her when she woke up and saw that she had slept later than normal. A note by the bed said Ben was taking Daxx and Izzy to town to pick up breakfast. Then they'd come back, get Ella, and head to the park for a picnic. Based on the time Ben had scribbled on the bottom of the note, they had left just fifteen minutes ago.

Ella picked up her phone and scrolled through the texts sent between her and Charlotte last night. Ben was the main topic, but Ella had held herself back from saying anything about Charlotte hitting on Ben multiple times. In answering Charlotte's nonstop questions about what he did over the past few days, Ella found herself feeling protective of a lot of what Ben had shared.

This morning, feeling emotionally drained, the last thing Ella wanted to do was call Charlotte, but if she didn't, she would just keep replaying the imagined conversation in her mind, over and over.

Charlotte answered on the second ring. "So? Start where you left off. You guys went to the beach yesterday."

"You hit on him more than once." So much for easing into it as she had planned.

Silence.

"What am I supposed to think, Charlotte? What am I supposed to do with that?"

"Did it cross your mind that maybe Ben misinterpreted something?"

"No."

"Well, I don't know what you want me to say. I don't think I did. I told you about the one time. Why wouldn't I tell you about other times if they happened?"

Ella started feeling confused. She hadn't even considered questioning the truth of it.

"You're going through a lot," Charlotte said. "This feels like an unhealthy distraction from what's really going on here."

"That doesn't even make sense. What do you think is going on?" As soon as Ella said it, she had a bad feeling about giving that kind of opening.

"It's not normal what Ben did. And neither is your reaction."

Ella had no idea how to respond. She didn't know if she agreed or disagreed.

"How can you think any of it is normal?" Charlotte said.

It hit Ella then, the disconnect she was feeling—and why. "Maybe normal wasn't working for us."

Charlotte laughed.

"What's that supposed to mean?" Ella said.

"Nothing," Charlotte said. "It doesn't matter."

"Okay …"

"Fine. I'll just say it. You and Ben think you're special."

"What? What are you talking about?"

"You do! Normal for everyone else isn't quite good enough for you. Anyway, that's not the point. This August … do you even know if she's real? What if he's making the whole thing up? What if he imagined it?"

"*What?* Are you kidding? Where's this coming from?" Ella said.

"Normal, healthy people don't go do what Ben did and then come back and tell a fairy-tale story that—I'm sorry to say—sounds way too good to be true."

"I … no … Ben's just …"

"Ben's just what? What are you afraid to say because you know it's true?"

"What are you doing, Charlotte?"

"What are *you* doing, Ella?"

Ella was so confused by the ricocheting thoughts competing for her attention. Eventually, she just said, "You don't know anything."

Charlotte was quiet before she said, "Maybe I don't, but at least I'm not in denial. This is such dangerous ground, Ella."

"It sure is. I'm going to go now." She hung up.

9:38 a.m.

When they got back from town, Ella was working in her office, which surprised Ben, considering how strongly she felt about not working on weekends. She seemed off, but he couldn't pinpoint how.

She went to the park with them, but the picnic fell flat, far from what Ben had pictured. Ella seemed distracted and on edge as time ticked forward, and when Ben asked her if she wanted to talk about what was on her mind, she said it was nothing, just that work was piling up and she had a lot to get done. Ben wasn't convinced that was it; he could feel the distance between them growing again.

He offered to keep the kids at the park so she could go back and get some work done, and he wasn't at all surprised when she quickly took him up on it.

When he and the children went back home an hour later, Ella wasn't in her office working. She was at the kitchen table—just sitting there.

Though she said hello to Daxx and Izzy with a forced smile, it was Ben she kept looking at. He had seen that look before.

Shit. His mind started racing, and he forced it to stop— to wait. For just a minute.

He set Izzy and Daxx up with a puzzle they never tired of, and then he and Ella went to the backyard.

Neither of them sat. Ella stood facing Ben, her hands at her sides. This was defenses-down Ella. Not good. She had made a decision and was ready to live with it. Ben knew this Ella well. What he didn't know was what kind of decision she had made. But he had a bad feeling—which was confirmed when Ella said, "I've been thinking about what you said, the honesty thing, and how it's really the only way to move forward."

Her words, Ben realized, should have flooded with him relief—they were both on the same page, honesty as a priority—but instead, his world felt like it was starting to tilt again. He knew what needed to happen next; he should ask Ella what she needed to be honest about. He should take a deep breath and open himself up to whatever it was. Instead, his radar tuned into something he didn't want to name, and he felt himself going into fight-or-flight survival mode, so he started talking—so quickly there was no way she could get a word in.

"I totally agree," he said. "There are things I need to tell you. There's this part of me that got, well, I guess it got ripped open. It's one of the things I talked to August about, one of the things she just got me talking about and then helped me with. She called it unfinished business because it was still stinging. She told me the pain came for a reason."

"Which pain? What are you talking about?" Ella said.

Ben told Ella about the boy who ate lunch alone. By the time he was finished telling the story, Ella was quiet. Ben wasn't sure how to read her reaction. He hoped she understood, that she got it.

"That's not who I want to be, Ella. I don't want to just let someone sit there in pain like that." He felt uncomfortable and too exposed, but he pressed forward, against his instincts. "August referred to the whole thing as *the stinger*. She explained that my response to it was like

209

someone who's allergic to bee stings, except mine was an emotional and mental response, not a physical one."

Ella sat on the step. "So you're allergic to … what? I don't understand."

"No, it's not exactly like that." Ben shook his head, searching for the right words. "Sorry, I'm not doing a good job with this. When she explained, it made so much sense."

"What did she say?" Something shifted in Ella's face; it became softer and gentler, and he felt encouraged as she said, "Do you remember?"

Ben closed his eyes and put himself back at the house with August. "Hold on … yeah … I remember. She said it was a power thing. When you're allergic to something, you feel small next to that thing." He could hear her voice, her words. "And that thing, it looks so big to you because it has so much power over you—at least that's what you think."

He opened his eyes and looked at Ella. "So, when you're allergic to something, you feel like you have no power over that something. *It* has all the power. The way August explained it, I had such a strong reaction to the boy eating alone because I felt like I had no power to do anything about it. There wasn't a thing I could do about him and his pain. But then she said that wasn't true—that it wasn't true at all. And then she said something that really hit me: pain doesn't take away your power; it shows you where you forgot you have it. She compared it to a game of hide-and-seek, saying you wouldn't look for a person unless they were hiding. Sometimes, according to August, we do strange things to call attention to what it's time to see. We play games with ourselves. She said I have to start healing the pain I see and feel or I'm going to lose myself under the disguise of pretending it's not there and I don't see it. Do you get it, Ella? Am I making any sense?"

Ella was looking down at her lap. The longer she took to answer, the more Ben understood. His heart sank as, finally, she said, "Is it possible that you … need help?"

She had managed to lace a tone of pity into the accusation.

Ben didn't answer. He knew which Ella this was.

10:16 a.m.

Stop it. Don't do this, Ella begged herself. She stood, an old feeling surging inside her, one so demanding and toxic she started unleashing it instead of sitting with it and looking at it as she knew she should have, projecting it as quickly as possible instead of facing it, knowing—knowing so deeply—it was only making things worse. What she had put in motion took over, and she felt like she couldn't stop it.

"Why don't you invite August over?" she said. "Why don't you call her?"

Ben just stared at her, not saying a word.

So she went on: "Allergies? You've never been allergic to anything. An *emotional* response? What does that mean? Do you hear yourself?"

10:19 a.m.

The pain in Ben's gut was sharp.

"Who is she, Ben?" Ella continued. "Who the hell is August? How can you remember every little thing she said?"

Ella went on, and Ben tuned her out. It was hard to catch his breath, and a surge of heat intensified inside him. How could she do this? He was being raw and vulnerable, and she *knew* it—and still she was in attack mode.

Screw this. That's exactly why I left.

Why did he have to say another word? He didn't have to explain *anything* to her, and he sure as hell didn't have to stand there while she spewed her toxicity at one of the few things he knew was good and true right then. There were so many things he wanted to throw out at her, how she—

Okay ...

But there was something demanding his attention more than his anger right then. It wasn't that it was louder than his anger; it just rose higher in his consciousness.

The heat that had made his skin start to feel prickly subsided as he realized this was a potential turning point, one of the things he and August had talked about.

He had never realized it before—*the heat of the moment*, what that expression meant. This was it. This was the opportunity.

Abide-by number six: say and do things that make you feel more like you, not less like you.

He deliberately slowed his breathing with deep inhales and exhales, though not obvious enough for her to see; he wouldn't expose himself to her like that. He wouldn't share that part of him.

He silently told himself what he needed to hear right then, that he was okay ... and he felt his emotions back off a little.

This was about him being true to himself, he decided. It had nothing to do with Ella.

Finally, he looked at Ella and cut off her tirade by calmly saying, "August is real. And everything I said happened. All of it—every word. I don't know how I remember everything she said, but I do." Suddenly, a thought came to him. It was so clear and obvious he didn't question it for a second. "The thing is *you believe me*. I know that. This isn't like you, Ella. Something else is going on. Your reaction ... that thing you just did—it's about *you*."

She sat there staring at him, not saying a word.

Another thought came to him, one that resonated deeply. He put it into words as best he could: "What do you need, Ella?"

Most of him didn't care what happened next. He had never before felt the soaring, exhilarating freedom he felt in that moment. Without causing any damage, he had spoken his truth.

10:29 a.m.

Ben's words sent Ella's emotions reeling. It felt like—right then, just for the moment—he knew her better than she knew herself. It threw her off balance. She needed space, as much as she could get. It felt like their backyard was closing in on her, and the thought of going inside and being around the kids made her feel even more claustrophobic.

Elizabeth Day

Finally, she said to Ben, "I need ... I'm going to the beach," and without waiting for a response, she was on her way, walking, wondering if this was how Ben's steps had felt that Tuesday.

When she reached the sand fifteen minutes later, Ella kicked off her flip-flops and made her way to a cluster of boulders away from other people. She sat down and leaned against the warm rock, her face up to the sun.

Please help me.

Nothing.

She said it again.

And again.

Please help me.

She opened her eyes, looked down at the sand, and started squeezing and releasing handful after handful. It felt good—the grit of the sand compressed against her palm and then dropping between her fingers.

A surprising thought came to her as she released another handful. She was jealous of Ben, of where he was emotionally, personally—in every way now. She envied what Ben and August had—the raw connection. Nothing held back.

She was pretty sure August was real.

She has to be. Right?

The question was left hanging, no one to answer it but herself. She wasn't ready to. If there was nothing wrong with Ben—absolutely nothing—what did that say about *her* mental state?

Her thoughts bounced back to what she knew for sure about Ben. Ever since he came back, it was nothing like she had imagined it would be. She and Ben kept veering off in unexpected directions—because of him. He was different. He was unapologetically himself. That was it, she realized. He had faced his demons. He had laid everything out on the table. There was nothing to hide and nothing to be afraid of. Even the things that didn't make sense yet, even all the uncertainty ... Ben seemed fine with all of it. He had helped himself, and now he was trying to help them.

She, on the other hand, felt fine with very little. If Ben didn't go back to Starfish, what was he going to do for work? It was bigger than not going back to Starfish—she could feel it. Her guess was he wanted out of the corporate world. Then what? What did that mean for the bills they needed to pay? The world they had built for themselves? What did it mean for *her*?

She felt herself moving farther away from clarity rather than closer to it.

An awareness came to her: *Stop thinking so hard.*

A crab stuck its head out from a hole in the sand and then scurried up and out. Just as quickly, it darted sideways, back and forth, then back down into its hole. There were dozens of other crabs doing the same thing. She let herself get lost in their movements, their routine.

And then a realization came to her: *I want to feel like me again.*

It was so simple. And she knew that was at the core of it all. As she sat with that, watching the crabs make deliberate movements, the sandpipers tiptoeing across the sand, and the pelicans soaring and swooping, she realized a freedom they had, one she had taken away from herself.

215

It was the same freedom Ben had now—and the biggest obstacle to her knowing happiness in the way she wanted to.

She got up and began slowly making her way home, knowing what she had to do.

12:42 p.m.

Ben was on the couch, reading to Izzy and Daxx. He looked up when Ella came in through the screen door. They were about to have a conversation that would change things, for better or for worse; he could feel it. The children hugged Ella and told her about the puzzle they had put together and what was happening in the mouse book Ben was reading to them. He was trying to gauge her, trying to figure out which Ella this was, but he couldn't pinpoint it. She looked at him then, and as he read her face and her body language, Ben told the kids they would read more later, that they could watch a movie now. He put on the one about the kangaroo family that lived in the tree house, because it always made them laugh, and then he walked out to the backyard, knowing Ella would follow him.

Ben took a deep breath, waiting for Ella to begin. He wasn't going to try to stop her or shift her attention. He saw where it led when he tried that last time. Bracing himself, he accepted there was no way to avoid what was about to happen, whatever it was.

"We've come so far … and you've been really brave, Ben."

Why is she crying? Ben's stomach tightened.

She was suddenly calm as she said, "I tried to tell you earlier. I tried to have the conversation … I really messed up. I'm sorry, Ben …"

His ears started feeling hot as her story spilled out, and some of the words he heard much louder than others. They were enough to tell him a story he couldn't believe was true: "Do you remember … from that Japanese company … my jewelry designs … they actually did … when they offered me … lied to you … I know—"

Of course Ben remembered. How could he possibly forget? Three years ago, when the twelve months they had agreed on passed and neither of them had grown their businesses enough, Ben let go of what he realized were idealistic but not realistic dreams and got a job at Starfish. Ella, too, had given it her all. She had been doing a ton of networking, and through both of their efforts, she eventually got a fifteen-minute sit-down with a chain of jewelry stores in Japan to pitch her design work. As she came to understand, and later explained to Ben, while the Japanese had done a stellar job raising a generation of math, science, and engineering geniuses, they hadn't given nearly as much time and attention to allowing creativity and ingenuity without framework or constraints. So, while they could perfect the assembly of jewelry and pretty much every systematic part of the production process, they were severely lacking in creative talent and were willing to pay a lot of money to buy that talent from elsewhere.

When she asked Ben to help prepare her for it, he did extensive research about Japanese customs and what to expect in a meeting like the one she was going to have. There were strict guidelines about body language, subtle gestures, and etiquette she needed to be aware of. They spent hours going over everything, and Ben played the part of the interested party, giving her the opportunity to practice her approach and her answers to potential questions.

The closer it had gotten to the meeting, the more real the possibility seemed and the more excited Ben was for her. She had told him how much she wanted it, and he knew she could do it; he had total confidence in her and made sure she felt that reassurance.

The day of the meeting, which took place in Los Angeles, a two-hour drive from their house, he couldn't focus. As the day wore on, he kept checking his phone to see if he had somehow missed her call. The plan was for her to call him on her way home.

Not having heard from her, and assuming the meeting had been delayed or was somehow still going, he was shocked when she walked in the door.

"Sorry I didn't call," she said, giving him a hug. "I just had to decompress." Ben found that strange but ignored it; he was eager to find out how it went.

"So ..." he said, "how'd it go?"

She sat down on the couch and took off her earrings. "I couldn't tell. I have absolutely no idea." As she walked him through the details of the meeting, he was distracted by how flat her voice sounded. He guessed she was just tired; it had been a long four months leading up to that fifteen-minute meeting—for both of them, all of it juggled with raw emotions from Andy's death just five months before. Ben totally understood Ella's sudden quiet moods, her withdrawing; he often felt the same way, though he tended to want to talk with her *more* in those times.

A few days later, when Ella told him she had gotten the call and that they weren't going to offer her a contract, he comforted her and promised her everything would be okay—that they'd figure things out. He told her how proud he was of her, acknowledging how hard she had worked.

And now, three years later, what Ella was saying ... there was no way.

She repeated it. "They offered me the contract, Ben. I'm sorry. I'm so, so sorry. I lied to you when I said they didn't."

"But wait—"

"I'm sorry." Her words were mixed with tears and choked-back sobs. "I turned it down."

"What?"

"I turned it down. Then they increased the offer ... more than what we were hoping for." She couldn't stop crying. "I still turned it down."

"Wait, wait, wait ..." Ben put his hands on his head and took a few steps back, away from Ella. This was not happening. There was no way she was telling him she lied about something that directly led to one of the biggest forks in the road they had ever come to, the one where he had to make the turn—and she didn't. There was *no way* she had lied about that, watched the repercussions, and held it in for *years*.

He looked at her. "What the *hell*, Ella?" His voice was a whisper. "You told me they turned you down when they *wanted* your designs—when they handed you your dream?"

"You don't understand, Ben." She sounded so desperate.

"I didn't have to quit my business? I didn't have to get the job at Starfish?"

"But, Ben ... you lied too ..."

"No ... no." Ben stepped back again, feeling the need to distance himself from her in every way, as far as possible. "Don't you dare mix the two up. Don't do that. *Don't do that, Ella.*"

"Okay, but ..." He hadn't heard this voice of hers in a long time, not since last time she knew she was wrong and was trying to talk her way out of it. "I knew it would be bad for me—for us, for the kids. I could see it, I could see the pressure building, how much would change when it went from my boutique business to a corporate venture with big money and huge expectations, and I could have done it, I know I could have, but when I pictured it, the more I looked, the more I saw how it would change me." She wiped her eyes, but the tears didn't slow down. "I'd *have* to change in order to—"

"Are you kidding me! You're trying to explain that to *me*? How you might've had to change? I know *exactly* what happened. You were worried you'd have to sacrifice who you are—so you let me do it instead. You didn't want to have to fit into a world where you don't give a crap about the things most people there care about, especially those you have to answer to every goddamn day, even on weekends and days off that you never actually have. So you had me do it. How could you be so ... Your lie changed the entire trajectory of my life!"

"Ben, I—"

"You don't even know what would have happened. We'll never know. We'll never ..." It was so hard to wrap his mind around the enormity of it all. "Why didn't you *talk* to me? We were a team! You broke us up three years ago, and I didn't even know it!"

"That's not what—"

"How could you not *talk* to me about it? Don't you realize how insulting that is? Do you have *any* idea? I don't give a shit about the job. You didn't tell me! You lied to me about something life-changing!"

"You would have convinced me to do it." Her voice was quiet. "I wouldn't have had a choice."

Ben shook his head. "You don't remember what we were like. My God, Ella, what lies have you told yourself for the past three years? How could you say that? How could you put this on *me*? Is that how you've justified it all this time?" She looked so different to him now. "Never, since the first moment I met you, did I have any idea that you were—"

Something stopped him.

Slicing, explosive words were begging to erupt.

You'll never, ever be able to take them back.

His stomach in knots and his fists tight, feeling like he could barely breathe, he walked inside, past Daxx and Izzy, and out the front door.

1:32 p.m.

Still standing in the backyard, trying to get a grip before going in, Ella was so relieved to see Ben come back just a few minutes later. He could yell at her, say anything he wanted, anything to catapult them over this giant obstacle she had placed in their path.

But he didn't say a word.

He walked straight to the basket on the kitchen counter where they kept keys, pens, and more and pulled out a pair of headphones. Then he seemed to hesitate, and she held her breath, hoping he would turn and look at her. But he grabbed a pen and paper and wrote something, then left the paper on the counter and plugged the earphones into his phone. He stopped, leaned over and kissed Daxx and Izzy on their heads, then glanced back at Ella before leaving, and she wished he hadn't, because the look in his eyes suggested he had no idea who she was.

1:54 p.m.

Ben felt grateful for the blaring music drowning his thoughts, leaving no room for anything but mechanical movements, one step after another, as far from Ella as he could get, each step taking him in the opposite direction. Looking down, he didn't see anything but the pavement below him—gum on the sidewalk, other people's feet and legs, a dog on its leash, an empty bag on the ground, the corner curb, asphalt, more feet in sandals, bare legs, a skateboard, a foot pushing off of it, up another curb, pavement, cracks … he kept walking.

He let the music fill all the space inside him, matching his anger, keeping up with his heartbeat, in tune with his heavy, fast steps, deliberate movement to and away, not stopping, not pausing, finding a different route rather than waiting for a light, waiting to keep going, no stopping. No stopping. No stopping.

2:48 p.m.

The children were building a fort with the couch and pillows while Ella was straightening up the house. There wasn't much to be done, but she was afraid that if she stopped moving, stopped being active, she might come undone and have a breakdown right there in front of Izzy and Daxx. When there was nothing left to clean off or put away, she picked up her phone and called Charlotte. Forcing a smile, she waved to the children and stepped outside to the backyard for some privacy.

The minute she heard Charlotte's voice, she said, "I'm so sorry how I left things our last conversation. I haven't been myself. Things just ..." *Get a grip. You did this.* "He left again, but this time he left a note saying he'd be back tonight."

"Shit. What happened? You guys seemed great yesterday. And apology accepted."

"We were. It's been okay, one step at a time. But then I told him something I've never told anyone." She told Charlotte about the offer from the Japanese company.

There was silence until Charlotte said, "Jesus."

"I know. It's not good."

"I have to ask—why did you tell him?"

"I had to. It was this thing between us. He didn't know about it, but I did, and I could feel it growing between us. I think he might have sensed something for a long time."

"Did he *tell* you he sensed something? That he felt there was something you'd been hiding?"

"No, but—"

"Then why did you tell him? One of my roles as your best friend is to call you out on your shit. And this, my friend, is a truckload of it. Of course this sent him over the edge. How could it not?"

Ella felt like she couldn't breathe. "I *had* to tell him. Ben and I can't move forward without honesty. It's the way we used to be, the only way to—"

"Make you feel better about yourself." Charlotte let out a loud sigh of frustration, which confused Ella. Why was this conversation so upsetting to her? Before she could ask, Charlotte said, "It gets to me—people pretending they're doing someone this big favor by being honest, but really they're trying to rid themselves of guilt, and so they're taking a bucket of this … this ugliness, and they're dumping it on the other person. The only person who feels better is the one who did the dumping. What good does it do the other person?"

"So you told me about hitting on Ben because … you wanted to make yourself feel better?"

Silence.

Ella went on. "But you didn't tell me about the other times you hit on him because … that would have been too much? *That* would have been dumping your stuff on me?"

"You're really gonna turn this around like that?"

Ella shook her head. "I'm exhausted, Charlotte. The only thing I care about right now is Ben coming home. I called you because I needed a friend. Not a judge. Not a lecture. I'm figuring things out. I've made a ton of mistakes. I don't know what I'm doing. I …" The tears came again.

"Jesus, I'm sorry." After a long pause, Charlotte said, "I'm tired too. I don't know how much help I can be to you right now, Ella. You … it's like you already have the answers and don't really want to hear what I have to say. And anyway, I have some stuff going on myself."

"Shit. I'm sorry. I didn't even ask how you were, what was going on with you. What is it? What happened?"

"I'm not in the mood, Ella. And I have to get back to work. Text me if Ben comes home. It's going to be okay."

As she said goodbye, Ella thought, *When Ben comes home*—when. *Not if.*

3:01 p.m.

Ben ended where his journey originally started, at the bus stop at the edge of town. He sat down on the bench and took off the headphones.

Suddenly immersed in the silence, he felt like he had dropped into another world.

It wasn't long before one thought after another rushed in to fill the silence.

He remembered comforting Ella after the deal supposedly fell through. He had been so sure they would say yes—to her creativity, her business acumen, her charm, her talent. He had believed in her, and after she told him they said no, it felt really important to him to make sure she knew that she was more than good enough, and so were her designs. The company just wasn't a good match; that was all. It was a conversation he tried to have again and again, wanting to make sure she didn't lose confidence in herself and her dream, but she kept brushing it off, not wanting to talk about it, saying it was best to just move on rather than dwell.

And then there were Izzy's art shows he wouldn't have missed for meetings that didn't matter. He was expendable and replaceable at Starfish. He'd seen it dozens of times. It didn't matter how good you were. People moved on, switched positions, found something better elsewhere, and suddenly the person everyone thought the company couldn't possibly do without was gone and forgotten, and someone new became the one they could never do without. *But they could.* Daxx and Izzy, they were a different story. Ben wasn't expendable and replaceable when it came to being there for Daxx and Izzy.

He thought about the meetings with Daxx's teachers he could have gone to. What would he have picked up on that Ella didn't? What could he have offered?

How many more times could he have picked Izzy and Daxx up from school and dropped them off? How many conversations would they have had during those minutes that would have added up to hours in the car together?

How many more meals would he have had with them?

How many more times could he have made them laugh?

He thought of random moments when he would catch a look in Ella's eyes; he sensed she was holding something back, but then it would be gone, that look, and he figured he had imagined it. He remembered the times he had asked, "Are you *sure* there's nothing going on?" She had assured him there was nothing. Eventually, he believed her and started doubting himself. It all came back to him—the times he had a feeling there was something false between them. But then he always wrote it off, convincing himself he was imagining things. He was paranoid. He was projecting. He was making a big thing out of nothing. It was him, not Ella. He needed to get a grip.

He tried to remember ... There was no decisive conversation. One day, there were so many exciting possibilities, so many possible paths, dreams they were running after together—for him, for Ella, for their family—and the next day, it was his responsibility to stop dreaming and get a *real* job with a guaranteed income. He was no longer his own boss, no longer in charge of his days, no longer in charge of his time. That was just the surface though. The real implications were much deeper, he was beginning to realize.

The anger was building fast, and his ears were ringing.

Stop. Stop, stop, stop—please stop.

As he fought the hatred that was trying to find its way in, begging to be felt, screaming that it deserved to be felt, as his fists tightened so much it hurt and he resisted the need to punch something, he desperately wanted to talk to August, but he knew he had to figure this out on his own; he couldn't go running to August every time he felt his world cracking.

He sat back, forced his fists open, relaxed his hands, and closed his eyes. Taking deep breaths, he pictured him and August on the rockers, and as he wondered what she would say, what advice she would give him, her voice came through loud and clear: "Oh yes, Ben. This one's a doozy, all right. So then, you have some choices now, don't you?"

3:23 p.m.

"I'll be right back," Ella said, leaving Daxx and Izzy in the living room, playing.

She went into the bathroom, closed the door, and stood with her back against it, finally free to feel the feelings she had been pushing down. Her throat felt tight, and she swallowed hard as the tears finally came. The weight of it all hit her, and she sank to the floor, cradling her head in her hands.

As Ella sat there staring at the tile floor, unable to stop crying, a part of her that had been quiet for a long time stepped up and took over, telling her to remember this feeling, to never, ever forget what it felt like to have her gut twisting in embarrassment and shame, her heart filled with sadness and regret.

Remember this loneliness, a part of her said. And she realized then how long she had been lonely. Since the day she told that lie.

Everything had been off since that day. All the electricity in and around her had been short-circuiting because the lie had severed a primary connection between her and Ben. Ever since then, the friction in what remained of their connectedness, their frayed attempts at the old closeness they used to have, they were bound to fail, or at least fall short, because there was something too big Ben didn't know, for three years.

And now he did.

She wondered whether Charlotte was right, if telling Ben had been selfish, if she had done it just to make herself feel better. The truth was she envied Ben's determination to be honest with himself first, then with her.

That was it, she realized—the missing piece—which was why her honesty with Ben had been so hurtful. She hadn't been honest with herself first.

Her whole body shaking, her head in her hands, she finally loosed the truths she had been trying to lock inside her the past three years, far from her consciousness. They finally had their say as she whispered to herself through hushed sobs, telling herself one bottom-line truth after another.

You lied and lied and lied …

You broke him …

You watched him lose himself …

You faked so much …

You tore us apart …

She continued admitting the scope of what she had done.

She made no attempt to stop her tears, only to quiet her quick, short breaths and sniffles so the children wouldn't hear.

Never forget what this feels like, she told herself again.

After a long while, she composed herself enough to go out and check on Daxx and Izzy, careful to avoid saying anything. Daxx would pick up on the sadness in her voice, and she didn't want to do that to him. Seeing that they were engrossed in a movie Izzy must have put on, Ella got a pen and some paper and returned to the bathroom.

She sat on the floor and wrote a letter to Ben. She told him the truth, why she turned down the contract—that she had been afraid of getting consumed by the business and losing sight of what was important, because, as she knew so well, life could change in an instant, as it did with Andy. "It's not an excuse. I know that," she wrote. "There is no justification. I only know it's something that impacted my decision. It was so fresh then, the pain of a sudden, permanent absence. It was so raw. Andy had died five months earlier."

She went on to say she didn't want to miss Daxx and Izzy's growing-up years. Of course Ben hadn't wanted to either. It was so wrong on her part. And selfish. She told him that what she was most embarrassed about and what she most regretted not telling Ben was the thing she feared most: with Ben being as good as he was with Izzy and Daxx, had she accepted that contract and taken her business to the level it would have required, she would have faded out of their picture and would have stopped being able to relate to them. She'd be the mom who tried to fit in, and they would have private jokes, the three of them, and memories she didn't share, and she'd be the serious working mom who came home from a business trip and tried to be playful and catch up on all she had missed. She'd have two different mind-sets, requiring that she ramp up and then thaw in an endless cycle as she stepped back and forth between a simple, kind world and one that required a constant assertion of power. She didn't trust herself to do that well—or even close to successfully. She knew something would give. And she was afraid it would be her relationships at home. She didn't trust the part of her that would thrive in the position and thirst for more.

She wrote that she was offering all the words to Ben only as an explanation, not as an excuse, not as justification. Then she went on to apologize for lying, for letting him think he was imagining a distance between them, for not admitting the guilt consuming her and affecting them every single day, for the time lost, for each moment lost. The list went on. When she had finished apologizing, she cried some more, this time because there was nothing left to say.

As she folded the paper and slowly wrote Ben's name on the outside, she knew the letter was way too late. Her apologies and explanations rested in the neat confines of a page, when the truth was nothing that could be contained anymore. The damage she had inflicted was everywhere.

4:04 p.m.

Ben hadn't moved from the bus stop.

What now? he kept asking himself. Every time he thought of Ella, the same surge of negative emotions just kept repeating itself, anger being the easiest one to identify. And when he thought about the past three years, every memory felt slightly distorted.

Ben thought of Ella standing in their backyard. He had looked at her right before leaving a few hours ago—really looked—and something was different; she looked like a stranger he didn't want to meet. It was one of the worst feelings he'd ever had. He wondered how two people who knew each other so well, who had been raising two children together, who had been through the death of a family member together, who had loved each other so well, who had always felt destined for each other and lucky to be together, how they could get to the point where they looked at each other like they didn't know who the other person was—and didn't want to.

"Well, fancy meeting you here."

Ben looked up, and his heart skipped a beat.

No way …

You knew it. You knew she'd show up. Why do you think you're here?

I can't believe this …

Yes, you can. You knew it. You knew …

Thank you thank you thank you thank—

"Well, don't just sit there staring at me like you've seen a ghost," August said, leaning over toward the open passenger-side window. "Come on over and say hello."

Ben walked to August's truck, taking in the moment.

"August," he said, unable to contain his smile. "It's so good to see you."

"Well, I would say the same, but you don't look … Well, that's neither here nor there, is it? This is a hoot. Something kept bugging me to drop off some more honey for Heather at the farmer's market. I had a feeling she'd need more today, and sure enough, she did. A lot more. Well, get in, Ben! Why are you still standing there?"

Ben got in, and August picked up where she had left off. "Anyhow, Heather invited me to lunch, but I just had this itching to get back home, and you know me, I follow my itchings. And then as I'm passing the bus stop, I thought, *Well, that poor dear looks about as lost as Ben looked that day—what the heck?* I realized it was you. What's wrong, Ben? Hold on. Let's get out of the bus's way. It'll be here soon." She pulled up about twenty feet, put the truck in park, and turned to face him. "Let's hear it."

"Seeing you—how you showed up again … I don't know. It makes me feel like anything is possible. It makes me feel good."

"Oh, you're going to make me blush."

"I'm serious though—I just feel so *different*. How are you, August? I've been thinking about you—wondering how you've been."

"I'm doing just fine, thank you. Go on now. Let me make myself useful. Let's hear why you're at the bus stop looking like you've lost your best friend."

Ben told her everything that had happened, from the time he arrived home all the way to his leaving again.

"I see," August said, nodding. "That's a pickle."

Ben smiled. "That it is."

"Well, my friend, the way I see it, we are where we are. Do you know for sure—for absolute certain—that anything leading up to this moment should have been different? Even though a lot *could* have been different—if he said, if she said, if they did, if you … you get my drift—the question is, are you where you belong in your life right now, *today*, Ben?"

"I don't know … I can't say yes. I *won't*. I'm not letting her off the hook like that. It doesn't feel right."

"I'm not talking about what happened before this or even what comes next," August said. "I'm talking about *today*. From here on out, you can do whatever you decide.

But before that, I'd caution you to ask yourself a most important question: am I happy to be where I am today?"

Ben looked in the side-view mirror and thought about it as he watched another bus pull to a stop behind them and open its doors. No one got out, and soon the doors closed, and the bus pulled away, continuing on. Ben turned to August and shared the answers that had surfaced. "I'm not happy to be where I am today with Ella, and I'm happy with where I am with Daxx and Izzy."

"And *you*, Ben? How about where you are with *you*?"

"If I'm going to be totally honest … I *am* grateful for the past three years and where they brought me, all the way to meeting you." He shook his head, a part of him roiling with anger, feeling like he was making what Ella did okay. Tempering the surge of frustration, he said, "But that—*none of that* changes how I feel about what she did."

August patted his arm. "Life goes so quickly, Ben. Some lessons are better learned as early as possible, and this is one of them: There are people who sting once and then are *very* careful not to do it again because they don't like being the stinger. Will they sting again? Oh sure, of course they will. But not like they did before. And one thing's for sure: they'll try hard not to. And they'll succeed. And they won't be perfect. There'll still be some zingers but not nearly as many stingers."

She smiled, seeming to be both present and far away in her thoughts, and Ben wondered what was on her mind. He was about to ask her, but then she went on, saying, "And then there are those who sting again and again and again. And you know what, Ben? They never recognize that they're the stinger. Those are the dangerous ones. Which is

Ella? Answer that. And then you'll know how to move forward.

"I never brought any stingers with me, Ben, not for too long anyway. I wanted more honey on my journey. You've gotta know who the stingers are—and who's stung you but would never want to again, even if they do. Because there's a big difference there."

Ben thought about it—and then decided to stop thinking so hard, realizing that might be the root of his confusion, the attempt to make sense out of any of this. He decided to just say what was in his heart, to get it all out and see where it led him. "She's not a stinger—I mean, she stung hard—this was a stinger, but *she's* not a stinger. It's not who she is." His stomach clenched, and his skin felt prickly. There was more, he realized: "The thing is, even if I could forgive her, I don't think I could ever forget what she did. It's changed everything," he said.

"It doesn't work like that, Ben. What I mean by that is *it really won't work*. If you're going to forgive, you *have* to practically forget, because as long as you actively remember, you're going to hold back something, even if it's just a little part of you. That little part is the part that doesn't want to get fooled again—because it remembers—and it'll be on guard and on watch 24/7. That's all it'll do. Nothing else. To have the kind of connection you've talked about wanting with Ella, there can be no holding back and no resentment. Not even a sliver. It's got to be all or nothing, Ben. Do you see that?"

He closed his eyes, nodding. "I do …"

"The real question is, can you forgive her?"

Ben looked at August. "I don't know. I honestly don't. Not for turning down the job—that's not what gets to me. It's that ..." Ben stopped, not wanting to fire up that feeling again.

August nodded and then seemed lost in thought as she looked out the window. After an unusual moment of quiet between them, she said, "I'd like to tell you a story about forgiveness."

When she didn't continue but turned to Ben as if waiting for a response, he quickly said, "Yes—please do."

August closed her eyes and took a deep breath. "I had a son ... Pete. Heather's little brother." She smiled. "We were living here by then." She motioned around them, saying, "Well, not in this truck of course. In the house. Henry was a music teacher at the middle school. I think it's still there. Granite Middle School?"

"Yes, it's still there," Ben said.

"Well, Henry, being the gentle soul he was, he rode his bike to work once a week, every Tuesday, about twelve miles. He wanted to make sure he saw what there was to see between here and there, things he wouldn't notice when driving. You see, Henry was a big believer in change—well, that change happens quickly, and sometimes before you even know it's happened. I think it was his way of slowing things down a little. You're smiling. Did you ride your bike to work too?"

Ben laughed. "No, I just think I would have liked Henry a lot. I wish I could have met him."

August patted his arm. "Me too, Ben. Me too."

"So then ..." Ben prompted.

"Yes. So ... I should back up. Henry had been trying to get me to learn how to drive stick. He was never someone to push his will on anyone, but he pushed hard with this one. I don't know why I pushed back. I guess I just didn't see the point and really didn't feel like learning. My hands were full with Heather and Pete, who were five and three then. Plus, I had my own car. True, it was sitting in our driveway and had been for a while, but we were saving up the money to get it fixed. In the meantime, I didn't need to leave home that often. Henry was always stopping at the store on his way home because a block of ice was usually on the list."

"A block of ice? What for?"

"Well, we didn't have the propane refrigerator back then, so we used a big cooler. An ice block would last a few days, three at most, and then it needed to be replaced."

"Wow," Ben said. "I can't even imagine living like that, especially with two little kids. That's impressive, August."

"You're so kind. But it didn't feel that way. It just felt simple, and we were all about simplicity then, Henry and me. Maybe that's part of why I just kept putting off letting him teach me how to drive his truck. I guess I had no need to." August stopped and looked at Ben. "You're good to listen to this old lady talk and talk."

"Are you kidding me? I love listening to you," he said.

"So then, where was I ... yes ..." She stopped again and looked at him as if weighing what to say next. "I don't know how good I'm going to be at this, Ben," she said, her voice soft. "I haven't told this story in a long time. I'm just not sure I'm going to be very good at it." Her voice had a slight quiver, and her sudden sadness made Ben nervous.

He took her hand and said, "It's okay, August. I'd really like to hear your story. I think you can tell me."

With the way she looked at him, Ben felt like she needed him to say something else, to say more.

"You can take as long as you need," he said. "You'll do fine."

August nodded, took a deep breath, and then began with new resolve. "It was a Tuesday morning. I was helping Heather make Play-Doh, and it was time to add the food coloring. Pete just loved that part—not any of the rest. Not the mixing or waiting, just adding the little drops of color. So we always let him do that step. 'Go on out and get your brother,' I said to Heather. He was outside playing. He loved to take his little matchbox car and run it up and over and down the pile of logs, over and over ..." She looked down and then at Ben, a tear sliding off her cheek. She pursed her lips, then whispered, "This is hard for me, Ben. This is very, very hard for me."

"You're doing great, August," he said quietly, nodding, his sadness for her steadily building.

August leaned back against the seat and closed her eyes for a moment.

"Heather ... she went outside to tell Pete it was time to add the color, and then I heard her screaming. *'Mama! Mama!'* she yelled. I dropped the bowl and ran outside. 'He's not answering me, Mama!' she said. Over by the woodpile, little Pete was on the ground, not moving. I knelt down and scooped him into my arms. He was breathing, I could feel it, but his color was bad ... it was very bad, and his breathing was so slow ... and I couldn't wake him up.

You see, I didn't know it then, but Pete was having an anaphylactic reaction."

She looked down and wrung her hands in her lap. "I didn't know he was allergic, that a bite from a black widow could ... if he wasn't treated right away ... and I didn't know what to do. We had no phone, Ben!" she said as if she was trying so hard to explain, as if it had just happened. "We didn't have a phone, and the car, my car was broken, and the truck ... Henry's truck was there because he had ridden his bike to work, and I could have put my little boy in the truck and driven like hell to get him to the hospital ... only I *couldn't*. I couldn't, Ben, you see? Because I didn't know how to drive stick because I hadn't listened, I hadn't listened to Henry when he urged me to learn ... and so I told my little Heather who was scared to death and crying so hard to go inside and just wait, to just wait there and not move while I went for help ..."

August tried to choke back tears, but they kept coming. "So I ran ... I ran like hell down the driveway, down the dirt road, my little boy in my arms, and I was crying, I was crying so hard it was blurring my vision, and I could barely breathe as I lifted one foot and then the other, faster, as fast as I could go down that road, and I knew it was going to be too late, I knew it the way a mother knows things, so I held him closer to my heart, willing him to feel it, to feel my heart beating for him, begging my lungs to breathe for him, but I could see his face turning blue, Ben, I could see it happening, and I knew my baby boy, my precious boy was dying in my arms ..."

"Oh my God, August," Ben said, taking her hand again. "Oh my God, I'm so sorry. I'm so sorry ... I can't imagine ..."

Ben tried to think of what to say, how to ease her pain as she let the tears go, no longer holding back.

"That's good, August ... Let it out ..."

She squeezed his hand and nodded.

When she had composed herself, she took a deep breath and let out a long exhale. "I'm sorry to put you through that. I ... without knowing that part of the story though, the rest of it just wouldn't make sense." She reached into the center console and pulled out a small package of tissues. She wiped her eyes and let go of another long breath. "You see, Ben, you know where this is going, right? You know what I'm going to tell you?" She looked at him.

That's when it hit Ben, what she was trying to tell him. He shook his head. "No, August. It wasn't your fault. It wasn't."

"It *was*, Ben." She ran both hands along the steering wheel. "Had I done the right thing, the responsible thing, and learned to drive this truck back when Henry asked me to ... I might have been able to save Pete. Instead, Henry and I lost our son, and Heather lost her little brother. And Pete ... my baby boy lost his life."

"But, August—"

"Now hold on. This isn't about me—this story. It's about the importance of forgiveness. You see, Henry did something courageous. He acknowledged what I *knew*, that there was indeed something I needed to be forgiven for. And then he did something heroic: he forgave me." She took another tissue and wiped her eyes. "Oh, Ben, we were both in so much pain, in such deep grieving ... but a few weeks after the worst day of our life, Henry made me sit down, look him in the eye, and listen to him well. He said the words that became my lifeline, words I've played over in my head thousands of times since.

"'August Rose,' he said—one day he had just added Rose to my name—'I can't hear the music anymore. And I can't make music anymore. I can't live like this. I forgive you. I forgive you, August Rose. Now you need to forgive yourself. And you can't go taking days or months or years to do it, because then the music will never come back, especially for me and Heather.'

"You see, Ben, he begged me to forgive myself so that he could hear Pete's voice in his head and, as he called it, the music of his laugh. He said, 'I feel like I can't breathe without it. I need to hear Pete's laughter again. That's all I want to hear, August Rose, and I can't do it by myself, and I sure can't hear it with all this blame going on. It's so loud. *Please*.'"

"Oh, August ..." Tears slid down Ben's cheeks. He let them fall, not knowing what to say, trying to process all the emotions he was feeling.

August went on. "You see, he gave me a way to make things better, for him and for Heather—he convinced me that the only way I could ease the pain they were in was to forgive myself. Imagine that. That's a *good* man, Ben. We could have spent a long, long time being destructive and angry, me at myself, him at me, but because of his insistence on forgiveness, we, the three of us, spent a lot of time just being very, very sad. I don't say *just* as in it not counting much; I mean, thanks to Henry, we didn't have to deal with anything on top of the overwhelming sadness. We missed our little Pete. We missed him so much it sometimes had one of us doubled over in pain, the tears never seeming to end. But there was no anger, Ben. No hatred. Not a mean word spoken. And so we hurt *together* ... and eventually, we healed together."

Ben looked at August for a long time before saying, "How did I get so lucky to cross paths with you? I want Ella to meet you. She would love you, August. And she'd see it, all of this ... and she'd understand."

Smiling, August slowly shook her head. "No, Ben. It's *you* Ella needs to meet, not for the first time but again. And *then* she'll understand, and so will you."

After

Ella poured lighter fluid over the charcoals in the hibachi, then lit a match and threw it in. She looked at Ben. "Ready?"

"One second." Scanning the piece of paper he was holding, he quickly reread the words he had written. Something was telling him it wasn't time. "I'm not sure ..."

"You don't have to do it," she said.

"No, I want to ... I just feel like ... Can I read it to you first? I feel like if I don't say it out loud, in front of someone, something will be left unfinished."

Ella rubbed her hands and then put them over the flames. "I think I get it. You want a witness—for his sake."

"Yes, exactly." Relief washed over him. It was becoming their normal again—them *getting* each other, that click that seemed to happen every time either one of them generously heard past the other person's words or saw beyond first glance. "It just needs to be said out loud, in front of someone other than me."

"I'd love to hear it." She sat back. "Whenever you're ready."

Ben took a deep breath. "Okay," he said. "Here goes." He glanced down at the paper, then hesitated and looked at Ella. "I know you won't, but I want to say it anyway—please don't judge anything I've written here. Don't even feel like you have to say anything after I read it."

Ella nodded. "Okay. I promise."

"All right."

She smiled. His encouraging, strong, kind Ella—she had been back for a while now.

Finally, Ben read to Ella:

I don't know what your name is, so I'm not sure how to address you, but I saw you sitting alone one day at your school during lunch. Every day since then, I've regretted not asking if I could sit with you, or not even asking, just sitting down across from you. I wish I had said something to you, anything, just something so you would know you were noticed.

I need to say I'm sorry. I'm sorry I didn't do anything that day. I'm sorry I walked away and pretended I didn't notice.

Every time I picture you sitting there alone, I wish you could have given that pain to me. It wouldn't hurt me the way it might be hurting you—it's a time and experience and age thing. I'd feel it for you if I could. Or if you preferred, which I have a feeling you might, I'd feel it with you. And then after we felt the rawness of the pain, of whatever's happened in your fifteen or sixteen years to leave you so alone, we wouldn't stop there. We'd make our hands into fists and squeeze with all our strength, and after the tips of our fingers dug into our fisted palms, we'd finally release the tightness in our throats, and if tears came out in embarrassing torrents, we'd let them. And then after we said everything we've wanted to say—how we feel about life, about everything—because no one's judging, we'd be able to look at each other, two would-be strangers, and it would start to come back, an awareness ... we'd start to remember who we were before the pain—who we are. And I'd listen as you'd tell me, first one word, then two, and then you wouldn't be able to stop—words, who you are. I'd see myself in you, and you in me, and as you talked, I'd see you sit up tall. I'd see you move the hair out of your face, and I'd see your smile for the first time. And I'd ask you to tell me more about who you are and why you're here, and I'd thank you over and over because I'd feel so lucky to have gotten to meet you.

I'm sorry I didn't do any of that. I'm so sorry I kept walking.

He looked up at Ella.

"Yes, Ben," she whispered. "Yes."

"I think it's time," he said. "Do you?"

She nodded.

Ben set the paper on the burning coals and watched as everything he had poured out began the process of transformation into ashes, to be carried on a breeze into the moonlight.

He looked to Ella, unsure what to do next. So much had led up to this point: days of sharing, long and thoughtful silences, layers of self-reflection, detailed apologies, tear-filled and vulnerable explanations, deliberate eye contact again and again, quick gut-instinct decisions, and necessary pauses. They had found their way to this moment but hadn't looked past it to what might happen next.

All Ben knew was that this was it; the process was complete. Writing, reading, and burning the letter was the final step in what had been a series of pivotal releases, one after another, always ending in the need to forgive themselves, he and Ella taking turns. This last piece was his, epitomized by the boy whose name he didn't know—the sadness, the aloneness and fear, the global archetypes he felt he had tapped into—the experience was in his past now. He could feel it. Every aspect was either a part of him now, fully integrated and no longer distinguishable from the whole of who he was, or he had let it go and left it behind, having learned what he needed to from it. Change was in motion, leading him forward.

Ella was staring at the fire and seemed mesmerized by the shrinking paper. Finally, she said, "I'm holding so tightly to you, Ben, right beside you. I think you're brave. I think you're the bravest man I know."

He watched her staring at the fire as she talked, the flames shooting higher now, the paper and Ben's handwriting curling in on itself.

Ella went on. "Do you know how much it moves me and inspires me—God, it inspires me—that seeing a very sad boy having lunch by himself was enough to send your world off its axis?"

With a *pop*, sparks flew.

"The truth is," she said, "beneath everything else I've felt during this whole thing, there's always been a deeper stirring, even when I couldn't admit it or explain it, and it's this: I *love* that you started walking, that you took those first few deliberate steps out of Starfish that day. And I love that you *kept* walking when I know—I know you, Ben—it had to be so hard not to turn around and come home that Tuesday. I love that you faced the uncertainty straight on. You dove so deep, Ben." She shook her head, and he could see her mind at work. "God, you dove deep. Right down into the dark, terrifying depths."

Ben wanted to say something, but no words came, and he realized it felt good just to be, to listen and allow. To really hear her.

It seemed to take effort when Ella pulled her attention away from the fire, and when she did so, she looked at Ben. "There is no husband better than you. There's no father better than you. No better example for Izzy and Daxx." She smiled, leaned over, and put her hand on his cheek. "I'm the luckiest person I know. Thank you for sharing your letter, for trusting me enough to." Choking back tears that came more often now, though softer and gentler than they used to, she said, "Thank you for everything, Ben."

"Come here," he said. Taking her hand, he led her a few steps away from the hibachi, and they lay down on the grass—Ben on his back, Ella curled up next to him, her head on his chest. Looking up at the sky through the jacaranda branches, he intertwined his fingers with Ella's.

Now he could take the next step.

* * *

"Aren't you coming with us?" Daxx asked Ben.

He handed Daxx the bag of sand toys and said, "No, buddy. I'll meet you there in a little while. I have to make a call first." He looked at Ella, and she smiled. His reassuring Ella. Turning to Izzy, he said, "You've got the towels. Anything else you need?"

"Snacks," Ella said. "I've got them."

He gave each of them a hug and said he'd head down to the beach after he was done with his call.

"You'll do great," Ella said in his ear as she hugged him again.

When the screen door closed, with the three of them on their way, Ben looked at the time. He had a few minutes before Danny would be calling. Ben had emailed him, apologizing for leaving Starfish so abruptly and hardly being in touch except to say—forever ago—that he needed to take some personal time and that he wasn't sure how long it would be. In the email, he had asked if Danny would be willing to have a short conversation with him; he felt the need to make things right and tie up loose ends there before he was able to move on to whatever was next. Danny had sent back a quick reply, not friendly but not harsh either, setting up a time for the call.

When his phone rang, Ben inhaled deeply, exhaled, and then answered.

After quick pleasantries, Ben said, "Danny, I really appreciate you taking the time to talk to me."

"I'm glad you're okay, Ben. I don't want to beat around the bush here. There are some pretty wild stories going around about why you left so suddenly and what you've been up to for the past six weeks, seven weeks—whatever it's been. What happened?"

Be yourself. Just be yourself. "That's a good question," Ben said. "I'm not sure how to explain the start of it, but things are getting better—much better."

After a pause, Danny said, "Okay, well, that's not giving me much, Ben. Not a lot to go on there. Let me ask you this: why did you want to talk to me? It would be helpful if I understood why we're having this conversation."

Relax. Just be real with him. "I wanted to apologize—more than just in an email. You and Jules were really good to me. I'm sorry I left so abruptly. I wasn't thinking about how it would affect you and Starfish and everyone who had to take over my responsibilities. You're a good company with good people, and I really appreciate my three years with you. Please let Jules know too. I just wanted to say I'm sorry and thank you for everything."

Danny let out a sigh. "I'm not going to say it was easy when you took off," he said. "It took some maneuvering, but we got everything covered. You're not easily replaceable, Ben; I can tell you that. There's a hole. I haven't figured out where, but there is one."

No words came to Ben, so he stayed silent.

Danny then said, "It's not like I can offer you your old job back, but … I don't know. There might be a place for you here in a different capacity, if you're interested. You change the dynamics, and people like you—even after that stunt you pulled. I can't make any promises, but think about it. Let me know if you come up with anything. Just something to think about. I've gotta run. Give my best to Ella. She's good?"

"She's great, yes. Thanks."

"Good. All right, Ben. Be in touch."

"I will. Thank you, Danny."

Ben put the phone on the table and sat down. That wasn't at all how he had expected the call to go. He had been focused on just trying to be himself and get the apology out. He had wanted a feeling of completion at Starfish, on a note that felt right. Danny had cracked a door open for Ben, the last thing Ben anticipated. The thought of returning to Starfish still felt wrong though. He couldn't see himself fitting into his old role; he didn't *want* to.

Still, something had changed. August was right. He was being Ben, the real Ben, and people were responding to that, just as August said they would. First Ella. Now Danny.

* * *

Ben drove to August's house to stop in and see how she was doing. He also wanted to invite her over for a barbecue so she could meet Ella, Izzy, and Daxx. He was starting to enjoy the fact that she still didn't have a phone, that to talk to her, he needed to make the effort to go see her.

After helping her collect fresh honey, they sat on the porch and drank iced tea made with chamomile from August's garden and ate almonds that Ben had brought for her, dipped in the fresh honey.

Ben caught her up on the progress he and Ella had made, and August told Ben about Heather stopping by more and more lately. "I think there's a change taking place for Heather, a bit of a … tweaking," she said. "Something's happening. This old lady can feel it."

"You're not old, August. You're so far from old."

"I think we're all the age we need to be. My Heather included. I just have a feeling a change is coming for her. She's good about knowing when it's time, just like Henry was. I wonder what's next for her. She has so many talents. There's so much she can do." She smiled and sipped her iced tea. "What are *your* talents, Ben?"

"Oh … I don't know anymore, August. I mean, I'm not sure. I'm figuring it out," he said, twirling an almond in the honey to get an extra coating.

"Do me a favor, Ben—do everyone a favor. Don't rule anything out. Talents come in all shapes. The ones you're meant to use, they're not always what other people think they are."

"What do you mean?" If there was one thing he had learned, it was that under each layer of words from August, there were layers of wisdom. He just had to ask to hear it.

"Just because you're good at something doesn't mean it's what you're here to do," she said. "There are lots of things I'm sure you're good at, but there are just a few that you're good at and *enjoy*. There's a difference. You see?"

Ben smiled. "Abide-by number one: taste what you're doing." He clinked his glass with hers. "And number six: do the things that make you feel more like you."

August patted his arm. "Oh, you flatter me that you even remember that. Thank you, Ben. You're so kind. So good."

"It's easy with you, August. I don't know why. It just is. I have a question though. Let's say I figure out what I like to do, and it's something I'm good at. What if there's no way for me to make money doing it—or at least enough. That's kind of where I'm at right now."

"Ha!"

"What?"

"There's always a way, Ben. *Always*. Think about it."

Her unshakeable confidence made his world of possibilities feel like it was expanding right there and then, and he was sure that if August kept saying things like that and he kept trying to believe them, the possibilities would never contract again.

She looked at him. "Everything starts working when you're in tune with you. 'Can't you hear the difference?' Henry used to ask me that, playing a few notes on an instrument he hadn't finished tuning. I couldn't hear it. Not for the life of me. But I could feel it when one of us was out of tune with the other, and it was usually because one of us was out of tune with ourselves. If you're out of tune for a long while, and you're spending too much of your time doing something that feels scratchy, you'll get irritated pretty quickly, and you'll look for things and people to blame. Pretty soon, you won't be a lot of fun to be around. That's someone who's really out of tune. Something has to change. It just has to. That's no way to go through life."

"You're right," Ben said. "It's not."

With the push of her feet, she set her rocker gently in motion again. "I'm sure you've seen it, Ben. You can just tell, can't you? The people who are in tune with themselves? And then those who aren't—they just seem to get bothered too easily. And their smile, when you see it, it's got a distance to it."

Ben could picture it. He remembered what he was like a few months ago, when his smile felt tight, when his default expression was far from relaxed. "Yes ... there's an edge to them. It's like, even when things are good, something's not right."

"Want to know what I think?" August said.

"Of course," Ben said, smiling.

"I think the challenge is to ask yourself again and again, *who am I? Is this who I am?* And to honestly answer. Oh, that's where it's at, Ben. Can you see it? When you act like you, who you really are—when you spend your day being you, it just all falls into place. When you're in tune with you, it's exactly like that beautiful thing you just said: even when things go wrong, everything is somehow right. Powerful stuff, Ben, this being in sync with yourself. That reminds me. Hold on right here." August went inside and came out with the Maglite. Handing it to Ben, she said, "I can't look at this without thinking of you."

Ben smiled. "And that's bad?"

"Oh, no," she said, sitting back down in her rocker. "It's just that it feels like it should belong to you. Ever since that night—do you remember, Ben? When you shined it up there to the moon and your light came through?"

Ben would never forget. "Of course, August, but you need a flashlight. I can't take this."

"Oh, nonsense. I never use this one. I have others. Henry had it as a weapon more than anything, which is funny because I can hardly even imagine my Henry actually using it like that. He'd talk the ear off an intruder before anything else. Anyway, I don't need it, Ben. And it feels like … well, maybe you could use it, as a reminder."

Ben rolled the flashlight over his open palm, feeling its weight. "If you're sure, August."

"I'm sure."

"Okay, thank you." He clicked it on and then off again. "You know, I think our tunes can change. Maybe that's what you're sensing with Heather, the change you were talking about."

"Sure could be. I like that. It just might be time for a different song for my Heather."

He set the Maglite down and said, "I've been thinking. I'd love for you to meet Ella and Daxx and Izzy. And I'd love for us to meet Heather. How about we all get together next Sunday? Come to our house for a barbecue?"

August clapped her hands together. "Oh, Ben. Really? I can't think of anything I would love more."

Thrilled, Ben went inside to get a paper and pen so he could write down their address, along with directions. He couldn't wait to tell Ella.

* * *

As Ben pulled into the parking spot, Ella ran her finger along the wind chime on her lap and said, "I hope he likes it." She and Ben had come up with the idea together and then, over the course of several afternoons, had gone to two other bike stores and a hardware store to get everything Ella would need.

"I think he'll love it," Ben said. "*I* love it."

Ella smiled. It was definitely a departure from anything she had ever made before, and she had to admit she was really happy with how it turned out. Lately, she had felt a shift taking place in her work, a letting go of old patterns, styles, even colors, and an opening to new possibilities. She was starting to feel inspired and creative in a way she never had—at least not for a long time. Some of her old clients weren't nearly as excited as she was about some of her new designs, and she lost a few of those clients, but she decided, thanks to Ben's constant encouragement, it was okay.

They had barely opened the door of the bike shop when Ethan said, "Hey, you guys!" He hurried over from behind the counter and pulled Ben into a bear hug, saying, "Good to see you, man. I'm glad you're back."

Ella couldn't stop smiling.

"Thanks," Ben said. "It's good to be back."

Ethan took a step back and looked the two of them over. "Seeing you two together … I mean, I've only known you apart. I like this. This is good. You two look different together … better." He started laughing. "You know what I mean. It's just good to see. What can I do for you?"

Ella handed him the chime. "We brought you this. We both wanted to thank you. You were really pivotal for us— two strangers who found their way to you, and you didn't treat either of us like a stranger."

"We're so appreciative of everything you did for us," Ben added. "You took a big chance on me, this crazy guy who just walked into your store one day and then ... wouldn't really leave."

Ethan laughed, patting Ben on the back. "Speaking of that," he said, "I have a check for you. But let me look at this beauty first." He lifted the chime high and smiled and shook his head. "Unbelievable." He touched the different elements—the curved spoke, the layers of two-inch-long bike chains, hung in circles, the hanging hex keys and bike-repair tools. "And look at this, front and center," he said, turning the Japanese spoke wrench.

Ella basked in the moment, hearing the chime sing its songs, seeing Ethan's reaction, and standing next to Ben, holding his hand.

"You made this?" Ethan said.

"She did," Ben said, the pride in his voice making Ella's heart surge.

"This is ... amazing." Ethan looked at Ella. "Thank you."

"My pleasure," she said. "It really was."

"Follow me," Ethan said, leading them to the counter, where he carefully laid the chime down. He reached behind and pulled out an envelope.

As Ethan tried to give it to Ben, Ben stepped back and put his hands up. "I can't," he said. "I just can't take it."

"You worked for me, Ben. I'm not someone who takes that for free. It's just not right."

"Please," Ben said, "I don't want to make you uncomfortable about it or anything. It's just that the time I spent here was so ... I don't know ... *good*—it had nothing to do with money or work or business. It was like a retreat, this getaway, and I just want to keep it exactly as it was. I don't want to change anything, and getting paid for it, it just feels like it would change what it was."

Ethan looked at the wind chime on the counter. "Okay, Ben," he finally said. "I get it." He folded the envelope and put it in his pocket.

A couple walked in and approached the used bike section.

Ella said, "We don't want to keep you. Thank you for everything."

"Not at all. You're good company, you two. You're welcome anytime." As he walked them out, he said, "Any exciting plans for the day?"

Ella and Ben looked at each other and started laughing.

"We have no idea what's next," Ben said.

Ethan smiled and nodded. "That's the way."

* * *

Ella was relieved that when she gave Charlotte a hug, the awkwardness from being out of touch for a while dissipated. "Thanks for meeting me," Ella said.

"Well, I've pretty much thought of you *every* time I've passed here," Charlotte said as they sat at the only empty table in the Blue Express. "So, yes, Ella, I've thought about you a lot lately."

Ella rotated her coffee cup, feeling the warmth of it on her fingertips. "I'm sorry. I know I was caught up in my own life and didn't give a lot of thought to what was going on for you."

Charlotte sat back and let out a forced laugh. She shook her head. "*Nothing* was going on for me. I realize that. I'm actually seeing a guy—a therapist." She pointed at Ella. "Don't go thinking this is all about you—our friendship unraveling. It's something I had been thinking of doing for a while. It's good. It's good to have someone listen."

"How'd you find him?"

The barista brought over Charlotte's latte. As soon as she turned away, Charlotte said, "His office is just down the block, across the street. Here's the crazy thing. I'm sure I've seen the place a hundred times, but then early last week, it was like I *noticed* it for the first time. Weird—I know. I felt pulled, so I thought, what the hell. And I went. Had my first session that day."

"Can he see through you? I mean, you know all the games we play—even with ourselves." From the look on Charlotte's face, Ella realized it may have been insensitive to be so blunt. "What I meant is, is he good?"

"Good enough. I don't need to be on the Autobahn with this. A snail's pace is good for me. I can't move through things as quickly as you and Ben seem to be able to. You guys are good, right?"

Ella sipped her coffee, thinking of how to answer. Why was it so challenging to just be herself? "Yeah ... we're good, but we have some pretty big unknowns. Like what he's going to do for work. We've got savings that'll last us a little longer, but the sooner we figure it out, the better. And ... I'm going to meet August. She's coming to our house this weekend for a barbecue. Izzy and Daxx are really excited."

"Are they? What do they know about her?"

"Ben's described her as being like a fairy godmother, so who knows what in the world they're expecting." Ella

laughed. "But I'm really looking forward to meeting her—
finally."

Charlotte just smiled—a silent smile that said plenty.

"Hey, you should come," Ella said. "You can join me in
seeing for yourself that she wasn't an apparition."

"I'll pass, but thank you." Charlotte fidgeted with the
sugar packets and then finally locked on Ella's gaze. "Don't
look at me like that. I'm just not feeling it. There'll be a lot
going on, you guys getting to know each other, a whole big
group thing, and I'm more into one-on-one right now. No
offense."

Ella nodded. "I understand. If you change your mind,
let me know. The kids are helping me plan the menu. It's
going to be a good one."

"You can do this, Ella. You don't need me there."

"Okay ... I didn't mean—"

"Things have changed. There's just not a lot of space
for me right now." She drank the last of her coffee and then
pushed her cup away.

"That's not true. There's plenty of space. We—"

"Every time you say *we*, you mean you and Ben. And
you say it a lot."

Ella wasn't sure what to say to that. "I wish I was a
better friend to you. You've been a really good friend to me.
I wish I knew how to do this better."

Charlotte sat back in her chair, and Ella sensed it was to
put a little more distance between them. "You're both
different since that whole ... episode. It's just ... I don't
know. I don't know anything anymore. But I'm figuring it
out." She looked at her watch, though not long enough to
even see the time. "I gotta go. Thanks for the coffee. Next

time it's on me. I'm guessing you guys are saving every penny right about now. Tell Ben and the kids I said hi." She gave Ella a quick hug and left.

It was wishful thinking, Ella realized. The awkwardness hadn't dissipated; it was growing just as quickly as the divide between them was deepening.

* * *

On Sunday morning, as Daxx and Izzy were making a welcome sign for August and Heather, and Ella was cutting cabbage for the coleslaw, wondering out loud whether they should set up to eat inside or outside, considering there was a 50 percent chance of rain, a framed photograph next to the couch caught Ben's eye. He paused in the midst of making the barbecue sauce, feeling pulled in by the photo of him and Ella on the beach four years ago. It was such a candid shot of them laughing. In the past few years, every time he glanced at that picture, it felt like he was looking at an old version of them, a young and maybe even naive version. But not anymore.

"What are you smiling about?" Ella asked.

The list was growing, but Ben said the first thing that came to mind. "I'm excited for you guys to meet August. I think—"

The knock on the screen door drew his attention. Outside was a woman Ben didn't recognize.

Daxx jumped down from his stool, ran to the door, and said, "Are you August?"

Ella hurried after him and opened the screen door as the woman introduced herself. Ben had to strain to hear;

her voice was so soft. When he heard "Heather," he felt a subtle panic.

As they made introductions and Ella offered Heather something to drink, Ben's internal conversation was getting louder and louder, wondering why Heather was there without August and why she was five hours early. He felt the room closing in on him as he looked at Daxx, who was wide-eyed with curiosity, and Izzy, who was in awe of Heather. And when his eyes focused on Ella, the look she was giving him was urgent, prodding him to focus. Feeling unsteady, he sat down at the kitchen table.

Heather, who—oddly to Ben—seemed as comfortable in their home as they did, pulled out the chair next to him and said, "May I?"

He nodded, realizing Heather was exactly as he had pictured her, though August had never described what she looked like. Her energy, her presence—it was so like August's but still her own. He couldn't pinpoint what the difference was. The similarities, on the other hand, were obvious. There was no rush about her, no awkwardness even though Ben hadn't said a word yet.

She smiled, looking at him and holding a long glance before she said, "My mom said something about you that I think is beautiful." She paused, still smiling but seeming to gather herself. "She said you're the one who turned your mind down so you could hear your heart. That's how she's referred to you since the day you two met. 'My Ben,' she'd say. 'He can hear his heart so much better now.' And then she'd smile and shake her head, loving every bit of your conversation she was reliving. She's talked a lot about you, and it's good to finally meet you."

Breathe, he reminded himself. *Look at her. This isn't about you. Look at her.* He tried but couldn't pull himself out of the daze swirling tightly around him. "Thank you," he barely managed to say. He purposely avoided looking in the direction of what he knew would be Ella's incredulous, what-in-the-world-is-wrong-with-you stare; he understood that she didn't understand yet.

"I'm sorry to just show up like this," Heather went on. She looked at the children and smiled at them. All eyes were on Heather; she seemed so calm, Ben would later remember. "I had the directions you left for my mother, but there was no phone number on it, and I didn't want to just not show up when I knew you were expecting us this afternoon. You see ... my mother passed away in her sleep last night."

"Oh ... oh, no ..." Ella immediately went to Heather and hugged her. "Oh ... I'm so sorry, Heather. I'm so, so sorry."

Izzy quickly followed, offering Heather a hug with no words, looking so sad it made Ben ache. He couldn't guess what Izzy's sadness was about right then, but for him, the awareness that she would never meet August—and August would never get to know Izzy—

"Dad?" Daxx said in a loud whisper, the look on his face questioning. Ben nodded, and the tears fell. Daxx went and hugged Heather too.

"Are you okay?" Ben asked Heather, his voice shaky, willing himself to focus on *her* well-being. He swallowed hard. "I mean, I know that's a crazy thing to ask, but ... how are you? Was she sick? I just saw her a few days ago. I ... What happened?"

Heather wiped her tears and said, "I'm okay. I had a feeling this was coming … I'm not too sure how to explain it." She looked at Ella—seeming to draw strength from her, Ben noticed—and then looked back at Ben. "Something changed, and I think it had to do with meeting you. You helped her find peace, Ben. I'm not sure how you did it."

"Oh, no …" Ben shook his head. "I did nothing, Heather. Your mother is one of the most generous people I've ever met. She did all the helping. When I …" He looked at the children, who were hanging on his every word. "I was hoping I could start giving back. Today … today was going to be the beginning. We were going to cook for her and host her and take care of her the way she …" Ben took a deep breath.

Heather said, "There was something about meeting you, Ben. There really was. She didn't tell me specifically what it was, but I could tell. You brought her a peace she never had." Heather got quiet, as if she was remembering. "I could see it in her eyes. They were so *clear*. So beautiful." Heather smiled. "She wasn't sick; in fact, she seemed to have more energy than usual. We had a nice long conversation yesterday, and then I spent the night. We were going to make some jam to bring to you today. We always have fun coming up with new ones, and my mom … well, you know how much she loved sharing." Heather paused. "I knew something was wrong when I woke up. I could feel it, so I went right to her room, and …"

"Oh, honey," Ella said, reaching over and holding her.

"I'm so sorry," Ben said, his throat razor-tight.

Daxx put his head on Ben's shoulder.

265

As he put his arm around Daxx and pulled him close, August's words kept replaying in his mind: *pain doesn't take away your power; it shows you where you forgot you have it*. But he couldn't process it. Nothing made sense.

He hugged Daxx with both arms, and Daxx held on tight.

* * *

Ella and Heather were picking flowers from the yard for August's life celebration. Heather had decided to move back to the farm and make it home again.

As she knelt down and separated a tangled clump of weeds to find newly blooming flowers beneath them, she let out a laugh that gave way to tears … and then eventually she smiled. "My mom used to say, 'Now, Heather, that's how you end up with nothing but *weeds*—by mixing up your *wants* and your *needs*.'" She looked at Ella, her face hopeful. "Do you get it?"

"Um …" Ella tried to pinpoint what Heather meant.

"That's okay. Telling jokes isn't really my thing either. I always have to explain them. If you take the *w* from *wants* and replace the *n* from *needs* with it … you get *weeds*." She smiled then, seeming a little flustered. "Anyway, my mom was always pointing out the difference between needs and wants, telling me to want whatever I wanted, to let the list be long or short, but when it came to *needs*," Heather brought the bouquet to her nose and inhaled deeply, "she always said, 'Have just a few. Travel light. Travel well, my feather.'"

As they walked back to the house, Ella said, "I'm so sorry I didn't get to meet her, but I'm so grateful to have met you. And, Heather, anything I can help you with, anything you need—someone to talk to, someone to help with the yardwork and gardening, please call me. It feels so good to be here at August's old place, your place now. I'd be more than happy to keep having excuses to come by and pitch in. You have no idea how much it helps *me*." Daxx and Izzy ran by them, chasing a butterfly. "And the kids just love being here."

"I'll for sure take you up on it," Heather said. "I have my hands full here. The timing feels right to have made this move, but ..." She looked around, seeming to take it all in. "Well, I'll figure it out. It helps to know that I'm not alone. You and Ben and the kids, you're a great family. Thank you, Ella—for everything."

"It's my pleasure. You should know—you're doing such a great job with all of this."

As they sat on the rockers, organizing the flowers, tying them in bundles, and watching the children run around, Ella said, "This is going to sound strange, but ... I'll back up. On our way home yesterday, Daxx asked me why you weren't sad that your mom died. I didn't know how to answer him because—I get what he's looking at, what he sees, and I don't want to invalidate that. I *know* you're sad. Of course I do. It's just that you do seem to have this ... this peace, and it's so different from how undone I was when my brother died. One second, he was such a huge part of my life. Then—like that—he was just gone." She shared the details of how Andy died, finishing with, "I couldn't function. I just totally shut down."

"Oh, Ella ... the circumstances are really different—*night and day*. It's no wonder it turned your world upside down. It would've done that to mine too. This passing ... my mom's ... it's so different from what you must have gone through." She paused in the middle of tying the chamomile flowers on her lap. "Each death is different." She looked at Ella. "Did that come out right?"

Ella assured her it had, realizing how much death Heather had experienced—her brother, her father, and now her mother. Her heart ached at the thought of Heather being orphaned. Though she had mentioned different friends, none had come around in the past few days, at least not when Ella, Ben, and the kids were there.

Heather ran her fingers along a buttery yellow hibiscus petal and said, "I know this won't last more than a few hours before it starts to wilt, so I felt kind of bad cutting it, but ... I don't know. It's like I just want to savor it up close, to keep it so close to me for a while, and it's somehow easier to do because I know I only have a short time with it."

"I get it," Ella said, gathering another small batch of wildflowers from the bucket. "I have a feeling you're one of those people who's really good at getting all there is to get out of the moment."

Leaning back in the rocker, Heather said, "I don't know about that. Ever since my brother died, I think about death all the time. So, pretty close to my whole life. It's just *right there* in the front of my mind. Does that seem morbid? I promise you it's not. I just ..."

"It doesn't sound morbid," Ella said. "I understand—I really do. After Andy died, the subtlest things changed, things I never expected. It's like I can't say goodbye to my kids, to Ben, to anyone I love without this awareness that it could be the last goodbye. It stops me sometimes. I think, *What if this is the last conversation we have?* Sometimes that changes what comes next. It's just part of who I am now."

"Yes! Yes, that's just what I mean," Heather said.

Ella added another finished bundle to the pile and turned to Heather. "But your peace, where does that come from? For me, time healed the pain—a lot of time." She grabbed another bunch of loose flowers. "To be honest, I'm sad to say I've just become numb to it; it's not that I've come to *peace* with it."

"I'm not sure where this peace I feel comes from," Heather said. "I miss my mom so much. There's this big space inside me that feels so hollow. There are so many things …" Heather smiled. "I'll miss her 'forgetting' to take her apron off after she was done cooking or planting—she used the same one for both. Long after she was done, she'd still be wearing that apron, and I eventually knew it was best not to remind her that she was still wearing it. She knew. And when I brought it up, it just made her have to pretend she didn't realize it, and then she would slowly … so slowly, she'd reluctantly take it off. Eventually, I stopped pointing it out."

"What was special about it? Why'd she leave it on?"

Heather shook her head. "I don't know. It never felt right to ask. It could have been because it had seven pockets, and she really did love pockets. It could have been because it was a Mother's Day present from me and Pete. I don't know. All I know is she always found excuses to wear it even when she didn't need to."

Ella wondered if August had worn the apron around Ben; he had never mentioned it.

Heather went on. "I'll miss the way, when my mom talked to me … it felt like there was nowhere she'd rather be, nothing she'd rather be doing. Do you have someone like that in your life?"

Ella felt gratitude fill her as she nodded and said, "Yes. Ben does that for me."

"That's so important. My mom was always so interested … and interesting. We just talked so easily. I'll miss our conversations … and, now that I think about it, all the comfortable silence between us. She was a really good mom. The best kind. Can I tell you something?"

"Of course. Please," Ella said.

Heather looked off into the distance with a smile, and Ella wondered what she was seeing. "After Pete died, he used to come play with me. Maybe I imagined it as a way to cope, or maybe it was really him." Heather looked down. "I don't know, but sometimes I'd catch glimpses of him, or I'd hear him—I'd look all around then and whisper, 'Pete? Is that you?' It was kind of confusing, to tell you the truth. But most of the time, I just knew he was there with me, laughing, chasing things, racing things, all the things we used to do together. Looking back, I think maybe he was there as long as I needed him to be, until at some point I knew everything was going to be okay. The same thing happened after my dad died. I'd hear a flute or an oboe, and I knew it was him reassuring me." She shook her head. "Or maybe I imagined it all. I don't know."

"Oh, I'm sure you do know," Ella said. "And you can trust that."

"I felt like they were telling me it's not over when we die, that it only gets better. The pain of missing them doesn't go away, but the awareness of how short this life is becomes more vivid, and it makes me want to enjoy it and do with it what I feel moved to."

Ella closed her eyes and felt surrounded by a blanket of warmth. She wanted to lean into it and pull it close around her.

"I think we're here for the blink of an eye," Heather said, that peaceful feeling seeming to slip into her words again. "Who we are is *so* much bigger than this. Don't you think, Ella? And when we die, we—who we are goes—on and on and on."

"I like thinking of it that way," Ella said.

Pulling another flower out of the pile, Heather said, "It would be like if the hibiscus could go back to the moment before I cut it ... when it thrived." She seemed sad as she twirled the flower between her fingers. "I have a feeling we go back to our essence. Here, maybe we just do our best. It feels to me kind of like a big, beautiful experiment. A wonderful and heartbreakingly sad one at times. But it's not our everything." She tied a bow with the string and then made final adjustments to the arrangement. "I picture my mom there, back in our everything, with my brother and my dad. I'll be with them again when it's time. That's got to be how it works." She looked at Ella. "Even though it hurts so much not to be able to have her here physically, she's everywhere, Ella. She has to be." She pointed. "In that butterfly. In that falling leaf. In that eucalyptus bark. Just like my brother and dad. And your brother. I *really think so.*

Have I just convinced myself? Is there any chance it's true? It's true, isn't it?"

Ella wiped the tears running down her cheeks and said, "I'm the one who's supposed to be comforting and helping right now—and look at me. I'm a mess."

"We take turns, all of us," Heather said, getting up and giving her a hug. "I think, in the end, we just want to know it's going to be okay. That *we're* going to be okay. I think we are, Ella."

* * *

As they drove home from August's life celebration, Ben thought about all the people there, from so many different walks of life, and the ways August had touched their lives. What Heather had arranged was really more of a get-together, and through her constant introductions of one person to the next, she got strangers talking—and the topic they naturally went to was August, the one thing they for sure had in common.

Ben talked to August's mailman, who introduced himself as Jake and explained, "Without fail, she was *always* there to meet me at the mailbox. Rain or shine. She knew all about my twin daughters, just soaked in everything I could think of to tell her, and I always filled her in on my progress toward getting my pilot's license—just single-engine. Nothing fancy." He stroked his chin and seemed lost in thought for a moment. "Oh, that August. I'm sure gonna miss her. What about you? How do you know her?"

Each time Ben told his story to someone new, he remembered different details, and it struck him how life-changing his interactions with August were.

The grocery clerk, Janet, told Ben to guess how many times August anonymously paid for the groceries of the person behind her in line.

Ben had guessed three.

"Try *sixty*-three," Janet said. "August knew how to make a stranger's day." Ben couldn't figure out how that would work, her paying anonymously.

Janet explained, "Well, she always came in my line—we had it down pat. If she paid with a card instead of cash, I knew she wanted me to use it to pay for the next person. She'd just go on her way, not even looking back, then pick up the card from me the next time she was in. A long time ago, she explained that she had a special bank account for times like that—that's all she ever used that card for." Janet shook her head and smiled. "I'm gonna miss her spunk." She looked at Ben then, as if something had just occurred to her. "How'd you know her?"

And so it went, one exchange after another as a handful of the people in August's life got to see how they were all connected. Ben loved that he got to hear stories about Henry too, as anyone who was friends with August seemed to have been Henry's friend too.

It really was a life *celebration*. It was hard to feel sad in such a wide-open outdoor space, so close to the comforting energy of the house, with chirping birds and the constant buzz of August's bees providing the music.

"It was well done, wasn't it?" Ella said.

"I was just thinking—"

"Look!" Daxx said as Ben turned into their driveway. "A bike!"

"With a bow …" Izzy said.

Ben looked over at Ella; the look she gave told him she was as clueless as he was.

A tandem bike was parked close to the front door, and it had two bows on it—one on each seat, both orange. Ella and Daxx could barely get their seat belts off fast enough. As soon as they were unbuckled, they scurried out of the car and over to the bike.

"Can we ride it?" Izzy said.

"I'll go on the back, and you can drive us," Daxx said to her.

"Well, hold on … there's a note," Ella said, picking up an envelope with Ben's name on it and handing it to him.

Ben opened it and looked at Ella. "It's from Ethan." He sat down on the stoop and read the letter out loud:

Hello, my walking friend. You wouldn't let me pay you, and I respect your reasons, but you did a lot of work for me, and I've given a lot of thought to how I can thank you. I restored this tandem with you and Ella in mind. Now, I'm including instructions that I always give to my customers who buy tandems. I've collected them over the years from talking to riders—old, young, new, and experienced. As I was reading over them (it's been awhile since I took a look at them), I was hoping you wouldn't think I meant anything too personal by them. They're just …. well, I like them, and I think you and Ella will too. So here you go. Ride by sometime and say hi.

Bring along some of Ella's business cards with you, if she has any. Everyone's asking where I got the coolest chime they've ever seen.

How to ride a tandem:

1. It's not the same as riding a bike by yourself. Remember that.

2. Focus on the person you're riding with—not the bike, not what you just passed, not even where you're going. That's how you have a good ride.

3. The person in front is called the captain; the person in the back is called the stoker. Know who's who, and keep taking turns from one ride to the next.

4. The captain is responsible for straddling the bike and holding it steady for the stoker to get on. Expect some adjustment and awkwardness when the stoker gets on. The stoker is the first to sit and put their feet on the pedals.

5. IMPORTANT: Once the stoker is on, any bike movement made by the captain will make the stoker very uncomfortable and tense—unless the stoker decides to trust the captain fully, in which case the stoker will then go with the flow and refrain from putting their foot down, realizing it's not necessary, they're safe.

6. The captain decides which foot to lead with, right or left. While the captain is still standing with both feet on the ground, hands on the handlebars, the stoker is the one who backpedals until the pedals are set to begin (the starting one at knee height). To avoid a wobbly start, the captain should remain standing, one foot on the ground, one on the starting pedal, and then start pedaling before sitting down.

7. The captain is in charge of communication. "On" means start pedaling. "Off" means take your feet off the pedals. Only the captain is able to see bumps in the road ahead, which counts for anything that's not completely flat, so it's the captain's job to alert and prepare the stoker by saying, "Bump." The stoker's experience is dependent on good communication from the captain.

By the time Ben had finished, the children had lost interest and were inside. Ben looked at Ella and had no doubt she was thinking the same thing he was. He put his arm around her and said, "How did we get so lucky to have such good people show up in our lives?"

* * *

Two weeks later, Ben and Ella's fourth tandem ride went much better than the first three had. As they reached their destination, Salamander's, without any falls or tense moments between them, Ben felt good about their progress. He was surprised that he liked being both the captain and the stoker, and Ella had said she liked taking turns as well. There were challenges and pluses to both positions, and he was still so busy trying to figure them out that he didn't have a preference yet.

After their sandwiches arrived, Ben told Ella about his meeting with the high school principal. After many early-morning and late-night conversations with Ella, Ben had decided one of his next steps was to look into volunteering at the high school, this time as a true mentor. He was thinking an hour or two a week. "So I talked to the principal—a great guy, by the way. You can tell he really cares about the school and the kids. I found out I worked with his sister at Starfish."

"Sometimes I forget how small this town is," Ella said.

"No kidding. Anyway, he said, without having a student there, I can't volunteer unless it's through a vetted agency. The problem with that, as I learned, is that these are established agencies and businesses with already-set agendas. They're not interested in creating new clubs. They're all about growing what they've already set up."

"Well, you don't have to create a new club, do you? Do you know what the other clubs are? Can't you just help out with one you're interested in?"

"Nope." Ben shook his head. "You'd think it would be easy to volunteer. It's actually not. Even if there was a club I was interested in helping out with, I'd have to go through that agency or business, not the school. It could take months. And it's not usually done like that. They send their own people."

Ella pulled some of the sprouts from her sandwich and put them on the side of her plate. He guessed she was going through the options in her head, just as he had—no, he didn't want to become a teacher or a counselor or get a job within the school system. It wasn't even about how long it would take. It just didn't feel right. He wanted to volunteer. He'd figure out how to make money, what he would do for a job, after he figured out this part of what was pulling at him.

Ella looked pensive. "Something doesn't feel right."

"What do you mean?"

"It shouldn't be this difficult."

"I don't know. Maybe I'm going in the wrong direction, and that's why it's not working."

"I disagree. Everything we've talked about—it all keeps pointing to this, to working with students. Does it *feel* like the wrong direction to you?"

"No … it doesn't," Ben said. "That's the thing. That's why I'm confused. It feels totally right—but all the signs are pointing to no, this isn't going to work."

Ella seemed a million miles away, deep in thought, until suddenly she said, "Okay. How about Starfish? What about going through them?"

Doing his best to keep the unexpected surge of irritation out of his voice, he said, "I thought about that too, but if I go through Starfish, I have to actually be a Starfish employee, which means I'd have to work there again." It made him a little uncomfortable that she would even suggest he return to Starfish. In their hours of conversations, hadn't he made it clear he didn't want to go backwards? That was one of the few things he was actually sure about.

"Well, what about if you did something different for them—totally different from what you did before ... something more *you*. A job you create for yourself. Danny *did* say there might be space for you. Remember?" Her eyes lit up, and she said, "Imagine if you could do anything you wanted there, Ben—no limits. Imagine you could play *any* role you wanted to."

"Like what? What kind of role?"

"What do you *want* to do? If you could do anything at Starfish, what would it be? If Danny and Jules had you create your dream job there, what would it look like?"

He felt possibilities expanding. "Anything?"

"Anything," she affirmed.

His world was getting bigger, going from black-and-white to Technicolor. An idea came to him. "Okay, I'm just going to throw this out there. I haven't thought it through or anything."

"Tell me ..."

"One of the things I saw when I was at Starfish was wasted talent. A lot of people don't realize what they're good at—*really* good at. And so many positions are so structured—you have to do A through Z; there's no possibility for delegating G, H, P, and R through X. Why not? There's someone whose good at *every* one of those things—and they *love* doing it, even though it's someone else's most dreaded part of the day. I used to sit there in meetings, thinking about it, daydreaming really. If I could do anything, I'd help people find their real talents and then figure out how to translate that into the work they're doing—or transition into a more appropriate role in the company. I'd create new teams and restructure them so that most of the time everyone's doing what they're best at—and they love doing. Nothing would be wasted, nobody's energy misspent. The problem is I have no training in that. Or experience. And I don't even know … Why are you shaking your head?"

Ella leaned back in her chair and smiled. "Don't do that to you. If I did that, you'd be furious."

"Did what?"

"If I shot down your idea that quickly. You barely got it out before you started talking about how it can't work." She reached across the table and grabbed Ben's hand. "Let's back up—back to the idea."

She leaned forward, looking him in the eye. "I can't think of anything more perfect. You would be so good at a job like that, and everyone would benefit." She let go of his hand and sat back. "Oh my God, why didn't we think of this before? The school, Ben!"

"What do you mean? The high school?"

"Yes! You could do the same thing there, run a group, sponsor it, however it works, as a Starfish employee. Rather than using the kids like you guys did before—no offense, that's how you explained it to me."

"No, I know. Go ahead …"

"You would actually mentor them, *give* to them—you'd guide them and help them find what they're good at, just like you're talking about doing at Starfish. Get to know them, work in a small group setting, I don't know … but I can see it, Ben. Can you?"

He could—a hint of something slowly, finally coming into focus.

All he wanted to do in that moment was stand up, lean over the table, and kiss Ella. So he did.

* * *

"Okay, I'll talk to you later, Charlotte." Ella hung up as Ben came in the door.

Hanging the car keys on the hook, he said, "How is she?"

"Mostly good, I think. It's hard to tell. There's still a big disconnect."

"Well, I think you're doing a great job," Ben said. "I know it's not easy."

"To be honest, I don't know how long I'm going to keep trying. It's starting to reach a point where I'm not sure it's healthy."

The look on Ben's face suggested he didn't disagree.

"Talk to me," Ella said.

"You've said a number of times you don't want to 'drop' her or 'abandon' her, and I get that, but if someone's toxic and you keep them in your life, you're dropping and abandoning you."

"But is she actually toxic?"

"You're a really happy person, Ella. And almost every time you interact with her, it drains your energy and takes you a little while to recover. I think it's an extension of abide-by six—give your energy to people who make you feel more like you, not less like you."

She got up from the couch, gave Ben a hug, and said, "Thank you."

"For what?" he said.

She kissed him before saying, "I wouldn't even know where to start. So … how'd it go with Jules and Danny?"

His smile reached his eyes.

"That good?"

He nodded.

"I knew it! Tell me! Tell me everything!"

"I can't wait to—but one second. I'm gonna say hi to the kids."

"They're out back."

"Okay. Be right back."

While Ben went out to the backyard, Ella thought about all the hours she and Ben had put in over the past two weeks, coming up with a proposal detailing his ideal job, including the details of how it would work, what it would look like, and how it would benefit Starfish. Ella had played devil's advocate, pulling no punches so he could cover all bases and consider all possible glitches, then address those in his proposal, which, once finished, he emailed to Jules and Danny. They had requested a meeting with him after that, but Ben couldn't tell from the flat tone of the email whether they were open to the idea or if it was going to be a we-need-you-to-stop-contacting-us kind of farewell meeting. Ella had read the email and had no idea what to expect either.

Ben came in and got two beers out of the fridge. He opened them, handed her one, and sat down. "So … I followed your advice—starting out by explaining how what I wanted to do would benefit them. I got so into it … and you know what I realized? It was easy to have the conversation because I believed every word I was saying. There was no way the conversation could turn out badly—I wasn't trying to convince them of anything. I was telling them what I *know* to be true. They'd either be interested in it—or not."

"And? What did they say?"

"They didn't even hesitate. I start next week."

"No way! Your proposal *rocked*."

"It did—thanks to you. There's one thing though."

Ella felt her stomach tighten. "Salary?"

"Yes."

"Shit. We should have put it in the proposal. An exact compensation should have been part of it. I *knew* it."

"We couldn't," Ben said, so calm, the opposite of how she was feeling. "It had to be in person. We were right. Trust me. I had to say an amount I could stand by."

"Which was?" Ella had tried to keep her tone even, but it wasn't working.

"I told them I was willing to get paid next to nothing to start, to show the value of this idea and since I have no formal training in it. Danny started to say no, but Jules cut him off. She said I didn't need to start at 'next to nothing' but that a much lower pay than I was used to might be a fair starting point for something this new. I agreed. I'm sorry. I'm not sure how this is going to play out for us financially. I know we don't have a lot of time left. I was thinking on the way home I can also get a night job at—"

"Just … hold on … I need a minute," Ella said. She was getting better at it now. She had learned from Ben, who had learned from August. She was more easily recognizing when her instinctual reaction was an old one. When her response was simply out of habit, it felt overplayed, like a broken record. It was 100 percent predictable. She was learning to pause before following through with that kind of reaction, to instead take her time and choose how she wanted to react, and those moments of conscious decision were starting to reshape everything.

As soon as Ben had brought money up, she had started to react how she always did, but she caught herself this time.

The burning tension she was feeling was a reaction she had had so many times in the past—immediate irritation mired in a deep fear of running out of money, of not having enough, which always turned into a surge of anger and heavy worry. Nine out of ten times in the past, it had led to sharp words hurled at Ben or passive-aggressively dumping guilt on him, suggesting—without saying it—that he wasn't doing enough or should be doing something better than he was. It had never made anything better, and it always drove a wedge between her and Ben. And every wedge took time to recover from.

Ella made a decision.

"What number did you come up with?" she asked.

Ben gave her the low figure.

Ella took a deep breath. "And that feels right to you?" Her voice was calm now, her tone sincere.

"Yes. For now."

"You don't feel taken advantage of?"

"Not at all. Think about what I put them through with leaving—no notice, not taking care of anything. Just walking out. Now, they're not only allowing me back, they're giving me a shot at my ideal job. My *dream* job— which I have no experience in."

Ella nodded. "Okay. If you're really fine with it, I trust you. I trust that it's right. We're okay for now; that's all we need to know. The rest is going to work itself out." She checked in with herself. Yes, this was right. It felt good. "I *know* it's going to work out. This is what you're meant to do, Ben, and the rest will work itself around that. They're going to see your value in this new position so quickly money won't be an issue. And let's take worst-case scenario, that they don't see it. *You* will have seen it, and you'll know you deserve to be paid well for it."

"In the meantime though, I can't ignore the financial reality," he said. "I really think I should get a second job at night in case this doesn't work out. Plus, it'll bring in at least a little more in the meantime."

"Then we'll never see you."

"I know, but—"

There was no way she was going to let his fear get in the way, not when he had come this far. "Ben, you should hear yourself talk about people, what you see in them. How about that lady who was planning Starfish's events when she should have been the company representative who *went* to events, because *that's* where she shined. She was a networker, not an organizer, you said. And Jules and Danny were so sorry to lose her, right? Didn't she leave because the job just wasn't working for her?"

"Yes ... I forgot about that." She could see the wheels spinning in his mind.

"Oh, Ben. You're going to be so good at this, and *everyone's* going to benefit. And we need you too—me,

Daxx, and Izzy. That's why a second job won't work. We need you more than we need the extra money. Let's commit to something—to stop worrying about money. It's never helped. In fact, it's messed up a lot of things. Instead, let's just commit to helping each other be who we are, whatever that looks like. We can reevaluate a month from now, six weeks from now—whenever. And if we decide I'm totally wrong, we'll go back to worrying about money and letting it be the deciding factor in the decisions we make. But until then, it takes the back seat. *We're* the drivers. You and me— together."

He put down his beer and gave her a hug, not letting go, not saying a word. It came to her in that moment— what a gift the tandem and its instructions from Ethan were.

* * *

It was the fourth Tuesday in a row that Ella went to the farm to visit Heather and work in Henry's old wood shop. Four weeks ago, she had stopped by to check in on Heather and see how she was doing. Heather had offered to show Ella around the rest of the property. In all the times she had been there while getting ready for August's life celebration and then trying to help Heather with the estate details after that, she had never actually walked the whole property.

As Heather guided her around that afternoon, Ella felt like she was touring famous places she had read about—but they were well-known only between her and Ben: the hammock among the stand of trees, the beehives, the winding paths through the wildflower fields. She felt August's spirit, she was sure of it, and it made her smile.

What she wasn't prepared for was how Henry's wood shop made her feel. When they reached the farthest corner of the property, they came upon the square shack. Heather finally got the door open, and when they went inside, Ella felt like she had stepped back in time to someplace enchanted and magical. It was dusty and earthy, and something Ella couldn't pinpoint about it moved her. Was it *whimsical?* That didn't seem to fit what she knew about Henry.

Heather seemed right at home introducing Ella to the different tools Henry had taught her how to use. She touted the importance of the moisture meter, explained the roles of the different-sized chisels, and talked about discerning when to use a router versus a jigsaw. Then she pointed out where, up on a shelf, the first recorder Heather had made was on display. Heather told Ella how thrilled her dad had been that Heather wanted to learn to make instruments.

"Do you do it anymore?" Ella had asked.

Heather had looked around the old shop and smiled. She slowly shook her head. "I don't. I loved it when my dad and I would work together, and I just loved learning from him. He was such a good teacher—the best kind because you could tell he cared as much about what he was teaching as who he was teaching it to." She picked up the recorder and dusted it off with her sleeve. After playing a few notes, she gently put it back. "It just stopped being my thing after a while. I really can't say why. I guess I stopped being excited about it." She looked at Ella. "Do you think that's sad? It feels a little sad saying that while standing in here."

Ella sat with it for a moment and then said, "It doesn't feel sad to hear it. In fact, nothing in here feels anything but … *good*."

Heather closed her eyes, took a deep breath, and smiled. "My dad. It's what he did here, the energy he put into it. It stayed even though he's gone."

Ella responded as best she could, but she had trouble coming up with the right words to describe just how powerfully the space moved her, how inspired she felt standing there surrounded by Henry's tools and the coils of wire and the pieces of wood of every shape, size, texture, and shade—browns, whites, yellows, grays, and reds. And the dust everywhere, she loved it. She wanted to write her name in it.

"Ella," Heather had said with the kindest smile, "would you like to explore your talents here? Have a go at it?"

And that was how it began. Every Tuesday morning, Ella and Heather had a standing nine o'clock appointment. Heather would spend some time teaching Ella how to use another tool and then leave her be, free to make herself at home in the old wood shop and use anything there. Ella let loose and experimented with all new materials, including old keys, broken glass, wire, and nails, in addition to wood blocks, cuttings, planks, shavings, and more. The time flew by as she created a series of wind chimes.

Though Ella was going to the wood shop more and more now, not just on Tuesdays, their Tuesday routine stuck. After the lesson, while Ella's creative juices were flowing, Heather would prepare lunch. It always included something from the garden. Ella's favorite was the roasted red pepper and eggplant tapenade, served with crusty

French bread—and honey of course. Ella still couldn't get over how alive the honey tasted, so different from any she had ever bought. She finally understood why Ben had been so enthralled.

On this fourth Tuesday, as she and Heather sat in the kitchen, enjoying a turnip, green been, and tomato salad with hard-boiled eggs and fresh bread, Ella filled Heather in on the changes in Ben. "He's just so energetic. I mean, he wakes up so happy, and it's like he can't wait to start the day. He comes home from Starfish relaxed and feeling good—or fired up and excited. Those are the nights we end up staying up late fine-tuning how to translate what he's doing into the high school group he's starting to mentor next week."

Heather paused, put her fork down, and seemed to really take in Ella's words. "That must make your whole house so happy," she said. "I'm so happy for him—and you and Daxx and Izzy. How are the little munchkins?"

"They're doing great. Daxx has been showing his mischievous side lately." Ella laughed. "And it's … I don't know." She realized there was nothing funny about it and wondered why she had just laughed. "He's testing us, figuring out limits and boundaries I think."

Heather dipped a piece of bread in the honey. "I can't picture it. How so?"

"Like when Ben comes home, he'll ask Daxx and Izzy to come out and throw the ball around with him. For no apparent reason, Daxx suddenly started saying no, acting like he didn't want to—when we know that's *all* he wants to do. I catch him staring out the window at them, but then he'll deny he wants to go out. He shuts down in his sadness, and I don't know what it's about."

"Oh no! And he has such big feelings."

"Exactly. I don't know what's going on. It's like he feels the need to have his say and stand up to us, but it's not for his benefit."

"You're doing a great job. Don't you worry, Ella. We'll just all keep an eye on him. I'll pay closer attention on Saturdays when you guys are here. Whatever's going on with him, it's not going unnoticed—you've made sure of that. It'll get figured out. We'll keep looking and talking and being patient till we understand better."

Heather had a way of doing that, Ella realized, of caring so deeply about something that mattered to someone else. She'd never known anyone quite so good at it.

They talked about how Heather was adjusting to life on the farm; it felt good, she said, to be home. She was taking things one day at a time. It was a quiet, introspective time for her, honoring the memories of her family and finding the courage and clarity to discover what was next for her. In the meantime, she loved spending time with the bees and working with the flowers, herbs, and vegetable gardens.

Ella shared how her chimes were suddenly more in demand than her jewelry. Working in Henry's old shop had inspired her and brought out a deeper level of creativity. She loved the idea of her art creating music. She had also volunteered at the children's school to make wind chimes with the different classes for the Art Masterpiece program.

"If you need a helping hand, I'd be glad to do it with you," Heather said. "It would be good to get out and be around people a little more than I have been—especially around little ones."

Ella said, "Absolutely! I'd love it. I can get you set up right away. Thank you. I always think I have it under control, but then things never go as planned, and having someone there to help, it would be so great."

Heather bit her lip and then smiled. With the absence of words, Ella saw something in Heather's eyes and had a clear realization.

Ella would think about it not just the rest of their afternoon together but also the whole way home, and it would dominate her conversation with Ben late into the night. She would go to bed that night with the realization still vibrating inside her: *we all need to be needed.*

* * *

After reading Daxx and Izzy the story about the hippo that always made them laugh, Ben came back to the kitchen table and said to Ella, "They're ready for you. By the way, Daxx is in no mood to sleep yet, so expect lots of questions about anything and everything."

Ella barely looked up from the paper she was reading, one of many that were strewn across the kitchen table. "One second …" she said, her eyes riveted to the page.

"What is it?" Ben asked.

He had been as transparent as possible with the high school students in the peer group, without compromising Starfish's credibility or making Starfish look bad. He had explained what hadn't worked with the previous group. Without quite saying Starfish's motive had been mostly about looking good in the community and for their board, he admitted it didn't have the integrity he and Starfish wanted, and it wasn't accomplishing for the students what they had hoped for. It was too much of a one-way street, with Starfish on the receiving end. That was about to change.

Ben hadn't known what to expect; he wasn't sure how the eight students in the peer group would respond, especially when he explained the new objective: to help them discover their strengths, talents, and passions and then guide them into positions that channeled those skills—now, today. No matter what it looked like. And he was very clear about that: who knew how it would look for each individual student? Before explaining it, he wondered if they would be bored by the idea. Had they already heard that a hundred times? Had computerized surveys already told them which careers they were best suited for?

He hadn't expected the group to double in size, then triple, and be twenty-nine and growing by the fourth week, which was when the students voted on the group's new name: the Way Finders. Their finalized—for now—mission statement read: "Find each student's individual way and celebrate it." Now in the sixth week, they were well into the process of figuring out their talents. Nothing excited Ben more than a student's face when they realized that spending their time doing what they loved and were good at benefited everyone. He couldn't wait to tell Ella that Rachel, a junior with supposedly no direction, showed Ben a logo she had come up with for the Way Finders, without being asked to. He'd never forget the look on her face when he suggested to the group that Rachel take the lead role in branding for the group. When they asked what that entailed, he said, "Let's find out. You tell me. Rachel, what are your thoughts?" And they dove in, talking, brainstorming, wondering, trying, figuring out, and discovering.

In the process of finding each student's place in the group, he felt strongly about handing off the leadership role to one of them—a team, actually, but a point person to start—someone to take his place so that he could step back and let them run the show, stepping in only to encourage, guide, and mentor as necessary. He had asked them each to write a personal statement. It could be about anything— whatever they wanted. He let them know it was to help him get to know them better and to help him discover who might thrive in a leadership role. He and Ella had been reading through the statements for the past two nights, narrowing it down.

Ella finally stood up to tuck the children in and handed the paper she had been reading to Ben. "You found your leader." Smiling, she gave him a lingering kiss on the cheek and then headed to Daxx and Izzy's room.

Ben sat down, leaned back in the chair, and read:

To Mr. Ben: This one day after school, I was leaving campus after choir practice, and as I went around the corner on the way to the girls' bathroom, a guy was beating the crap out of this boy on the ground. He was just lying there. His face was bleeding, and he was holding his stomach, looking so defeated, like he had given up, looking right in my direction, and he saw me. It all happened so fast. I looked at the two jerks who were standing a few feet away. It was obvious they were there to make sure no one interfered. And then I looked around and saw other people like me, everyone quickly looking away. There were maybe four or five of us there. I'm sure everyone was thinking the same thing I was: *we have to do something*. But no one did anything. No one even took their phone out to video it because the two guys watching would have had that phone in two seconds. But what if all of us took our phones out at once? They couldn't have gotten them all, right? Of course I didn't think of that till later. And when I couldn't sleep that night because all I could see was that boy's eyes focus on something in the distance as he's getting another kick to his side, I thought of something else I could have done—I should have done. I should have stopped. I should have closed my eyes and started singing "Amazing Grace," singing it at the top of my lungs. Now that I think about it, I don't know if I've ever sung it with my eyes open. I go somewhere else in my head when I sing it. No one knows this (except you now), but I changed a line of the song. Instead of singing, "how sweet the sound that saved a wretch like me," I sing, "how sweet the sound that loves a girl like me." I can't help it. So many good feelings fill me and seem to spill out with that song—they're overwhelming but in a good way. And I'm not thinking any bad thoughts about anyone or anything when I sing it. Just a whole lot of big and powerful good feelings. Speaking of big, I can make my voice big and loud, Mr. Ben. I'm just figuring out how to make it pretty, not ugly. I used to say some ugly things. I think it's pretty when I sing though. That's what Mrs. Peters said anyway. She's my choir teacher. I should have sang so, so loud the second I saw what was happening. It would have made them pause, wouldn't it? You can't beat the shit out of somebody while you're hearing that song. So, Mr. Ben, I don't know how I fit in this group. I don't know what kind of leadership role I can play, but I want to find out. I want another chance to do the right thing. I'm hoping this is it. Because I can't stop thinking about that boy.

Ben set the paper on the table and looked at Ella, who had returned.

She pulled her chair closer to his, smiled, and said, "Look what you've done, Ben. *Look at you.* I'm so proud of you."

He didn't know how to tell her she had made it all possible. He took her hand and held it against his cheek. "Thank you," he whispered.

* * *

Ben handed Ella a check. She barely glanced at it before putting it on the table, her focus back on the article she was reading in the newspaper.

Ben realized in that moment how much had changed in the past eight months, from the time he walked out of Starfish, to returning to Starfish and starting an entirely different career, to now. He had just handed Ella the biggest check that had ever been made out to him. Jules and

Danny had taken him out to lunch to celebrate how he had more than proved himself in the previous six months; the check was to make up for how underpaid he was during that time. Starfish had benefitted in ways Jules and Danny hadn't foreseen but which Ella had predicted. She had been right. Starfish had never gotten so much good press—and all for free.

Eight months ago, Ella would have stared closely at the check, deposited it immediately, and then started a conversation about what promises Jules and Danny had made for future payments. Did this mean a new salary? Was he no longer probationary? How much were they talking? Instead, she was absorbed in the article. It was about the Way Finders and an app they created, called *I'm Here*.

Ben smiled.

Something had prompted him to tell the students the story about August and the flashlight she gave him, how she had made him stand up and hold it that night, pointing it at the sky, feeling what it was like to give off light, to be light. He told them how he felt in that moment, the lesson August was teaching him. He never knew what to expect from the students, something he was coming to appreciate more and more. That particular day was no exception. The bell signaling the end of lunch rang, and everyone dispersed quietly, rather than with the energetic conversation they usually left with. There was no closure that day, and he was unsettled by that as he left campus, keeping an eye out for the boy who had changed his life. He had yet to see him. Not alone. Not with a group. Nowhere. That too unsettled him.

And then his meeting with the students the following week happened.

"Mr. Ben," Jasmine, their leader, said, "we need to talk about the flashlight. We've been thinking …" Apparently, the students had been talking about it.

Five months later, *I'm Here* was up and running—basic but running. A number of the students had been paired with two Starfish employees who acted not just as mentors but as teachers and active participants, volunteering their time and expertise. They loved the idea behind *I'm Here*. Matt, Starfish's number-one tech guy, remembered what it was like for him as a high school student. He worked with the students who couldn't get enough of code and gigabytes—Kyle, Evelyn, Nadine, and Jared—and the five of them created the app. Carly, Starfish's marketing genius, would never forget what it was like to be overweight in a Southern California high school. She was thrilled to work with Connor, Sophia, and Sam to get the word out about *I'm Here* to the other students.

Ben remembered the day it was scheduled to go live at 6:00 p.m. He, Matt, Carly, and the Way Finders met before school, during lunch, and then again after school, going over last-minute details and reassuring themselves and one another.

The questions had bounced back and forth, and Ben sat back and took it all in, appreciating the fact that, except for the obvious gap in ages, anyone listening wouldn't have been able to differentiate the students from the Starfish mentors; they were all asking and answering, everyone equally invested and excited … and nervous. Ben couldn't remember the last time he felt such a good nervousness.

Every time Ben thought of a question, someone else asked it:

"Have we made it clear it's a serious app, not to be used lightly?"

"For sure. We've hammered that message."

"And they know when to use it?"

"I'm definitely confident about that."

When you feel alone and need reassurance that you're not, Ben repeated for the thousandth time in his head. They were aiming for an audience of ages twelve to seventeen. The California public schools had been surprisingly accommodating, allowing them to get the message about the app out without endorsing it themselves.

In everyone's nervousness, the questions continued, even though they had been asked and answered in the previous months.

"What if no one uses it?"

"It's already had more than three thousand downloads."

"No, but that's a good question. What if no one uses it?"

"Is that a bad thing? Wouldn't that actually be a good thing?"

"We've been over this. It'll get used as it's needed. We have to trust that."

"I think we all need to take a deep breath and let go."

Ben was hopeful that if there was a teenager out there who felt alone—for any reason at all—they would open the *I'm Here* app and click the "I'm Here" button.

Clicking that button made a statement. It said, "I'm here. I matter. I count." Those were the words actually written under the button. What wasn't written was the understanding that the person who clicked the button was struggling and needed to know they weren't alone.

After clicking the button, a map of California would come up, and when another student with the app responded to the call for help (which they knew about from the beep their phone gave), a light would show up on the map, and a message would be sent through the app to the person who pressed the button: "I'm here with you" or "I'm here for you," whichever one the responder chose. The whole thing was anonymous, and the map just showed the basic proximity of the responder.

With every response, another light would show up on the map, and the button-presser would receive another "I'm here with you (or for you)" message. To make sure at least one person responded, the Way Finders had created a schedule, assigning response duty to cover twenty-four hours of every day for the first month.

The app was programmed to reset three minutes after someone pressed "I'm Here," at which time that student would receive a text with a supportive message and three hotline numbers to call. The wording of that message had taken them weeks to craft, after consulting with different professionals, including a handful of psychologists, and a significant number of other students.

There was still plenty they hadn't figured out, including how to allow for more than one person to press the "I'm here" button at the same time. They were okay with that conundrum for now, since the other person needing to know they weren't alone would know it—and would become one of the responders supporting the person who pressed the button. They also wanted it to allow for a variety of languages, not just English and Spanish, and they had plans for the map to expand to the whole country and eventually to a map of the world—filled with lights. This was a start though.

The day it was being launched, eventually all the questions that could be answered had been. That's when Ben stood up and said, "I couldn't be prouder of every person in this room." He talked about each person, emphasizing the unique role they played. And then he just smiled and nodded because he couldn't say more without getting choked up.

And now Ella was sitting there at their kitchen table, a huge smile even though tears were running down her cheeks, reading the article about the high school students and the *I'm Here* app they created, sponsored by Starfish.

I'm Here was working.

The number of responding lights was growing every time the "I'm Here" button was pressed, which was now at an average of seventeen times an hour. Students from 127 different schools were using it already—obviously taking it seriously.

As Ben waited for Ella to finish the article, he thought of the boy sitting alone at the lunch table—and how brightly his light had shined on Ben without him even knowing it.

* * *

After Ben, Ella, Daxx, Izzy, and Heather finished lunch, the children went out to explore the property to find a good spot for a tree house. Heather had enthusiastically okayed the plan, saying she was more than happy to help build it. She agreed it was just what the farm needed—an outstanding tree house. As she and Ella sat in the rockers on the porch, Ben excused himself, letting them know he was going to visit August's gravesite, as was his routine.

The ten-minute walk took Ben past the vegetable and herb gardens, past the hammock, and then beyond the beehives to the small, well-kept family cemetery. August had been laid to rest between Pete and Henry, and all three plots had mason jars overflowing with huge, colorful bunches of wildflowers.

Ben took a seat on the ground, still not sure how to do this or what to say.

A bee buzzed around the wildflowers and then zoned in on a daffodil. Ben smiled. How long ago it all seemed. Little did he know when meeting August that he would never feel the same way about bees. And neither would Daxx and Izzy.

Most nights now, after reading to Daxx and Izzy, Ben would tell them an August story to close their day, and more often than not, bees were the main characters—thrilled bees, funny bees, forgiving bees, and bees with abide-bys.

Recently, Ben and Ella were in the driveway with Izzy and Daxx, who had been begging to try out the tandem. As a van coming down the street slowed down, nearing its intended address, Izzy climbed down from the bike—ignoring the rule about communicating that they had just taught her and Daxx—her eyes following the van with its brightly painted logo.

After it parked a few houses down, the owners came out and talked to the two men who had gotten out of the van. The neighbors pointed to the corner of their front yard, where hundreds of bees were concentrated around a hive.

As one of the men wearing protective gear began pulling a thick hose from the van, Izzy started walking toward them—so slowly at first Ben had no idea what was happening.

"No .... no ... no!" she cried, running full speed.

By the time Ben caught up with her, they were only a few feet from the stunned neighbors, who tried to explain to Izzy that there was no other way—they had looked into moving the hive, but it wasn't feasible.

Izzy turned frantically to Ben. "I don't know what that means!" she said. "What does that *mean*?"

Crouched down, holding her, he explained what feasible meant, but she cut him off. "No!" she said, crying. "No, Dad! Don't let them kill them. They—" She caught her breath and then quickly tried again. "Can we take them? Please!" she said, her tears soaking her cheeks.

Forty minutes later, emotionally drained, she fell asleep on the couch, her head on Ella's lap. Daxx was sitting on the floor, quiet, adding little lines behind the single big bee he had drawn, showing its zigzagging path as it flew away. The real bees were gone.

Ben could relate. He felt so much more deeply now. He noticed more and cared more. Just the week before, he was walking across the plaza, on his way to meet Ella for lunch, when a disheveled woman he guessed to be in her twenties was suddenly distraught, wailing because the handle of the paper bag holding her life's belongings tore off. The contents fell to the ground, and in her reaction to that, she let the broken bicycle she was walking tip over. She seemed so sad, like it was the most devastating thing that had ever happened to her. Ben thought of a lot of reasons to keep walking, but something bigger was in charge inside him now. It stopped him.

He went over to her and asked if she was okay. Sobbing, she told him everything he had just seen happen.

He said the first thing that came to him: "What do you need?"

She just kept crying and repeating the story, and eventually, he quickly walked away, promising to be right back.

When he came back to her a minute later with an empty bag bearing the logo of the nearest store, she quickly calmed down. She wiped her eyes and seemed present suddenly, fully aware of him for the first time. He handed her the bag.

"Okay?" he said.

She nodded and then quickly moved her things from the ground to the bag, including the pieces of the torn paper bag.

Ben picked up the bike and leaned it against the nearby sign pole, then said again, "Are you okay?"

Sniffing and getting her breath back, she nodded again, making momentary eye contact.

He smiled at her then, offering the deep assurance he felt, embedded in the pulsing love in his heart. In that moment, all the heartbeats of the world—even in their wildly different variances—somehow felt in sync, and he had no doubt the rhythm of life was fully supporting her.

The interaction felt complete.

When he met Ella for lunch, it didn't even cross his mind to mention it.

It felt like he knew no other way. He no longer had any desire to quell the silence, to be louder than the buzzing, to hide from himself or disappear into his thoughts. His thoughts had been playing a new role for a while now, one of taking directions from him rather than assuming the lead.

He remembered what Heather said when he first met her. *You're the one who turned down your mind so you could hear your heart.* It was true, he realized. And it was August who had heard his heart before he did—and then convinced him it was worth listening to, promising him it would never disappoint him. She had nudged him to do the scariest thing he had ever done—follow his inner compass, no matter what—and nothing had cracked open his capacity for happiness quite like it.

It felt good to sit there on the ground, his fingers aware of the crumbling dirt and the soft blades of grass as he acknowledged August's life and how it intersected with his. Feeling another surge of gratitude, he reached forward, put his hand on her grave marker, and said, "Thank you for finding me, August—and for being so sure I would too."

* * *

On Tuesday afternoon, Ella was finishing up for the day in Henry's old shop. She carefully hung the wind chime she had been working on for the past few days, the first in a new series she had yet to name. Each chime was a small, roughly circular mirror, created from broken glass. The simplicity of the design resonated with her, and its reflections sparkled in a way that seemed to celebrate life and whisper dazzling promises that—though wordless—she knew in her heart she could trust.

Throughout the day, she had experimented with different suspensions of each line, listening as one chime touched another, which then touched another, each contributing its unique sound to the connection being made. A few times, the resulting ting—the music created—made her catch her breath, the beauty ran so deep, and she knew those particular chimes were exactly where they belonged.

She started to close the door, then paused, leaned back in, and drew a heart around her initials in the sawdust on the shelf.

After saying goodbye to Heather, Ella walked down the long drive to where she always parked her car, close to the mailbox. As the bees buzzed by and two hawks dipped and soared to a music of their own, Ella contemplated the brilliant orchestration of her life. She could never have predicted where her mistakes would take her, where her vulnerability would lead her, and where forgiveness would gently land her. Filled with gratitude, she stopped and looked around, feeling the strength in her presence on a dirt road in the middle of nowhere—a limitless somewhere.

Acknowledgments

I'm grateful to the many people whose written works of art have taught me, inspired me, and nudged me.

I'm grateful to the musicians whose songs I played on repeat; their soulful artistry took me where I needed to go in a way nothing else could.

I'm grateful to Amanda Turner for boldly leading the way.

I'm grateful to Kaya McLaren for being her exquisite Soul Sister self.

I'm grateful to all who have been with me since the beginning of the Gusto emails in 2008, and all who have hopped in and out between now and then.

I'm grateful to those who, like Gloria Santoyo Ruenitz, are role models of poetic attention to detail and confident self-expression.

I'm grateful to Tama Kieves for her dedication to her life's calling. Her rich, precise wording has buoyed me, encouraged me, and propelled me.

I'm grateful for all the relationships that have broken what needed to come apart, healed what only an open heart can, and deepened my awareness of being fantastically alive in subtle and radical ways.

I'm grateful to Zoe and Indy, my light bearers ~ always.

I'm grateful to Chris, my kind anchor and love-filled stargazer, whose roles have always been so much bigger than he could possibly imagine.

And I'm deeply grateful to you.

Also by Elizabeth Day

Fiction
Living with Gusto

Nonfiction
Notes from Gusto: Break Free
Notes from Gusto: Relationship Reminders

For daily inspiration from Elizabeth Day, visit
www.TheGustoCafe.com.